ELEPHANT'S TRUNK

A Crime Novel

Jake Jacobs

ISBN 978-1-62806-442-1 (print | paperback)
ISBN 978-1-62806-443-8 (ebook)

Library of Congress Control Number 2025901785

Published by Salt Water Media
29 Broad Street, Suite 104
Berlin, MD 21811
www.saltwatermedia.com

Cover art by Tobie Jacobs

Elephant's Trunk

CONTENTS

AUTHOR'S NOTE

This is the third book in the Detective Brogan series, fiction crime novels based on experiences, and events occurring today. Using nearly forty years of investigative experience in law enforcement and the private sector, I feel honored to share my stories with you. They're a mix of true crime colored with fiction.

Senseless violent crime is on the rise across the nation. Some portions of my books have been described as scary. I hope none of my readers walk through life afraid, but I also hope they pay attention to their surroundings and use common sense in keeping themselves safe.

Walk with me through another exciting adventure in Sandpiper, Maryland. Take some time out for yourself and enjoy the read.

AUTHOR'S NOTE

[illegible]

1

CASSIDY & DILLON

Cassidy and Dillon's lives were just beginning. Both were eighteen and very much in love with each other, though they had no clue what love was all about. High school graduation had been a rush of excitement and the turning of a page. They were thrilled to take advantage of their newfound freedom and maturity. When their closest friends said they were going to Sandpiper Beach to celebrate, they jumped at the chance to join them.

Jennifer and Clay had always been their best friends. All four had known each other since grammar school. Clay had a used SUV, and Jennifer's parents had a two-bedroom condo where they could all stay. It was to be a long weekend vacation away from adult supervision. Their cargo included a case of beer and a couple of bottles of wine. The youthful flame of potential burned brightly.

The condo on 5th Street sat one block off the boardwalk with no water view, but the salty ocean air was intoxicating. Each couple had a bedroom and took full advantage of the privacy to have unbridled sex shortly after arriving. The dangers of getting caught in a parked car or someone's parents coming home early were no longer a consideration. Sex, without fear of getting caught, was a new experience. Cassidy and Dillon imagined this was the way it would always be. They couldn't keep their hands off each other, and affection flowed like a spilled bottle of wine.

It was May, and the weather was unusually warm; everything was perfect. In the afternoon, on the second day, the couples went to the beach with towels and small canvas beach bags. They spent the entire afternoon soaking in the sun. They all wore shorts and sweatshirts recently purchased at boardwalk shops. The water was still frigid from the receding winter months, so there was no way they were going to venture in for a swim. Around 5 p.m., they retreated to the boardwalk, where they scarfed down some pizza.

Dillon whispered to Cassidy, "I'm sensing Jennifer and Clay are looking for some private time. I think we should split up, what do you think?"

"I think you're right."

"Hey guys, I think Cassidy and I're going to go for a walk, how about we meet up later?"

Clay smiled as he jumped at the offer, "Yeah, that sounds good; we'll see you back at the condo. Have fun."

Cassidy and Dillon spent the waning daylight hours visiting the touristy shops and arcades on the boardwalk. At nightfall, most of the shops closed, and the foot traffic dwindled to a trickle. Summer store hours and big crowds were still a few weeks away. The temperature remained comfortable and prompted them back onto the beach. They still had their towels and sat on the soft, warm sand, watching the waves gently break on the shore. They were alone on the beach and began making out. His hand tangled in her hair as he deepened their kiss, "You taste so good." Cassidy rested her hand on his chest as one thing led to another. Having sex on the beach was a forbidden temptation they couldn't let pass. Dillon instantly started scanning the area and saw the dark outline of one of the rental chair shacks.

"Cassidy, follow me."

"Where're we going?"

"Come on, trust me, you'll see."

"Are you sure?"

The area was dark and secluded. In true Dillon style, his imagination started to crank up. Using the frame of the window on the shack, he proceeded to climb on top of the roof. "Come on, Cassidy, climb up."

"Are you crazy? I can't get up there."

"Look, grab my hand and put your foot on the frame. I'll pull you up."

Cassidy, a tall, thin brunette built for the volleyball she played in high school, was skeptical. Dillon did not disappoint as he pulled her right up onto the roof. They were about ten feet above the sand and fifty yards from the boardwalk, virtually invisible to the casual passerby. The thrill of being somewhere they knew they shouldn't be was stirring their sexual desires all over again. They both had a low giggle. Dillon spread out their towels and slowly began to lift Cassidy's sweatshirt off, and she lifted his. Cloudy skies obscured the moonlight.

Later, having re-dressed, they wrapped themselves in their towels and each other. The darkness, sounds of the surf, sex, and a long day in the sun lulled them both into a sound sleep. Dillon had already texted Clay a very short message,

"See you in the morning, Cas and I're spending the night in the dunes."

Dillon awoke around 4 a.m. with nature calling him to take a piss. He wet his finger and held it in the air, making sure he would not spray Cassidy while she lay sleeping. Peeing off the roof was liberating. His comfort level disappeared when he heard giggling behind him. He looked over his shoulder to see the vague outline of Cassidy sitting up and watching intently. Another bridge of intimacy crossed.

Cassidy said, "Me too, but not from up here. Help me down."

Dillon helped her off the roof. She moved off to the side of the building for privacy. When she reappeared, she was smiling and disheveled from her night on the roof. "You are so beautiful," Dillon said. Cassidy blushed and grabbed his hand as Dillon grabbed their towels and threw them over his shoulder.

"Come on, Cas, let's go for a walk." Cassidy's smile told him she would follow him anywhere. They walked to the waterline and continued quietly toward the inlet blocks away.

During their fifteen-minute walk to the inlet parking lot, they passed under the fishing pier. They didn't see a living soul. "Hey, Cassidy, let's stay on the beach a while longer. Let's turn around and head back the way we came."

As they approached the fishing pier, Dillon realized that under the pier, it was shaded from the moonlight, rendering it dark. He let Cassidy get a few steps ahead of him, then hooked his fingers into the back of her shorts. He brought her to a standstill directly under the pier and pulled her tight to him. She felt his erection pushing into her backside. She turned, "Really, again? Under the pier? We're going to get caught!"

"No, we won't, come on, it'll be fun," he grinned. She grabbed his hand and pulled him to her. Dillon quickly spread the towels out as Cassidy shimmied out of her shorts. Wasting no time, Dillon's shorts were off and tossed on the towel next to Cassidy. She laid on her back, and he laid on top of her. Their feet were just inches from the wet sand and gently lapping water. Dillon entered her slowly and began a rocking motion.

Cassidy was about to wrap her legs around him when she felt something wet and cold touch her left foot. She jerked her foot back immediately to see what it was. It took a moment for her eyes to process what she was seeing, "What the fuck!" *Is that a person touching my foot?* Cassidy's eyes strained to get a better look. She then realized it was not a hand but a dark stump at the end of an arm.

Her ear-splitting scream caused Dillon to pull out and fall back next to the body. His scream almost matched hers.

2

RUNNING FOR YOUR LIFE

Cassidy and Dillon were moving so quickly, it was as if they were a single entity. Grabbing towels, clothes, and the beach bag, Dillon and Cassidy turned toward the boardwalk. As they ran, Cassidy was crying while screaming some unintelligible mantra.

"Oh my God, Dillon! What was that? What do we do?" she wailed.

"Keep running," he wheezed. "For God's sake, we didn't even check to see if the person was dead or alive; we have to get help."

Dillon had stopped screaming and took Cassidy's hand to steady her as they ran. Dillon looked back once to be sure it hadn't been a mutual nightmare. A human-sized dark shape bobbed partially in the water and partially on the wet sand. The arms were stretched out as if the figure was trying to claw his way onto the beach. *There were no hands! There were no hands!*

Dillon continued to stumble forward and glanced over at Cassidy. She was crying and flailing her free arm in an effort to go faster. She was also half-naked! Dillon looked down to find himself in a similar condition. He jerked to a halt and stopped Cassidy's forward motion. He yelled to her, "We don't have any shorts on!"

Unable to remember who did what or how it came to be, they found their shorts and towels jammed in the beach bag. Twenty yards from the body, they both watched closely, transfixed on the form lying at the surf's edge while jerking on their shorts.

Dillon's thoughts spilled from his mouth. "This is like *The Living Dead*." They both were avid fans of *The Living Dead* movies. *Is that body going to get up and come after us?* They wasted no time and resumed their run for life. The deep, soft sand that hours ago had been so comforting was now inhibiting their escape.

All thoughts of maturity and adulthood had abandoned them. They were two kids running from a terrifying sight.

As they neared the boardwalk, a figure on a bicycle seemed to be watching their approach. Dillon recognized the man as a cop. For the first time, he thought, *We might live after all.* Cassidy was not thinking at all. She was just trying to put more distance between herself and the handless body.

Sandpiper Bike Patrol Officers usually traveled in pairs except for this evening when Officer Travis Jenkins's senior partner, Danny Hinkle, received a call from headquarters. "Officer Hinkle, your wife called and requested you report immediately to the hospital." Jenkins could hear the smile in the dispatcher's voice.

Danny stuttered, "It's time?" Then he grinned, "It's time! My son is being born." Barely mouthing, "See you later," he pedaled away as fast as possible without glancing back. Jenkins laughed. *I'll have to stop and pick up a stuffed bear or something before I visit.*

Jenkins graduated from the police academy in January. He was only twenty-one years old but was a strapping young man who imbued confidence. His assignment to the bike patrol started May 1st. Working the 11 p.m. to 7 a.m. shift was usually quiet. This assignment had a few advantages over car patrol, like being able to wear regulation shorts on warm, balmy nights as opposed to long uniform pants. In addition, Jenkins loved the added freedom and ability to access areas that patrol vehicles could not go.

After Hinkle pedaled away, Jenkins had resumed his duties of checking that all the businesses were closed by primarily shaking the door knobs for unlocked doors and the detection of break-ins. He had support from nearby vehicle patrol officers should he need backup. Jenkins never gave another thought about the fact he would be working alone for the last four hours of his shift while patrolling the boardwalk.

Jenkins stopped on the boardwalk and straddled his bike as he watched two figures emerge from the darkness, running from the beach. A panicked female voice reverberated across the early morning air. She was screaming, but her message was not understandable. A young man was holding her hand and running by her side. He seemed to be helping her across the sand rather than restraining her. The two runners shifted their flight path directly toward him. Officer Jenkins climbed off his bike, set the bike stand, and braced himself as he tugged at his ballistic vest and slid his hand down to his firearm.

Jenkins's attached body camera captured his activities during his tour of duty. It was a constant reminder for him to keep his cool no matter what the situation. *This might be one of those times.*

The teenagers arrived at an opening in the protective wall

that runs along the boardwalk. They were over a hundred yards from the ocean. The three-foot wall was to protect the boardwalk and businesses from the surf during times of extreme weather and seas.

Jenkins said nothing to the young couple as they stopped just short of the boardwalk. The two were now bent at the waist with their hands on their knees, trying to suck in oxygen. Both were disheveled. The girl's face was wet from tears, her eyes were bloodshot, and her hair was in desperate need of a brush. *I don't think these two are a threat or even at odds with one another.* Jenkins waited patiently to hear their story when they were ready to tell it.

The boy spoke first. "There's a body under the pier!"

"What do you mean, a body? Calm down, what's your name?"

"I'm Dillon Sullivan, and this is my girlfriend, Cassidy Wayne. We were down on the beach, and there's a body there under the pier. When we saw it, we ran up here to tell somebody. We didn't touch it! We just ran!" The girl said nothing but nodded her head vigorously in agreement with Dillon's description.

Jenkins spoke into the mic attached near his shoulder.

"BP 9 to Headquarters. Two teenagers report a body under the pier."

"Headquarters to BP 9, what's your location?"

"BP 9 to headquarters, Division Street on the boards. I'll enter the beach with them to the location of the body. Witnesses report they didn't touch the body, so they don't know if the person is alive or dead. I'm going to see if I can render aid. Have a backup unit come to my location. I'll report my findings as soon as I know them."

"Headquarters to BP 9, copy backup is en route. Fire

Headquarters, with medical personnel, will be notified and headed to the scene. Use caution."

Jenkins grabbed his flashlight from its mounting bracket, stepped into the sand, and said, "Show me what you found."

Dillon hesitated, and Cassidy started a low moaning, "No. No. I can't go back there."

In a stern but controlled voice, Jenkins said, "I need you to show me what you saw. Someone may need help."

Cassidy was shaking her head, and tears were running down her cheeks. "I can't. I can't. He doesn't have any hands!"

"What?" Jenkins said.

Dillon spoke in a low voice. "He doesn't have any hands. Both his hands are gone. It looks like they were cut off!"

A marked patrol car, blue lights flashing, roared up Division Street and stopped at the boardwalk. Officer Ronnie Hughes stepped from the vehicle and joined Jenkins and the witnesses. Jenkins knew Hughes from the academy; they had graduated together.

"Hey, Hughes, how's it going?"

"Doing okay, do you know what we have here?"

"All I know is these two came running up from the pier talking about a body; this is Dillon & Cassidy. Ronnie, why don't you take Cassidy to your patrol car and get her full information and a statement. Dillon and I will go down to the water. Keep her here until we have more information."

"Come on, Dillon." Dillon reluctantly manned up and went with Jenkins back across the sand. As they arrived at the water's edge, Dillon stopped about ten yards from the dark form, his voice shaking, Dillon asked, "Can I wait here? I don't want to see the body again."

Jenkins cautiously approached the body, still partially in

and out of the water. Circling to a position where he could observe the face of the person lying in the sand. His flashlight revealed a gruesome picture. This was definitely a dead body. The clothing and hairstyle appeared to be that of a male. The body was swollen, and the face was partially disfigured by crabs that still hung to the rotting flesh. It was impossible to tell the race or age of the victim as the flesh was black and blue and, in some places, green from exposure during its time in the water. Jenkins directed his flashlight up the outstretched arms of the victim and confirmed both hands were missing, just dark, congealed bloody stumps with darkened bones protruding at the wrists.

Jenkins had seen photos of drowning victims pulled from the water, but seeing it in person with the accompanying odors was too much. He felt the bile in his stomach begin to move towards his throat. He gagged and staggered a few steps back. He quickly shut off his flashlight and moved even further away from the body. It was his turn to suck in clean oxygen and get a grip on himself. *Whatever you do, don't puke on the crime scene.*

As Jenkins regained his composure, Dillon watched but remained silent. Dillon did not attempt to move closer or ask any questions. Without conscious thought, Dillon edged backward, fighting off the urge to run for his life a second time. *I'll never be able to forget this. I'm not sure I'll ever be able to go into the water!*

Moments later, Dillon heard Officer Jenkins speak on his radio. "BP 9 to Headquarters. We need Detectives to come to the scene. Alert the Medical Examiner. I'll secure the scene with one witness until further units arrive. Officer Hughes has the second witness at the boardwalk."

"Headquarters to BP 9. Assistance is en route, over!"

Jenkins approached Dillon with his flashlight on and tucked under his arm. Jenkins pulled a pocket-sized notebook and pen from inside his jacket. "Okay, you better start from the beginning. I need the who, what, when, and where. Tell me everything you know starting from when you got up yesterday morning. Don't leave anything out."

Dillon's shoulders sagged, and he bowed his head as he began to speak.

3

LOOK WHAT THE TIDE WASHED IN

The buzzing of his cell phone awakened him. Glancing at his bedside clock, he saw it was 6:05 a.m. He put the phone to his ear and answered, "Brogan."

"Brogan, this is Sergeant Cramer. We have a body on the beach at the fishing pier. Patty Ryan, Bob Carr, and the crime scene people are en route. The Medical Examiner has been notified and is on her way. We've got a few uniforms at the scene right now and will hold over the night shift for as long as they're needed. I have a note that the Chief will be in Snow Hill this morning. Do you want me to notify him? All I know is a couple of kids found the body and a bicycle patrol guy says it appears to have washed up after being in the water for a while."

"Sergeant, I'll take care of the Chief. I'll be with him in Snow Hill. Patty Ryan will be the lead investigator, so coordinate with her. I'll stop by the scene before I go to Snow Hill. I should be there within thirty minutes.

The sun rose on a ghastly crime scene. Hastily assembled five-foot collapsible mesh screens had been erected around the body. Crime scene technicians, the medical examiner, and the police worked side by side to determine what had happened to this unfortunate individual. A low hum of guarded conversations competed with the sounds of small waves lapping against the nearby pylons holding the pier.

Thirty yards from the body, beginning and ending at the water's edge, a half circle of four-foot metal fence poles, set at ten-foot intervals, had been driven into the sand by the crime scene investigators and fellow officers. Yellow police tape tied between them fluttered in a light breeze. Protecting a crime scene was first and foremost. The thin ribbon and watchful police officers made the message very clear. STAY OUT!

Onlookers bellied up to the tape to see what was going on. The breeze off the ocean carried with it the smell of death. The offensive odor prompted many of the nosey to gag and turn quickly away, not wishing to linger. Those leaving were quickly replaced by others who noticed the police activity from the boardwalk.

The media was mixed with onlookers just beyond the barrier. They were set up and filmed everything. Reporters blended with the crowd, seeking witnesses or information that might enhance their news stories.

"Hi, where're you from?"

"Do you know what's going on here?"

"Did you see the body?"

"Could you tell if it was a man or a woman?"

"Have you talked to the police?"

Many of the onlookers had their phones out, held high while videoing the action. Uniformed officers standing at the barrier were gathering names and looking at the identification of those they spoke to. There would be duplication, but there was never too much information obtained during these initial hours of an investigation.

At precisely 6:30 a.m., a tall, dark-haired man strode from the inlet parking lot along the water's edge. When he got to the taped-off area, he met and spoke with a uniformed officer. Only those standing close could hear the conversation. "Good morning, Officer Browning. How're things going?"

"Morning, Brogan. Everything is going pretty well. All your people are here, and so is the medical examiner, Vickery." Browning entered Brogan into the crime scene log affixed to his clipboard and noted the time of his arrival. He gently lifted the tape to allow Brogan access.

"Do you know if they've been able to make an I.D.?"

"No sir, I don't. I've been stationed here at the ribbon since I got here. I do have the names and contact information of a few people who were here before they put up the barriers. I also filmed who was here when I arrived. I'll download it from my phone and include it with my report."

No matter what your status or reason for being at a serious crime scene, a report was mandatory. It doesn't matter how innocuous these reports might be; they would be read and dissected by detectives looking for clues.

"Thanks, Browning. Good job, appreciate your efforts."

Brogan moved to the screens hiding the body and met Detective Patty Ryan. "Whatcha got, Patty?"

"Dead guy. Been in the water a while. No I.D. on the body and the crabs and water have made a mess of his face. Both his hands are missing at the wrists!"

"Homicide, you think?"

"Not jumping to that conclusion yet. He could've fallen off a boat and reached up to grab for the boat and met with the spinning prop. Vickery is still checking him out. He's definitely going to Baltimore for an autopsy and to help with the identification."

"Okay, Patty. I'm making you lead on this investigation. You know what to do. Tell Detective Carr he is to assist you with anything you need. I have a meeting in Snow Hill this morning, but I'll have my phone on if you need me for anything. If this turns out to be a murder or suspicious death, it'll still be your case. I have full confidence in you, and I'll brief the Chief on this. He's supposed to be at the meeting in Snow Hill. I'll tell him you'll be in Baltimore tomorrow morning for the autopsy.

"In the meantime, I'll call Charlie Connolly at the morgue and let him know you're coming. He's the liaison guy I introduced you to last year when we went up there together. He'll set it up, so you'll be the first examination in the morning. Be there by eight. Charlie has seen a lot of these cases, so pick his brain if you have questions. I'll see you tomorrow when you get back, and we'll get together on a plan. Be prepared to brief the Chief on what you learn in Baltimore. I'm going to talk to Vickery and tell her you're in charge. Any questions?"

"No sir, I got this."

Brogan could see Detective Ryan puff up with pride when he gave her the lead. He had mentored her and Detective Carr for years, and it was time to turn them loose. She was senior to Detective Bob Carr by only six months, but he knew Carr would give her his full support. *I'm confident she'll make good decisions and follow every lead that comes to light. Carr is ready to handle more serious investigations as well.* Sandpiper P.D. was being faced with a series of big-city crimes. It was time to grow the criminal unit. *I need to tell the Chief how I feel.*

Brogan turned from Patty Ryan to the woman crouched close to the body. "Hi, Doc. What've we got?"

Doctor Michele Vickery, the local medical examiner, turned to Brogan and smiled. "Not sure just yet. The body is in pretty bad shape, and he's definitely been in the water for a few days. I can't determine the actual cause of death from what I'm seeing. When they get him on the table in Baltimore, they'll be able to tell a lot more. These missing hands are especially concerning. I don't think a boat prop would make these clean cuts, but Baltimore will be able to sort that out. This is not where he died, so other than what's on the body, I doubt you'll recover any usable evidence."

"Okay Michele, I've assigned this to Patty Ryan, so she's in charge and will attend the autopsy tomorrow. Please share with her anything you find, or you think."

"Sure, Brogan. Never a dull moment in Sandpiper anymore, is there?"

"Sorry to say, you're right. I'm beginning to feel like I'm back in the Baltimore City Homicide Unit. Not a good feeling."

Brogan began his walk back to the inlet where his car was parked. He nodded at a man in a suit standing just inside the barrier and said, "Hi, Nelson."

Nelson Horn stood next to his gurney. Horn worked at the local funeral home and would be transporting the body to Baltimore per a prearranged agreement with the town.

Horn acknowledged the greeting by nodding his head and saying, "Hi, Lieutenant." Horn maintained a grave and practiced expression on his face.

Brogan wondered, *is that look something they teach in*

Mortuary school? Never seen Horn smile, but I've never seen him anywhere but at the scene of a death.

One of the news people stood a few yards from Brogan as he exited the crime scene. Normally, he would pass without comment, but this news person was a little different. As he drew near, he asked, "How're you doing Lynn?"

"I'm good, Brogan. How about you?"

"As you can see, we're a little busy this morning."

"Anything you can tell me for my show today?"

"Nothing solid. A male. Been in the water a little while. We'll know more after the autopsy. It's Patty Ryan's case. She'll be able to put together a press release sometime tomorrow. I'll be sure you get an early copy if it'll help you."

"Sure would. Thanks."

"Lynn, can you get your cameraman to scan the crowd a few times while you're here? You know better than most that criminals really do return to the scene of the crime."

Lynn Murphy paled and was visibly shaken by the reminder. Two years ago, she had been kidnapped from a crime scene by a serial killer and rapist. Unknown to others, Brogan and she had been lovers at the time. She was a local television newswoman, and they had hidden their relationship from everyone.

Brogan was able to save her at the last moment, but the incident left her scarred. Soon after that event, she and Brogan mutually decided to go their separate ways. She was now dating a lawyer from Salisbury. He had normal working hours, was extremely attentive to her, and she was fond of him. Dating a bad boy like Brogan had been exciting, but she now sought the companionship and safety of a more conventional relationship.

"I'll send you a copy of everything we get here today. Good seeing you again, be safe." Lynn turned to her cameraman. "Bobby, give me a lot of shots of the crowd while we're here. Email me a copy of the entire tape."

"Sure thing, Lynn," Bobby said without lifting his face from behind his camera.

Brogan felt bad for how his comment had come out, now seeing Lynn's reaction. "Lynn, you, okay?" Brogan whispered.

"Yeah, yeah, I'm fine. Shit still gets to me once in a while. Thanks for asking."

Brogan turned without further comment and walked to his car. He popped his trunk and pulled a white hand towel from the trunk. He took a few minutes to wipe off his shoes, restoring their luster. Once he was satisfied they looked good, and he wouldn't be dragging sand into his immaculately cared for vehicle, he entered and drove away.

Brogan prided himself on his appearance and his equipment. His new love interest, Kelly Hart, found these traits to be in line with the way she had always lived her life. Their relationship was growing with each passing day. She knew about Lynn Murphy but also knew that was old news.

About twenty yards behind the crowd, a man stood off to himself, observing the doings. A full gray beard, sunglasses, and a floppy hat were pulled down low, hiding his features. When a wheeled gurney was brought to remove the body, the man turned away and trudged across the soft sand. His hand slipped into his rear pants pocket and reappeared, holding a cell phone that he placed to his ear.

4
DET. LIEUTENANT WILLIAM BROGAN

William Brogan was the lead investigator for the Sandpiper Police Department (SPPD) in Maryland. His official rank was Lieutenant, and he reported directly to the Chief.

His police career began in Baltimore City, but local politics and corrupt politicians dictated he move on. As an ex-Baltimore City homicide detective, he brought a wealth of training and knowledge to the beach town of Sandpiper. His new home at SPPD was a dream come true. Now, ten years into this posting, he had established a stellar reputation as the top cop in Worcester County and maybe on the entire Eastern shore.

He went by only one name, Brogan. At forty-six, he remained engaged in martial arts training and daily exercise. Most people thought him to be a much younger man. His 6' plus height, athletic build, and thick dark hair completed the look of a self-confident man.

Brogan was dressed in his favorite blue Tom Ford suit and a starched white shirt. A 9-mm duty gun rested comfortably in his shoulder holster beneath his left arm. The jacket was tailored to conceal his gun. A fashionable striped tie and freshly polished shoes completed his uniform of the day.

Today, something was about to happen, but Brogan wasn't sure what. Sandpiper's Chief, Elwood Richards, had called him Sunday and directed him to report at 10:00 a.m., Monday morning, to the State's Attorney's Office in Snow Hill. The chief would not disclose the topic of the meeting but assured Brogan he had not fucked anything up and his presence was mandatory.

He left the crime scene at 7:15 a.m. and drove south on Route 113 toward Snow Hill. The meeting was still nearly three hours off. It would only take him about thirty minutes to get there. Brogan had time to grab some breakfast and a coffee. A breakfast and a coffee he would never have.

5

BURNING DOWN THE HOUSE

Brogan lowered the driver's window. May on the Eastern Shore of Maryland could be fickle, sometimes hot and sometimes cold, but today it was neither. The temperature was hovering in the mid-seventies and was predicted to stay there. This was a perfect day, and Brogan was enjoying every second of it, notwithstanding a body on the beach.

His unmarked, non-traditional police car was maintaining the speed limit. He was in no rush. The 2023 Toyota Land Cruiser was a drug-seizure-vehicle traded to Worcester County from the State's Attorney's Office in Carroll County, MD. A similar valued vehicle was sent to them from Worcester County. Trading seized vehicles was a long-used method of adding value to plain clothes operations, surveillances, and investigators across the State.

No emergency required his immediate attention. Brogan listened to a country radio station while keeping one ear on the seemingly unending chatter of the police radio. He drove out of Sandpiper on U.S. Route 50 and turned left onto State Route 113, heading south toward the county seat.

Man, I can't get my mind off of that body on the beach. It just might turn out to be a real who-done-it investigation, and I've given it away to Ryan. I'll stay deeply involved in this one. Leading is what I love to do, but sometimes, I should step back and delegate and trust others to do the job. I made the right decision by putting Ryan as the lead. She's up to the task, and it's her time to seek justice for someone who's no longer able to speak up for themselves. I need to let her do her job; I'll support her and not interfere.

Brogan made a call to his friend, Charlie Connolly, at the Baltimore City Medical Examiner's Office. His call went to voicemail. "Morning Charlie, this is Brogan. We had a body wash up on the shore this morning, and it's on the way to you. I hope you can see your way clear to post it first thing tomorrow morning. I've assigned my senior investigator, Patty Ryan, to the case. It's the first time I've let her run on her own, so if you can help her and make sure she doesn't miss anything, I'd appreciate it. She'll be there by eight, but knowing her, it might be seven. Call me if there's a problem or if you have any questions. Thanks."

Brogan's police radio, mounted and hidden under his dash, was set to monitor and communicate with all the law enforcement agencies in Worchester County. Sandpiper P.D. was always the priority channel when transmitting, but when they weren't transmitting, the other channels could also be monitored. His police radio crackled to life. Brogan recognized the voice of the Sheriff's Office Police Communications Officer, Ann Kurtz.

"Sheriff's Office to Car 47, you're needed to assist the County Fire Department at the scene of a reported house fire on Silver Hook Court in the Shady Lane Development."

"Car 47, Sheriff's Office, 10-4, I'm about five minutes out."

Brogan realized he was only about four miles away from that location. He slowed and pulled to the shoulder, awaiting Car 47 to report his arrival and status. A couple of minutes later, he heard the status loud and clear.

"Car 47, Sheriff's Office. I'm on the scene along with the fire department. There's a two-story dwelling showing smoke but no flames. Firefighters are preparing to approach the residence. I'll maintain my location and assist as needed."

Mere moments later, a much louder voice called on the radio.

"This is car 47, Sheriff's Office. Shots fired. I repeat, shots fired. One firefighter down. Shots coming from a front upstairs window of the house on fire. House number 622. A long gun is sticking out the window. Lights and sirens activated to identify police at scene. Additional shots have been fired. A wounded firefighter has been dragged behind a fire truck for cover. Four firefighters pinned down behind the truck. First aid is being provided to wounded firefighter. Extent of his injuries undetermined. I'll be out of the car assisting. We need an ambulance and more police!"

Brogan grabbed his mike and said, "Car 3 Lt. Brogan SPPD to Car 47, stay under cover. I'm six minutes out. Do you copy Sandpiper?"

"Sandpiper to Car 3, copy, I'll coordinate response with the Sheriff's Office and State Police. Backup and ambulance are en route."

Brogan spun the steering wheel to the left, checked his

side mirror, and stomped the gas pedal to the floor. The SUV responded with a tire squealing U-turn that pointed Brogan north on 113. He was only two miles past a side road that would take him to the crisis location, where all hell was apparently breaking loose. Immediately, thoughts of breakfast, the chief, and the state's attorney left him. He thought only of the downed firefighter and the operator of Car 47. *I need to get there and help bring this to an end.* Brogan slowed only enough to make a hair-raising, left-hand turn onto Vale Road that would take him directly to the scene. The first sign of wispy, white smoke was visible on the horizon.

The entrance to Shady Lane Development appeared on the right. As he turned into the community, a gunshot rang out. Silver Hook Court was the third road on the left. Brogan swung into the entrance of the deep cul-de-sac, but he held a clear view of the firetruck and the upper story of the house. Smoke was rising from the rear of the house. The upstairs front window on the right side of the house was open, but it was dark inside, and Brogan couldn't see a shooter. No smoke was coming from the open window.

"Car 47 to Sheriff's Office. The shooter's yelling out the window. He has hostages. He's threatening to kill his wife and kid if we don't pull back. Smoke is increasing, but still no flames are visible. I yelled to him that we couldn't move the truck and put firefighters at risk. He said if we leave the truck and move back, he won't shoot. I don't trust him. We'll be exposed if we leave our vehicles."

"Car 47, this is Brogan. Hold your positions and try to keep him talking if you can. Try to calm him down, if possible. Tell him you're waiting on a supervisor before you can comply with his requests."

"Car 47 to Brogan. Copy. Will hold with firefighters until further advised."

Brogan pulled a small pair of binoculars from his center console and brought them to bear on the firetruck. He saw four firefighters and a Deputy crouched behind the large wheels of the truck. The Deputy had his handgun drawn and a shotgun leaning against the tire. *They'll be safe as long as they stay put.*

Brogan backed out of the court just as a uniformed trooper driving a marked car arrived on the scene. Brogan signaled, and the trooper followed him down one block and made a right. They worked their way behind the house on fire and parked out of sight. Neither police car displayed emergency lights or sounded sirens that would reveal their current position. Before exiting his car, Brogan switched his police radio to the "black channel."

"Car 3 to headquarters, MSP car V-26, is on the scene with me. We'll breach the target house from the rear. Advise other officers at the scene to use black channel only." *Thank God they created a channel so police can communicate privately at a time like this.*

Trooper Irvin Blackburn met Brogan at the trunk of Brogan's car, and the men shook hands. Blackburn was fit-looking and a fairly big guy.

"I'm Irv."

"I'm Brogan."

Brogan shed his suit jacket and pulled his protective vest from the trunk, put it over his head, and fastened it into place. Brogan could see the trooper already had his vest on under his shirt. Blackburn wore no ranking stripes on his arm, which suggested to Brogan he was fairly new, possibly inexperienced as well. Brogan assumed control of the scene due to seniority.

"Blackburn, the important thing is to move toward the danger but to be smart about how we do it. I want you with me. We'll breach the house from the rear and work our way up to the second floor. Our objective is twofold. If the wife and child are present, do whatever it takes to remove them from the danger. Secondly, stop the shooter from shooting anyone else. If he doesn't surrender, or if he presents an immediate threat to us or others, we use deadly force. Any questions?"

Trooper Blackburn calmly replied, "Roger that."

Brogan associated that response with military personnel. *Maybe this trooper has more experience than I thought.*

"Blackburn, do you have a shotgun?"

"Yes, Sir, in the trunk of my car. Loaded and ready to go."

"Go get it and follow me. We're going in."

Once Blackburn had the shotgun, he followed Brogan, keeping the shotgun at high port. He also had removed his Stetson hat, revealing a military-style haircut. Brogan and Blackburn stayed in a crouched position as they moved forward to the rear of the house. They used trees and other vegetation to conceal their approach as they moved through neighbors' yards. Brogan pointed to a middle-aged man standing on his back patio and then gestured toward his house. The man got the message and retreated into his home through the back slider. *I bet other neighbors were watching but keeping themselves hidden.*

Brogan turned off the small radio clipped to his belt as they got close to the house. Blackburn had a shoulder mike, and he, too, disabled his radio so they wouldn't disclose their location.

Another shot rang out from the front of the house. *It sounded like a rifle. Definitely the shooter. No officer would fire into the home and risk innocent lives.*

Brogan was giving Blackburn hand signals as to where he should go and what he should do. Both of them ended up on the patio, flanking a rear sliding door. Brogan reached out one hand and gently pushed against the slider's handle. It soundlessly moved six or seven inches on well-oiled tracks. An orange cat shot out through the opening, scaring the shit out of both Brogan and Blackburn. Both officers looked at each other and nodded in unspoken agreement. Brogan pushed the slider wider and entered, Blackburn followed. The slider gave them access to a family room, which they cleared immediately. Both stood stock-still, listening and looking for possible threats.

In the dining room, under a window, a pile of cloth smoldered on the wood floor. The drapes were pulled down and set on fire. Smoke was rolling out a partially open back window from the dining room. There were no flames and no additional accelerants near the area. Both men turned from the dining room, considering the fire threat to be very remote compared to the gunman somewhere in the house.

They moved cautiously while they progressed down a hallway leading to the front of the house.

Brogan thought, *This is as real as it gets in the police world. There's an armed assailant in the house who already shot one man and who's shooting at the police with a rifle. He told police he'll kill his wife and child. Hell, I've no reason to disbelieve him.*

Blackburn remained calm and whispered to Brogan, "I've breached and cleared buildings before in Afghanistan."

Brogan got a little smile on his face, nodded, and tipped his head toward a staircase leading up to the upstairs. Both men moved together like they had rehearsed this maneuver a thousand times. The man upstairs had no idea what was coming his way.

6

CONFRONT THE SHOOTER

Brogan and Blackburn cautiously approached the staircase, which presented an increased danger of ambush. Before their guns would be at a level to deal with the threat, their heads would be exposed targets.

Brogan pressed his back against a wall for protection as he began his upward traverse of the carpeted stairs. Blackburn stayed at the bottom of the steps with his back pressed against the same wall. Blackburn's shotgun remained on his shoulder, and his eyes were on the area at the top of the steps where the shooter might present himself.

They could both hear the screaming rant of the gunman aimed at the firefighters and police officers assembled in the court area. The voice was partially muffled by the distance between the stairs and the room where he was making his stance. His yelling helped conceal any noise made by the deadly twosome making their way to his location.

Brogan reached the top of the steps and signaled Blackburn to follow. When both were safely in the hallway, they were confronted with two open doors. Quickly clearing the room on the left, they found an empty child's bedroom. The door on the right led to the shooter's location.

Moving ever so slowly toward the open door, the sound of the shooter's yelling became louder. It was difficult to hear what he was saying because his voice projected out the front window. His message was disjointed, slurred, and filled with expletives. *This guy is filled with rage and liable to do anything at this point,* Brogan thought.

Brogan crawled the last few feet to the open door. Blackburn had set aside the shotgun and drawn his service weapon to cover Brogan's actions. Peeking around the bottom corner of the door, Brogan saw the shooter with his rifle extended out past the window frame. The shooter's full attention was on his audience in front of the house.

Out of the corner of his eye, Brogan saw a young woman seated against the wall near the door. She was wearing a short nightgown that was ripped at the top, and her left hand held the garment together. Her right hand and arm cradled a small, dark-haired boy in her lap who looked to be about two years old. His eyes were red and as big as saucers. A second look at his mom showed her right eye was swollen and ringed by a red bruise on her cheek. *Looks like she'd received a beating this morning and is paralyzed with fear.* Neither hostage noticed Brogan, with their focus solely on the man at the window.

Brogan back crawled about ten feet while Blackburn continued to cover the doorway. Brogan stood and whispered to Blackburn, "A woman is sitting on the floor near the doorway holding a small child. The shooter's at the window. I'll get the attention of the woman and signal her to slide toward the open doorway. I'll pull her back and into the hallway. This can all go to shit if the woman won't or can't move to the doorway. I'll still go in, grab them, and pull them out, but be ready to take out the shooter."

A single nod of his head signaled Blackburn understood. The rules of engagement had been laid out; it was time to end this siege.

Brogan again crawled the distance to the doorway. Without fully revealing himself, he put his left hand just inside the room while continually watching the man at the window. Brogan saw the woman turn her head toward him, and he revealed his face to her while putting a single finger to his lips.

Brogan laid his left hand on the carpet and motioned for her to move to his location. The woman began to shift her position, sliding slowly toward the open door.

The shooter's litany of rage grew louder, and then he shot another round out the window. The woman jerked in fear, then continued sliding toward the open doorway.

I gotta move now. Brogan rose to his knees and centered the door. He reached in, grabbed the woman under both arms and dragged her and the child into the hallway and away from the door. In the next second, Blackburn centered himself in the doorway, with his gun in a two-handed grip, pointing at the shooter's back. The shooter saw movement and turned from the window. He swung his rifle into the room, presenting his chest.

No hesitation. Blackburn fired two quick shots, and the rifle flew from the shooter's hands. He fell forward and stayed still. Blackburn entered the room and slowly approached the downed man while watching for any movement.

Brogan had pointed the woman to the staircase, and she fled, still holding the child to her chest. Brogan's view of the suspect was limited because Blackburn's frame blocked most of his view. He did see the guy was face down, and the rifle lay near him.

Blackburn was only two steps away from the shooter when the man's left hand burst out from under him, seeking the rifle lying only a foot from where he had fallen. Blackburn took one step and kicked the assailant in the side of the head, knocking him out cold. Then he kicked the rifle across the room. Brogan surged toward the door with his gun in hand, but the action was over. The bad guy was down with a pool of blood rapidly expanding near his right shoulder.

Knowing there would be a full-fledged breach of the house, Brogan turned on his radio. "Car 3 to headquarters, the shooter is down, and the house is secure for entry. Requesting medical personnel to the second floor to treat the shooter."

Blackburn reached down and pulled the suspect's arms behind his back, handcuffed him, and rolled him onto his back. When the officer realized the unconscious man was bleeding heavily from the upper right portion of his chest and shoulder, he grabbed a pillow from a nearby bed and pulled the pillowcase off. After folding it several times, he applied it as a compress to the gunshot wounds. Medical personnel relieved him a minute later.

Because this was an officer-involved shooting, the case would be investigated by the Sheriff's Office, State Police, and the State's Attorney's Office. Brogan would be a primary witness to this righteous shooting. Blackburn displayed cool, unemotional courage during the entire situation. Brogan was glad he'd had the backup. Blackburn was justified in killing the man when he lunged for the rifle but had taken an action that spared the shooter's life. *Blackburn should be commended.*

When Brogan and Blackburn exited the front door of the

house, they saw the woman and child wrapped in a blanket and sitting in the rear of an ambulance while a paramedic administered care to her face.

A representative of the Department of Social Services had been summoned to the scene and was attending to the needs of the woman and child.

Brogan walked over to one of the ambulances and watched while they loaded up the injured firefighter. He knew Billy from many interactions at different crime and fire scenes over the years. The two had developed a long-standing, friendly banter over who was more important, cops or firefighters. He placed his hand on the man's shoulder and said, "How're you feeling, Billy? Paramedics say the bullet missed all the important stuff. You've lost some blood, but you'll be back dragging those hoses around before you know it."

Billy grimaced as he tried to smile. He whispered so none of the other firefighters standing nearby could hear, "Glad you were here today, Brogan."

"Yeah, I bet you are. But a state trooper saved your bacon today. Us cops appreciate what you folks do. Take care, and I'll see you soon."

Brogan gave a statement to a sheriff's office detective and touched base with a detective from the state police. He let them know he would make himself available to assist them with their shooting investigation involving the trooper.

Brogan hadn't fired his gun, hit, kicked, or killed anyone, so he was free to go. He found Blackburn and shook his hand. "Thank you, you did a great job today, and it'll be in my written reports. Call me if you need anything. Report it just the way it happened. You'll be fine."

Blackburn smiled with a simple reply, "Roger that."

7

THE AFTERMATH

Once the house was deemed secure from further shooting, the firefighters quickly entered through the rear and knocked down the hot spot of char on the floor. Fortunately, there was very little damage to the structure. The fuel for the fire had been the drapes pulled from the window. They were mostly consumed by flames. The flooring material hadn't ignited but caused most of the smoke.

Brogan retrieved his vehicle and brought it into the court. He sat and gazed out the windshield, watching the firefighters secure their gear in preparation to leave. They would return to their station with the marks of battle; one wounded man and several bullet holes adorned the right side of their truck. *Firefighters don't like dirt on their trucks; I hesitate to think about how they feel about bullet holes.*

Crime scene tape was strung around the property. Detectives and forensic investigators swarmed the area looking for evidence and documented everything with photos, diagrams, and measurements. Uniformed Officers were interviewing neighbors who stood on their lawns and driveways, gawking at the activity. A quiet neighborhood had been turned into a chaotic battlefield. A female Sheriff's detective, Deputy Sandra Dayton, joined the wife, child, and case worker from the Department of Social Services. She would probe into the history, background, and events that had led to this tragic event.

Brogan took copious, contemporaneous notes that he would use to construct a written report of his actions and the activities he'd witnessed during the shootings. He garnered the names of the shooter, Randy Long, his wife, Betsy Long, and their son, Tommy. The wounded firefighter was Billy Signmakr. The Deputy driving Car 47 was Deputy First Class Glen Beckels. The actions and interactions with Trooper Blackburn took up a large portion of his notes. Brogan gave great attention and detail to these notes as his report would be scrutinized by other police officials, attorneys, the media, and the general public who had an unquenchable thirst for blood and guts.

First, reports from paramedics said that Randy Long would probably survive his wounds, although the fate of his shoulder was very much in question. Once this was known, a few unscrupulous lawyers would beat a path to Randy Long's door, urging him to sue everyone from the governor on down in hopes of gaining financial remuneration for being a criminal. With the current state of affairs, it was even possible they would win. If they did, it wouldn't be because of anything written or left out of Brogan's report. Blackburn would be described as the hero he was.

Brogan called headquarters and spoke to Deputy Chief Trout, "I want to make sure the chief and state's attorney were updated as events unfolded at the shooting scene."

"Yes, they have, and you still need to attend the meeting in Snow Hill. The time has been moved to 3 p.m. Also, Detective Ryan briefed the chief about the body on the beach when she learned about your situation."

Brogan thought, *Nice! Patty took the initiative because I forgot. She's showing me my confidence in her isn't misplaced.*

Trooper Blackburn saw Brogan sitting in his car; he walked over and spoke to him through the open window.

"I'm glad you were here today. You can make decisions and sensible plans. It made a big difference when there was little time and no room for error."

Brogan responded, ignoring the compliment, "How're you doing, ever shot anyone before?"

"I'm fine, and yes, while I was in the Service, I shot a bunch of people. Most of them didn't make it after they were shot. I understand the need to take a life when necessary, and I'm okay with that."

"Would I be wrong if I thought you intentionally shot that guy in the shoulder today so you wouldn't have to kill him in front of his kid? You had a second chance to take him out and passed on that as well."

"Our departmental regulations direct us only to shoot when no other avenue is available, and then we should shoot to kill. Let's just say I might have to spend some extra time on the range."

"I don't believe you, but stick with your story and know you did the right thing. Sometimes, the rules don't apply in the heat of battle. The guy wouldn't have received the death penalty for what he did today, so the court will hopefully deal out appropriate justice."

Brogan felt confident. *If the first two shots into the shooter's shoulder hadn't resulted in his immediate disarming, the third shot would have punched a hole in his head. Blackburn knew exactly what he was doing.*

"Hope to see you again, and maybe we can catch a beer or a coffee down the road."

"I'd like that, thanks."

Brogan smelled of smoke, and his suit jacket laid wrinkled in the trunk of his car. With enough time before the meeting to start his day over, he drove home with the windows down in an attempt to get rid of the smell.

Brogan placed his dirty clothes in a garbage bag to prevent the smoke odors from migrating into his condo. He took a quick shower and changed into his Tom Ford pinstripe suit, white shirt, and blue tie, and was out the door with the trash bag in hand. It was headed for his trunk and eventually to the dry cleaners. Dropping into the driver's seat, he couldn't help but think: *This meeting better be important.*

8

THE MEETING

After stopping for a much-needed lunch, Brogan arrived at the State's Attorney's Office at 2:45 p.m. When he walked into the office, he was greeted by Pam Sampson, the receptionist, who maintained a smiling welcome to all those entering her domain. Behind her smile was a woman as tough as nails. "Hi, Brogan. Heard you were in a shootout this morning. Glad to see you look unblemished by the fray."

"Just a domestic that got out of hand. One of the firefighters got dinged up with a bullet in the leg, but he'll be okay when the docs patch him up. It was Billy Signmakr. He's a tough dude who'll be showing off his bullet wound in a few months. A trooper saved the day by taking down the shooter without killing him."

Brogan knew Pam would spread the word the trooper had made the right call. She'd tell the story like she'd personally been there, putting her stamp of approval on his actions. Public support would grow.

Pam maintained a vigilant screening of all visitors. Behind her were the offices of the county prosecutors, who worked day and night trying to put those most deserving in jail. These duties came with a guaranteed number of assholes who claimed wrongful prosecution. On occasion, one showed up at the office seeking to confront the prosecutor. Pam was well-schooled with both the panic button and handgun at her disposal.

"Come with me, Brogan." She led him to a large conference room down the hall. There were no windows, and the door was closed. Pam knocked, opened the door, and leaned in, "Brogan's here," she announced as she moved aside, allowing him access.

Brogan stopped short when he saw the assembled attendees. The State's Attorney, Rudy Carol, was seated near the end of the conference table. There was an empty chair to his right, and the next chair was occupied by SPPD Chief Ellwood Richards. Next was a who's who of local law enforcement in Worcester County. The Chiefs of Pocomoke City, Berlin, Snow Hill, and Tall Pines, as well as the Barrack Commander of the Berlin Barrack of the Maryland State Police (MSP) and the Sheriff of Worcester County, were all present. All eyes fixed on Brogan.

It's not my birthday, so I must've really messed up. Maybe I'm getting the boot for stirring up too much shit over the last couple of years. I'm not confessing to anything, and I know my lawyer's phone number by heart.

"Have a seat, Brogan," S.A. Carol said, pointing to the empty chair next to him. Smiling, he continued, "You've cost my office a small fortune today. This morning, I had two boxes of donuts and coffee for our meeting. You getting in a shootout, which delayed the meeting, meant I had to take all these folks out to lunch. This group was happy to get a free lunch from me, so you've upgraded your status with them a notch."

"Sorry, Rudy, shootouts trump donuts." Laughter filled the room. S.A. Carol paused and then smiled.

"Relax, Brogan, we've got a proposition that I hope you'll find interesting.

"First of all, great job on this morning's results. We were all briefed throughout the ordeal and concurred it could have turned out badly without your intervention. How's the trooper handling his role in what happened?"

Brogan turned and faced the MSP Commander and spoke directly to her, "Lieutenant, you should be very proud of Trooper Blackburn; his cool and unemotional actions were paramount to the success we achieved. I was pleased to have someone of his caliber as my backup. In my opinion, the shooting of the suspect was justified and prevented possible death or serious injury to myself and the other two civilians being held hostage. My report will reflect very highly on his performance today. He's a good man. You and the State Police are lucky to have him."

The barrack commander, Lt. Tawana Milton, nodded to Brogan and replied, "Thank you for that synopsis. I'll personally meet with him and share what you've said. I'll also ensure the shooting team is aware of your comments."

"Yes, please tell whoever is handling the shooting investigation that I'd be happy to meet with them and answer any questions they may have."

S.A. Carol regained the focus, "Moving on to the purpose of this meeting and why I called all these commanders together. For some time, this office has been monitoring an uptick in violent crimes and a parallel increase in illicit drugs on our streets. My office firmly believes this is no coincidence. While we're fortunate to have great cooperation among our law enforcement agencies, we believe there should be a tightening of the State's Attorney's Office's relationship with all the agencies by providing additional resources and coordination in the prosecution of major cases. During a major case, each agency should have equal access to the State's Attorney's Office and be able to call for legal and investigative advice as they move cases along."

Brogan nodded his head. *He's right; this would be a great enhancement to overall law enforcement.*

"I've gone to the County Executive and the Board of Commissioners and pled my case for the creation of two investigator positions in my office. They've acknowledged the need and will provide immediate funding for one position and then a second position during the next budget cycle in four months. I have a letter from both the Executive and the Board committing to their position on this request. I told them that these positions needed to be funded at a level that would draw the very best talent to help all of us succeed in fulfilling our promises to our constituents.

"I've met individually with everyone in this room and suggested that you be our first selection to fill one of these positions. Reluctantly, even Chief Richards has admitted that your talents are being under-utilized while serving just the town of Sandpiper."

Chief Richards chimed in, "Yeah, it took a lot to admit it, but Rudy is right."

Brogan leaned forward. *I don't know where this is going, but it sounds very interesting.*

"Your actions in stopping a serial murderer and the more recent human trafficking case have proven to everyone here that you'll be an added value to our crime-fighting efforts if you're free to have county-wide jurisdiction. It's important that someone from my office becomes involved in major cases as soon as they're reported. You'll not be investigating these cases, but you'll act as the eyes and ears of the state's attorney's office and a guiding hand to all the investigative units in the county. This includes our drug task force, currently led by the sheriff's office." *Damn! This is big.*

"If you agree, you'll be given the title Chief Investigator for the State's Attorney for Worcester County. You'll be provided with a car from the S.A. office and an office in the Sandpiper PD building located on the second floor near my prosecutor. Your salary will be commensurate with your title. You'll be allowed to carry your time and benefits with you to your new position. You'll remain armed as long as you qualify each year, and you'll have full arrest powers. These conditions have been discussed and approved by the county's department of human resources and the county's administrative attorney. What do you think, Brogan?"

Rarely was Brogan at a loss for words, but this was one of those times. He was flabbergasted.

"I'm flattered to be considered for such an important position, and it catches me completely off guard. It sounds like an idea that could have a great and positive impact on law enforcement in our county throughout the coming years. Would it be okay if I gave it some thought over the next day or two?"

"Of course. I know it's a lot to take in, coming out of the blue as it has. But if you look around, you'll see you have one hundred percent support from each of the leaders here. They feel that their investigators would also benefit from this arrangement. You can help the entire county if you agree to our proposal.

"Lastly, and to help you make up your mind, your proposed salary is on this slip of paper I'm giving you. I believe it's fair compensation for what's going to be asked of you. You'll be eligible for salary increases yearly with every new budget. Additionally, you'll be the final decision-maker when we hire the next investigator. When that time arrives, the new investigator will be subordinate to you, so it should be someone with whom you have personal trust and faith. I have total confidence in your ability to make the selection.

"Please call me when you've made your decision, and I'll share your answer with all those present here today."

With that, the meeting was over. The sheriff, barrack commander, and each chief approached Brogan and shook his hand, then offered sincere words of encouragement and support. Chief Richards pulled Brogan aside. "The Mayor was consulted before I made my final decision. To quote the mayor, 'Hell, he's all over the place anyway, so let the county pay for him. I know his heart will remain with Sandpiper.'"

Brogan chuckled to himself. *Yes, there's wisdom and truth in the Mayor's words.*

Richards whispered to Brogan, "If you give this a try and it doesn't work out, you've always got a place to come back to. SPPD will always need a crack investigator. And knowing you'll be just upstairs if I need an ear, I'm good with it."

9

A BIG DECISION

Brogan sat in his car for a few minutes. Still stunned by what just happened. *I need to call Kelly. What'll she think of this new opportunity? She'll support me, whatever I decide. But she thinks things out and may have questions or concerns I haven't considered. A new position will impact both of us.*

I won't soon forget this day: a body on the beach and then a tumultuous shooting and rescue operation. Now, I've been offered a life-changing opportunity that provides career growth!

I need to clear my head and think long and hard about all aspects of this new job.

Brogan pulled the folded piece of paper from his suit pocket where he'd stashed it. He slowly unfolded the paper, and his eyes grew wide. The pay increase was far more than anticipated. His decision suddenly became clearer, but he still needed to run this by Kelly.

I could retire and be comfortable in a few years. Expectations and goals will be set high, but I'm up to the challenge.

Should I call Kelly while she's visiting her mom and dad in Baltimore? Hell, yeah! This is way too important not to share right away. If the news about the shooting and hostage rescue in Worcester County made Baltimore news, she'd be blowing up my phone soon enough anyway.

Brogan hit favorites in his phone, tapped Kelly, and heard the call go through. Her voice gave him a warm feeling.

"Hey, Brogan. You missing me?"

"Yes, I'm missing you big time, but that's not the reason I'm calling right this second."

"Okay, what's going on that's more important than missing me?"

"Nothing's more important, but I need your input. I've got to make a big decision, and I want you to be part of it."

"Now you have my full attention. What's happened? I've only been gone two days."

"It's been a day! First of all, there was a body on the beach this morning, but Ryan is investigating that, then a shooting and a hostage rescue after that. I was there, but I didn't shoot anybody. A young trooper did all the shooting, and I was sort of his backup. No one was killed. A mother and her child were saved when a domestic turned terribly wrong. Oh, yeah, a firefighter got a bullet wound to the leg, and the house fire was put out before there was much damage."

"What the fuck, Brogan. Sounds like there was a war going on, and you were in the middle of it, as usual. Are you okay?"

"I'm better than okay, and that's why I'm calling you. I had a meeting today in Snow Hill and was offered a new position as Chief Investigator for the State's Attorney's Office of Worcester County. Rudy Carol offered me the job, and Chief Richards and all the other chiefs, the sheriff, and MSP barrack commander were there in full support of me assuming the new position."

"I'll fill you in on the job details when I see you. I didn't tell you the best part. It comes with a starting salary of one hundred and sixty thousand dollars.

"Brogan, this is amazing. Woo Hoo, did you tell them you'll take it?"

"My head is spinning, and I'm still bowled over by the opportunity. I asked for a couple of days to give them my decision. You're the first and only person I've told. What do you think?"

Brogan could almost see Kelly grinning through the connection.

"Wow, wow, wow! This is great, Brogan. I'm so proud of you, and this is a wonderful opportunity. I've always known you were well respected as an investigator, but this recognition is there for everyone else to see. I'm coming home tomorrow, and we can celebrate. I don't see any downsides. Tell them yes. Tell them Kelly says yes. What a hoot!"

"I thought you weren't coming home for a few more days."

"Are you kidding me? Mom and Dad will be just as excited as I am, and they'll understand I need to be with you. I love you, Brogan, and I'm so happy for you. I have to get off the phone and tell them. You deserve this. Congratulations."

Kelly ended the call. Brogan sat in his car, staring at his cell phone. *That went better than I thought.*

As Brogan had done often in his life, when he had a tough decision or wanted to think about something, he took a ride. No destination in mind. He often spent hours exploring new roads and new areas of the Eastern Shore while contemplating his next move. He dropped the gear shift into drive and began his latest drive.

10

A QUIET MEAL

Heading south from Snow Hill, he soon found himself crossing into Virginia. *This looks familiar, this is the place where I almost died. Thanks to Kelly's intervention, I survived. Now, I'm faced with a positive circumstance, and again, I called Kelly for her input. Life is full of twists and turns.*

Time had slipped away; it was 6:00 p.m., and his stomach growled, bringing him clarity. Time to get something to eat. *I need a quiet dinner and a beer.*

Brogan focused on where he was and immediately recognized he wasn't too far from a small restaurant he'd found on an earlier exploration of the area. It was family-owned, located off the main road, and depended on locals to keep its doors open. He had been surprised by the venue and the quality of the food they offered.

When he arrived, it was as he remembered, sitting at the far end of a small strip shopping center. It was called *Our Place.* Brogan's habit was to park his car away from his destination with it backed into a slot for a quick departure. Cops learn quickly that backing out of a parking space is a hazardous maneuver that is easily avoided. Police also like to have an edge wherever they go. Parking a short distance away and remaining anonymous was one of Brogan's ways to keep that edge. Even with his non-traditional vehicle, he didn't wish people to associate him with a particular car. He set the alarm and sauntered to the restaurant.

Brogan was met by a smiling young woman at the hostess stand. "Hi," he said, "I'd like a table for one."

"Of course, of course. My name is Teresa. Would you like to eat in the bar or one of our booths along the far wall?"

"May I have the last booth in the corner? I like the privacy."

"Yes, sir, you may. Please follow me." Teresa pulled a menu from a stack on top of her stand and led Brogan toward the booth.

When they arrived, Brogan slid into the seat, placing his back against a wall, which gave him a full view of the restaurant.

"Sir, Beverly will be your waitress, and she'll be with you momentarily to take your drink order while you study our menu. She'll also tell you about our specials this evening. Is there anything else?"

"No. Thank you, Theresa."

Brogan scoped the interior of the restaurant to refresh his memory from his prior visit. Low-volume music played from hidden speakers. It didn't interfere with conversations but added to the ambiance. Dishware clinked quietly at the small number of occupied tables. Brogan was the best-dressed man in the place, as most others were dressed casually. Brogan grinned. *This is a hidden gem. I remember the prices for the entrees at this little place were higher than most places, but I think it works to keep out the riff-raff and encourage a more subdued and respectful clientele. I'll be able to have a quiet dinner while considering my future.*

He was surprised there were only three tables taken and a young couple having drinks at the bar. He couldn't remember if they'd served alcohol last year, but they were serving it now.

Beverly, the waitress identified by her name tag, came and presented Brogan with a pleasant smile. "Howdy, what can I get ya to drink?"

"I was thinking about a beer. How about a Coors Light draft?"

"Yep, I can do that while you decide what you'd like to eat, I'll be right back."

True to her word, Beverly reappeared with a frosted glass of beer. She cocked her head as she said, "Make up your mind? Or would you like to hear the specials?"

"Nope, I'm good with the menu. I'll have an open-face beef sandwich with green beans and French fries, and can you smother it all in brown gravy?" *The calories in this meal are gonna add an extra mile to my run tomorrow, but this is a celebration, although a lonely one. I wish Kelly was here.*

The food arrived quickly and was served piping hot. A glass of water was placed next to his beer glass. Brogan's decision-making stress slowly lifted as he began his meal. He mulled over the new job, creating ifs and what-ifs, and quickly resolved each in his mind. *Kelly was absolutely right. This is an easy decision. Go for the gold ring when it's offered to you. I'll call Rudy tomorrow and give him a yes. I need to meet with the chief and address the selection of a new lead investigator for the P.D. Good thing I gave that body on the beach to Ryan. She might end up running the whole show. Anyway, I'll be upstairs if she needs help. Damn, things are moving fast.*

As Brogan's bill arrived at his table, he noticed the young couple at the bar paying their tab and preparing to leave. He placed cash, including a nice tip, with his bill under the edge of his plate and stood to leave.

When Brogan arrived at the front door of the restaurant, he nodded at a stocky gray-haired man standing near the end of the bar. Brogan wasn't sure, but presumed he was the manager or possibly the owner. The man nodded back and said, "Thanks for coming in."

Brogan stepped through the door, and his attention was immediately drawn to a loud female voice saying, "Darren, get off his car. What're you doing here? You know I have a restraining order out on you, and you're not supposed to get near me."

The man she was talking to was leaning against a dark blue Chevrolet four-door sedan. He had a long-neck beer bottle in his right hand and took a long pull. Brogan thought, *Who is this stringy long-haired lanky motherfucker?*

"Fuck his car and fuck your restraining order. We need to talk, and we need to talk now. Tell this fucker to take a hike. I'll take you home."

Brogan saw that it was the young couple from the restaurant, and the guy who had been with the girl was looking wide-eyed and unsure of himself.

"Who's this guy, Betty?"

"He's an asshole who thinks he owns me just because I went out with him a couple of times. He's a loser and won't leave me alone. That's why I got a restraining order against him."

"Hey buddy, can you get off my car? This is the first time I've been out with Betty, and we're not looking for any trouble."

"Yeah, well, sometimes trouble comes looking for you. Did your girlfriend tell you she's a whore?"

The young girl closed the distance between her and Darren and said, "I'm calling the cops, and you're going to jail."

"The fuck you are," Darren said as he lashed out and backhanded her across her face knocking her to the ground next to the car. Her date rushed forward and bent down to help her.

Behind him, Darren turned his back on the restaurant and raised the beer bottle intending to break it over his head.

Darren felt a searing pain in his right wrist as it was grasped and savagely twisted. Bones cracked, and tendons tore as the hand did almost a complete rotation. Brogan delivered an elbow to his temple while retaining his grip on Darren's wrist. Darren either passed out or was knocked unconscious by the blow as his legs gave way, and he hung momentarily suspended. Darren's entire weight was now hinged on his right shoulder. Brogan pointed to the sky, defying gravity, and dislocated Darren's shoulder. He then released his grip, and Darren fell to the ground and remained motionless. He wasn't dead, but the next day, he'd probably be praying to die. Between his wrist and his shoulder, he would spend the next few months in slings and casts.

Brogan turned to the girl who had been helped to her feet by her friend. "Are you okay?"

"Yes, sir, I'll be alright. Thanks for helping us." The boy stepped forward and said, "I'm Joe. I appreciate what you did for us."

Brogan noticed the old man from inside the restaurant was standing on the porch with a baseball bat at his side. "Son, I know that kid on the ground. He's a no-good son-of-a-bitch, but he's also the son of the local sheriff. I saw what you did, and he had that and a whole lot more coming to him. I'm going inside and call the state police so they can handle this. I suggest you be long gone before they get here. We got no cameras, and nobody inside saw a damn thing. I didn't see shit either."

Betty said, "Some stranger stepped up and put him down. It all happened so fast we didn't get a good look at him. We think he left in a pickup truck." Joe nodded in agreement.

Brogan gave them all a long look, turned, and walked away. When he reached his vehicle, he looked back to see they had all gone inside and left Darren lying in the parking lot.

Brogan drove north, heading home. *This has been one hell of a day. Guess I'll be scratching that restaurant off my list for the foreseeable future. Kinda' glad Kelly wasn't with me for dinner. She would've really hurt that ass-wipe.*

11

THE ANNOUNCEMENT

Brogan seemed to have a little more bounce in his step as he strolled into the Sandpiper P.D. on Tuesday morning around 10 a.m. He had been up early after a very restful sleep, a run on the beach, and a workout in his second bedroom, now converted into a mini-gym.

He grabbed the papers stacked in his mailbox in the communications room and acknowledged PCO Maggie Scott, who was working the radios. Sergeant Cramer was the Duty Officer again this morning.

"Hi, Maggie. Hi, Sarge. Everything peaceful this morning?" asked Brogan.

Before Sergeant Cramer could speak, his phone rang, and he gave it his immediate attention.

"Hey, Brogan. All quiet today, but I heard you had an eventful day yesterday with the body on the beach and then the fire and shooting. Everything worked out, so I hear. Oh yeah, Det. Ryan called in and said she was in Baltimore for the autopsy," Maggie said.

"Yeah, it was an unusual day, but it did all work out." *If she only knew about the day I had!* "Is the Chief in this morning?"

"Yes. He's in and not on his phone. Small miracle. I'll screen his calls while you meet with him."

"Thanks, Maggie." Brogan chuckled to himself and moved down the hallway to the chief's office.

Brogan tapped on the door. "Morning, Chief. Have you got a minute?"

"Yeah, sure, Brogan, come on in and grab a seat. Are you over the shock of our meeting yesterday?"

Brogan closed the door behind himself and dropped into one of the two seats in front of the chief's desk. "Chief, I've thought about the offer and discussed it last night with Kelly. She's supportive, and I've decided it's the right thing for me, so you're the first to know I'm taking the job."

"Good, Brogan, I thought once your head cleared and you'd given it some thought, you'd see the benefit to everyone if you said yes. I already spoke with Rudy this morning, and he told me that he has another car ready to be transferred into our department. And if I'm agreeable, he'd like to see you keep the car you're driving since it has the necessary radio equipment and fits with your new assignment. I gave him my thumbs up. Would you be happy with that arrangement?"

"Absolutely, Chief, I love my car and would've been sorry to give it up."

"Okay, then we're all on the same page. The next issue is who's going to take your place here at the P.D.?"

"I know this is your call, Chief, but if I was making the selection, I would promote from within and put Patty Ryan in charge. She's got the skills and demeanor to handle the job, and I believe she'd do well. I'd also suggest you promote Detective Carr to supervisor and the number two person in the criminal unit. This city is growing, and with it, so is the crime picture. We're no longer a quiet little beach town. This place has become a year-round destination and attracts more tourists and full-time residents. The Criminal Unit needs new growth and a couple more detectives selected from the uniformed ranks. I know all this comes with a price tag, but protecting and serving is what keeps the economy growing. The investment in the police department will bring untold benefits. On the Eastern Shore, people still love their police and will support this move, even if it costs them a few more cents in taxes. Everyone wants to feel safe, and our excellent reputation will bode well for the Mayor and Council if they get behind you on this stuff."

"All valid points, Brogan. I have a meeting with the mayor this afternoon and will address all your suggestions. If I can win him over, I think the city council will also support these expenditures. I'll let you know how it goes."

"I'm going to call Rudy Carol as soon as I leave your office and give him my decision. Give me a timeline I can share with him as far as my actual reassignment. What works for you? Don't forget I'll be right upstairs and will help you with whatever transition you and the mayor decide."

"I think a week or two will be enough. That'll also give you a little time to clean up or close out anything you're personally working on at this time."

With that said, Brogan stood and offered his hand across the chief's desk. The chief stood and shook Brogan's hand. "Brogan, I'm going to draft a memorandum to all our staff announcing your move and hopefully the reassignment of our investigators. It won't go out until you give me a date when you'll report upstairs and until I have something final from the mayor and city council on possible funding for promotions and transfers within the department. We have money in the budget, but things go better when everyone thinks they're in the loop. We might even hold a news conference with the S.A., mayor, and other law enforcement heads and politicians in attendance. This'll help sell it to the tax-paying public. I'm happy for you, Brogan."

Without further ado, Brogan left the chief's office and walked directly to his office to notify S.A. Carol. Brogan was on a new career path and couldn't wait to get started.

12
CLEAR CASE OF MURDER

At noon, Patty Ryan fronted Brogan's office door. Brogan looked up and waved her in and to a seat.

"Hi, Detective. How was the morgue this morning? Before you answer that, let me call the chief and have him sit in so we don't have to repeat this story twice."

Moments later, the chief came in, closed the door, and took a seat next to Ryan.

Detective Ryan referred to her notes before speaking, "This is a clear case of murder. The doctor has declared this is a homicide, and the cause of death could be either blunt force trauma or blood loss by the severing of the hands. Both actions are clearly intentional and would've resulted in death. The victim was severely beaten about the head and shoulders. He had a fractured skull in multiple places, crushed bones on both sides of his face, including a fractured jaw.

"The fractured skull and brain hemorrhaging may've caused his death, but the hands were cut off while he was still alive, and that would've resulted in massive and immediate blood loss sufficient to have killed him.

"His wounds to the head and face were caused by multiple

instruments, including fists and other weapons that may have been a bat or a round pipe at least four inches in circumference. The hands were cut off using a very sharp single-blade instrument such as an axe, hatchet, or meat cleaver.

"I photographed everything, including the clothes, which have been forwarded to the forensic lab for further examination. He had nothing in his pockets or any identifiable labels sewn to his clothing. The jeans he was wearing were Levi's, and his shirt was Under Armour. His underwear was Kirkland brand from the Costco box store. All his clothing was size large, and his waist was thirty-six inches. There was no belt, shoes, or socks on the body. The deceased is six foot even and weighs one hundred and eighty-five pounds. His hair is naturally brown. His eyes are brown, and he has no surgical marks or tattoos to help us with making an identification. The Doctor estimated his age to be between twenty and thirty.

"X-rays did show the deceased had a broken left arm sometime earlier in his life. The break definitely received medical attention as it had been set and healed nicely and completely. We'll probably have to use DNA or dental records to make a positive I.D. Dental records will be iffy as he's missing a lot of his teeth due to his injuries. Facial recognition by relatives or friends is not recommended, as he's been rendered nearly unrecognizable due to the beating and time in the water. They estimate he'd been in the water four to seven days. He didn't drown; he was dead when he hit the water."

Brogan looked at the chief and said, "What did I tell you?"

He then turned to Patty Ryan and said, "Well done and very thorough. What's your plan?"

Ryan thought, *Not sure what the comment to the chief was all about.*

Ryan laid out her plan. "Detective Carr is pulling all the missing persons' reports in Worcester, Wicomico, and Somerset Counties looking for possible matches. We'll check each of them out, comparing physical descriptions and other known information against our John Doe. If we don't find a match, we'll expand our search to other jurisdictions.

"We'll provide information to the media in regards to an unidentified body that was found on the beach. We'll hold back at this time that it was a homicide and the nature of the injuries. The kids who found the body are back in Baltimore, so I doubt they'll be sharing what they saw with anyone down here. We'll release vague information about the body, describing it only as a male with brown hair between twenty and thirty years old. This'll help weed out tips that'll waste our time.

"The medical examiner's office will let us know if any evidence is found on the clothing and the results of blood tests and further testing regarding drug consumption prior to death.

"It's expensive, but we can also request facial reconstruction to get a better idea of what this guy looked like before he was attacked. Several questions are nagging me already. How'd he get in the water? Why cut his hands off? Slow down identification or sending a message?

"We'll also coordinate and share our findings with the other criminal units in and around the county. We'll hold back just enough so that only the perpetrator would know certain information.

"Any other suggestions, Lieutenant? Chief?"

Brogan answered, "No, not at the moment. Let's see where your plan takes us and reconvene every afternoon at 3 p.m.

for updates and to tweak our plans. If you need manpower or other resources, let me know."

The chief added, "No, Detective. I have nothing. If you need me for anything, don't hesitate to come in and see me. Especially if Brogan's not around and you need an answer right away."

"Ryan, I know this is an important case, but don't forget to get some rest. A rested mind is sharper and less likely to miss something. I know because I don't follow my advice, and it gets me into trouble from time to time," Brogan commented.

Detective Ryan left the office, and the chief turned to Brogan and whispered, "I'm impressed. She may be just the person to take your place."

"Wow, it didn't take you long to find my replacement!"

The chief laughed as he went back to his office.

Brogan looked at his watch. *I suspect Kelly will be blowing into town soon, and she'll be all fired up and ready to celebrate. I think I'm ready, too. Maybe a nice dinner and some together time to lay out our plan.*

Brogan glanced at his watch again and then returned to his pile of paperwork, hoping to clear his desk before she called.

13

A DISTANT DANGER

Two weeks earlier, twenty-five hundred miles away and south of the U.S. Border...

The small cantina sat near the edge of town if you could call it a town. The cantina, a gas station, a small market, and a wooden church made up the heart and soul of this Mexican community. The main street remained a dirt road. Not much had changed here in the last fifty years.

It was 10 a.m. The cantina opened at 2 p.m., but for certain people, it was always open. Five of those people sat at a round table near the back of the building. Dust mites floated through the sunlit air from a few dirty windows. Even the light above the table was dim. The furniture was old, and the short bar was scarred with cigarette burns and years of abuse. The bartender, a short, rotund man with a quick smile that revealed smoke-stained teeth, brought a pot of coffee to the table with five mugs of varying shapes and sizes. He had been told there would be no alcohol served to these customers. He then immediately retreated from the cantina, locking the door on his way out.

The five people were members of the Calupoh Cartel. The name came from a Mexican Wolfdog known to be fierce and loyal to his pack. These cartel members lived by that code.

Four of them had been summoned to this meeting by The Boss, a nickname he earned when he killed a cartel boss in a bare-knuckle fight. The name his mother gave him was Julian Lopez, and he was a cartel sicario, an assassin who was moving up through the ranks.

The boss rapped his knuckles on the table just once and immediately had the group's full attention.

The boss spoke English clearly and decisively. "You've been selected for a special cartel mission. From this point forward, we'll only speak English, which is one of the reasons you've all been selected. You may recognize each other but may not know each other's story.

"Next to me, on my right, this dark-haired beauty is Ana Gomez. She's earned her seat at the table for killing two men who killed her boyfriend, who was also a cartel member. The killers were caught by other cartel members, brought to a warehouse, tied to chairs, beaten, and sentenced to death by cartel leadership.

"When I notified Ana, she asked me to take her to see these two men. When she confronted them, she calmly asked me to give her my gun.

"After I handed her the gun and without another word, she placed the barrel to the head of each man and blew their brains out. As you can see, she's beautiful, capable, and can be extremely violent when necessary."

The group looked at Ana and nodded in approval.

"Next to her is Diego Perez. This ruggedly built guy is good with his hands, a knife, or a gun. Diego follows orders without question and will die before surrendering. If Diego has your six, you never have to turn around.

"Next to him is Tomas Castillo. This unassuming guy is an expert in damaging any organization's communications or computer systems. He can bug a room, office, or car. He's proficient with tracking devices and other electronic gear, including small surveillance drones. He's fiercely loyal to the cartel."

Tomas grinned and gave a slight nod to the others.

"And the final person at the table is Sophia Garcia, better known as Razor. Don't let the appearance of this young woman fool you. The top of a straight-edge razor peeking out of her hip pocket earned her the nickname Razor, and nobody fucks with her."

Razor had a hatred of men that came from her dear and departed uncle, who brutally raped her after luring her to his small house in Texas when she was sixteen years old. She escaped his clutches just long enough to retreat into a bathroom, locking the door behind her. With no window for escape, she stood her ground with a straight-edge razor she found in the medicine cabinet. When he broke down the door, she wheeled the razor like something out of a horror flick. When she stopped swinging, her uncle lay dead at her feet. She drove herself away from the murder scene in her uncle's pickup truck while his shanty home burned fiercely in the rearview mirror.

When Sophia got home, she told her mother what happened. Sophia's mother cried out a confession that she had suffered similar behavior from her brother when she was a teenager. Her mother immediately contacted her sister living in Mexico and sent Sophia out of the country to avoid possible punishment.

Sophia lived with her aunt but found a home in the local cartel. Sophia found a certain amount of personal safety by portraying a masculine female. She sat straight in her chair with her eyes locked on the boss.

14

Cartel Business

The boss spoke, "When you leave here, you're to go wherever you're staying and pack a small bag with only your basic needs. If there's anything sentimental to you, you need to take it because you won't be coming back. Tell no one that you're leaving.

"The second reason you were chosen. None of you have ties to any people or any place here in Mexico. No one will care or miss you enough to ask questions about your absence."

The group looked at each other and nodded in agreement.

"You each possess skills and talents that'll be needed for the work we're about to do.

"Tomorrow morning, we'll begin a journey that'll take us across the border into the United States. I'll have passports, driver's licenses, and green cards for each of you that'll have your picture, real names, and personal information on them. The fact that none of you have ever been arrested in the United States is another reason you were selected. The cartel has paid one of our contacts here to scrub any criminal record you may have in Mexico.

"Do not carry any weapons with you for this trip. Everything needed will be given to us once we're across the border. Destroy your cell phones. You'll be given new burner phones. After we cross the border, you're to have absolutely no contact with anyone in Mexico. The only phone numbers in your burner phones will be for the members of this team and no one else.

"I can tell you nothing else at this time. This is important cartel business, and you'll have to trust me that all will be explained once we're in the U.S.

"If you have any questions, you need to ask them now. There'll absolutely be elements of danger during this assignment, but each of you has shown fear of danger is not in your makeup. Your loyalty to the cartel has always been unquestionable."

The crew sat up a little straighter in their chairs.

"I have personally selected each of you. From now on, you'll call me Julian. I'll be calling the shots, but I'm no longer the boss. We'll be a team, and I'll be a team member."

Julian looked at each member of his team, ready to field questions or concerns. There were none.

"Meet me back here tomorrow at 7:00 a.m. There'll be a van to take us North. If you bring a vehicle, leave the keys on the front floorboard. It'll be taken after we leave. You'll never see it again, but you'll be reimbursed for your loss."

Two days later, the team crossed the border by walking into the United States at the crossing in El Paso, Texas.

They staggered their entry and met at a predesignated spot just across the border. Once again, a nondescript van picked them up and took them to an auto body shop on the north side of El Paso.

At the body shop, Julian spoke with a Hispanic male in coveralls. The man gave Julian four sets of keys. Two sets fit a one-year-old white Chevrolet van that had a few dings and small dents but was otherwise clean and fully fueled with less than twenty thousand miles on it. The second set of keys was to a two-year-old Toyota four-door sedan. It was beige, clean, fully fueled, and also had less than twenty thousand miles on it.

While the vehicles were being checked out, Razor excused herself to use the restroom. Inside a stall, she lowered her trousers and underwear and retrieved her straight-edge razor wrapped in a condom and concealed inside her vagina. She slipped it into her hip pocket. *No weapons, but this is a personal item I couldn't leave behind.*

The Hispanic man was heard telling Julian, "All your requested supplies are hidden in storage boxes in the back of the van."

The team gathered in the lot behind the body shop, and Julian said, "Ana and Razor ride with me. Diego and Tomas follow in the Toyota."

The entire team assembled in the van, where guns and burner phones were distributed from the storage boxes.

Julian pulled packets of money from the boxes and gave each member a packet. "Here's ten thousand dollars each. Pay for everything in cash so our journey can't be tracked. Use your cell phone to call me only if there's an emergency. Diego, I'm going to give you the name of the city where we're going so you can enter it into your GPS. I'll give you the exact address only when we arrive in the city. Do the speed limit or just under. Don't attract attention or the police. If you're stopped, the credentials you've been given should get you through. Give us at least a fifteen-minute head start. We shouldn't see each other until we arrive in four or five days. I'll call you when we're stopping to eat, rest, or to stay somewhere for the night. We'll not be seen together or stay at the same place during our trip.

"Listen up. We're here on cartel business. We're going to set up a foothold in an area for a new distribution center for the cartel. We'll establish new delivery routes and disrupt and destroy any other drug gangs in that area. We'll take over. I know there're only five of us, but we'll remove the leaders of these local drug gangs with such violence that it'll scare compliance from the street dealers.

"I've never heard of this place, but our destination is called Sandpiper, Maryland. It's a beach resort with thousands of tourists and hundreds of bars. The perfect location to distribute product.

"The place where we'll stay and the delivery of the product have already been arranged. We'll use the cover of being painters and house cleaners when we arrive. We have magnetic signage for the van to use to blend in. Maryland tags will be there to put on these vehicles. The tags will be clean and match the VIN numbers of our van and car.

"Any questions? If not, I'll see you at the beach! Good luck." Julian smiled and entered the driver's seat of the van. The women jumped in, with Ana sitting shotgun and Razor grabbing a place on a removable bench seat behind the driver and passenger.

The van pulled out on a street heading east and out of El Paso. Ana set the GPS for a place called Sandpiper.

15

CELEBRATION

Brogan glanced at his watch and noted it was 4:30 p.m. before picking up his desk phone. “Brogan.”

“Hey boyfriend, guess who’s back in town?” Kelly’s excitement carried down the phone line. “When does the celebration start?”

“I’ve been waiting for you!”

“Wait no longer. I just dragged my stuff in from the car, and I’m jumping in the shower. I’ll be clean in about fifteen minutes. Why don’t you come over to the house, and you can tell me all about what’s been going on, and then we can go out and grab a bite to eat? Does your new job pay enough to take a girl out for food?”

“Yes, it does. You can supersize your fries and drink at McDonald’s.”

“Funny, man. Come on over and let yourself in. Duncan, the dog has been walked, so don’t let him trick you into letting him go outside again. He’s learned an obedient return after every outing in the yard earns him a treat. Now, he wants to go out every fifteen minutes just for the treat. Can’t wait to see you. If you leave the office now, I may just be coming out of the shower!"

"Now you're trying to get me to speed and break the law. Not a good thing to do for a guy in my position."

"I think I can offer you a better position. See you in a few." She hung up before he could respond.

Brogan wasted no time locking up his desk and heading out the door. He had worked well over eight hours yesterday, so he thought he owed it to himself to trim a little time off this workday. Besides, he was only a phone call away from being back on the clock.

Arriving at Kelly's house, he opened the door with his key and was met by the ever-excited Duncan, who was only too happy to bounce alongside Brogan as he followed the hallway towards Kelly's bedroom and bath.

The bedroom door was open, but the bathroom door was closed. Brogan yelled out a warning, "Man in the house."

There was no verbal response, but the bathroom door swung open, and Kelly stood there dressed as she had been at the time of her birth. Her hair had already been dried and styled, so she was not surprised by his presence. Brogan, on the other hand, was speechless but appreciative of the view.

They met with a long embrace and a deep kiss. Brogan turned her slightly and pushed her down on the bed. The celebration had officially started.

Duncan lay quietly on the floor at the foot of Kelly's bed. He had been taught not to jump on the bed when other people were already jumping on it.

After the initial celebration, Kelly and Brogan showered again and dressed casually for dinner. Brogan now maintained a couple of changes of clothing in Kelly's closet for emergencies.

They went to a restaurant called Liquid Gold and had a wonderful meal while tucked away in a corner that provided privacy. Brogan brought her up-to-date on the murder and the promotion.

"My god, Brogan, this is such wonderful news. Are you as happy as I am?"

"Yes. This is the chance of a lifetime to fulfill my ambition to make a real difference. I can't wait to get started. With Patty Ryan handling the murder, I'll have time to find out what the rest of the Agencies are up to. But as far as I know, the County has been very quiet, excluding the little shoot-out and house fire, which is, for all intents and purposes, a closed case." *It would be nice if the county was quiet for a while so I can get my feet on the ground. Nothing on the horizon that I'm aware of, so the timing is perfect. Keeping my fingers crossed. Maybe I'll be lucky. Unfortunately, good luck has always been elusive for me!*

16

Just a Note

The next morning, Brogan arrived at the P.D. at 9 a.m. A different sergeant manned the duty officer's desk. Sergeant Rodney "Eagle" Millstone sat straight in his chair. His uniform was clean and pressed to perfection. The nickname, Eagle, was derived from his shiny bald head. His self-deprecating humor made him a person you just loved to be around.

"Good morning, Eagle. Anything shaking this morning?"

"Hey, Brogan. I was shaking a little this morning, but this coffee and a donut have calmed me down. Oh, I got something for you."

Brogan looked curiously at the sergeant as he opened the top left desk drawer, retrieved a white business envelope, and handed it to him.

"What's this?"

"Not sure. A woman stopped by about a half hour ago and said she wanted you to have this. She said her name was Betsy Long, and you helped her and would know who she was."

Brogan recognized the name immediately. *That's the woman from the shooting. I still see her in a torn nightgown, pressed against the wall, trying to protect her son. I wonder what this is about.*

"What did she look like, Sarge?"

Millstone described her to a T and smiled widely as he continued by saying, "I had her show me her driver's license before I agreed to give you the envelope."

"Good move, Eagle. Nothing gets by you."

Brogan took the envelope and moved toward his office. He squared the envelope on his bare desktop. When he took it from Sergeant Millstone, he could tell by the weight and feel of it that it contained more than just paper. Had it been left anonymously, Brogan would have considered the possibility of a threat. *I have no idea what Betsy Long has left for me.*

Brogan removed a thin silver letter opener from his desk and ran it down the top seam of the envelope. He widened the envelope with two fingers and slid the paper out. When he did, a coin slipped from the folded paper, rolled around, and came to a noisy stop on the wooden finish of the desk. Brogan picked up the coin and examined it. It was about the size of a quarter and looked to be very old. The imprinted image was difficult to distinguish, but the printed words were definitely not English.

Brogan knew nothing about coins beyond those he carried in his pocket from time to time. His knowledge of foreign script was even more limited. He set the coin aside and unfolded the single sheet of paper.

Detective Brogan,

Thank you for saving my life and that of my son, Tommy. I truly believe Randy was going to kill us. I have decided I cannot stay here. Eventually, Randy will get out of jail, and he will come looking for us. I can't allow him to find us.

I'm going to stay with my sister in Oregon. She says she has room for us and will help me find a job and start a new life. Randy hates her and the positive influence she has on me. He never cared where she lived or what she did. I now consider that a blessing.

Randy was not always like this. Several months ago, he lost his job and became depressed. He started drinking and hanging with a rough group of guys. He'd come home late, drunk, wanting sex, and threatening both Tommy and me. Then he started hitting me when I didn't move fast enough or when I did anything he found objectionable. Of course, he would always apologize and say he was sorry when he awoke sober in the morning, but the pattern continued to worsen.

Three days ago, he came home drunk but all excited, saying we were going to be okay and he would soon have enough money to fix all our problems. That night, he gave me this coin. He said I was never to show it to anyone else or tell them about its existence. Apologetic again, he said I could have it made into a necklace after the secret got out. He would not tell me what the secret was or how he had obtained the coin. Like I said, he was drunk, and I thought he was full of shit, and this was just another one of his delusions while he was stoned.

I don't want this coin. I feel it's connected to something evil, perhaps a theft or some other criminal act. You are the only person I trust right now, and I'm giving you the coin so you might check it out. If it's nothing, I'm sorry for wasting your time, but deep down, I sense there is something wrong.

I'm ending my note with a phone number where I can be reached if you need me for court. I would be afraid, but I will come back alone if needed. I owe you that and so much more.

Betsy Long
438-555-9837

Brogan picked up the coin again and studied it closely. *Maybe this is connected to a crime. I'll show this to Stanley Berman; he's crazy about collecting coins and currency. I'll at least know something before I share it with the Sheriff's Office Investigators handling the shooting and fire. I doubt this is involved with that situation, but I bet it's involved with some wrongdoing.*

Brogan slipped the note and coin back in its envelope, taped it shut, and slid it inside his jacket pocket. He searched the contacts in his phone for Berman's number. He found it and punched in the call. As the phone rang on the other end, Brogan reminisced about how the two men had come to know each other.

17

A Coin Expert

Brogan met Stanley Berman shortly after Brogan had arrived in Sandpiper. The tall, thin man, wearing dark-rimmed glasses and clothing that looked well cared for but not normal beachwear, had wandered, seemingly lost, inside Jack's Restaurant, looking for a place to sit down. Somehow, he had gotten by the hostess stand and was attempting to seat himself. It is not an easy task at Jack's at 7:30 a.m. That morning, Brogan was seated by himself at a table for two, and the two locked eyes momentarily. Brogan, in a rare moment of fellowship, waved him over and said, "Need a place to sit?"

"Yeah, I've never been here before, but it must be something based on this crowd."

"If you want, you can join me. I just ordered, so I'll get the server to come back for your order."

"Wow, that'd be great if you don't mind. Extending his hand, I'm Stanley Berman."

"Glad to meet you, Stanley. I'm Brogan."

Once seated and their food orders placed, Brogan quickly began vetting his new acquaintance.

"Where you from, Stanley?"

"My wife, two kids, and I just moved here from Pittsburg. We were looking for better schools and a safer environment to raise our kids. I'm a CPA. The company I work for allows me to work from home and live pretty much anywhere I want. Beverly and I love the beach, so here we are. By the way, is Brogan your first name?"

"No, it's my last, but that's what everybody calls me. I'm a Detective with the police department here. You're not a wanted fugitive, are you?" Brogan asked jokingly.

"Not hardly. I get nervous when I see a police officer in my rearview mirror. You may be the first officer I've ever really talked to and, for sure, the only one I've ever dined with."

After their slightly awkward introduction, the conversation moved along smoothly. Stanley had revealed far more of his life than Brogan.

"As an accountant, I have a love for numbers and, by extension, a healthy interest in money. I've turned my career and personal interest into a hobby that occupies most of my free time. I'm a numismatist, collecting rare coins and currency. I have a small following of fellow collectors who seek my counsel on rare and ancient monies.

After breakfast, the men shook hands and agreed that it had been a fortunate circumstance that brought them together. They exchanged business cards and vowed to reach out if a need ever arose. Brogan had seen Stanley and his family once or twice since then, only to wave or say hi. Stanley had introduced Brogan to his wife and children. Both kids were now about eight or nine. This was the first time one of them had reached out.

After a brief conversation with Stanley, Brogan drove to Berman's house located just outside of Sandpiper. He parked in front of the small three-bedroom cottage with an attached garage. Brogan had never been there before and found Stanley home alone.

He met Brogan at the front door, "Come on in, let me show you my workshop."

Stanley led him through a very neat house. Brogan suspected that Stanley had done a quick pick-up before he got there.

"Brogan, this door cost me a fortune, but it's protecting a fortune, so it was worth it."

The door leading off the kitchen had an alarmed keypad lock. Stanley turned his back on Brogan, concealing the pad as he entered the code, and then pushed the door inward.

"Welcome to the Vault, Brogan!"

As Brogan passed through the door, he pushed it with his hand and felt its enormous weight.

"Steel, reinforced?" Brogan asked.

Stanley nodded enthusiastically.

Brogan *did* feel like he was entering a vault.

"I've had the garage completely retrofitted into a windowless safe. Only this interior door allows entrance and exit. I installed special interior lights that make it well-lighted, and the ventilation system I built keeps the room cool and dry. I've fortified the entire room and soundproofed all the surfaces."

Three large safes occupied a single wall. Brogan said,

"This is Worcester County, and those would normally be full of guns and ammo. What do you have in your safes?"

"My safes contain money of all denominations. Hundreds of items are housed here. Most are old, and all are rare, some coming from the early U.S. Colonial days. Some British coins from the same era are present. I have other foreign coins and currency stored here. Each item is sealed or protected in plastic with written information about each item detailing what it is, where it came from, and any known history the item brought with it. The other shelves hold my library of books about coins and currency. My long countertop has additional lighting and several microscopes and other devices I use for cleaning and examining currency and coins. This is my special space, and I've allowed very few visitors since its inception. Sorry, my counter-height rolling stool and one folding chair provide the only available seating."

"I'm completely blown away, Stanley. I pictured you as just a hobbyist with a small collection. You've every right to be very proud of what you've accomplished here. I think I've brought my mystery to the right place."

"What'd you bring me, Brogan? You didn't say, but I figured it must be something in my field of expertise."

"It's an old coin. Foreign, I'm pretty sure, beyond that, I don't know what it is."

Brogan fished a coin envelope out of a larger police department property envelope. Attached to the larger envelope was a Property Form listing Betsy Long as the person who brought it to Sandpiper P.D. Brogan had listed her local address on the form, and in the place for a phone number he had written, *See Brogan.*

An additional note was fastened to the envelope stating

if anyone asked about this item or tried to claim ownership, Brogan was to be notified immediately, and only he could release the contents. The description of the item was intentionally vague. It said, *Old Coin.*

Stanley laid a soft piece of cloth near one of the microscopes and watched as Brogan let the coin slip from the small envelope onto the cloth. Stanley leaned in close and asked Brogan, "May I touch it?"

"Of course. I touched it, and it appears it may've been touched a lot over its lifetime."

Stanley donned a pair of white cotton gloves. He picked up the coin and turned it over several times while looking at it with his naked eye. He then inserted a jeweler's loop in his eye and repeated the procedure while saying nothing. He then slid it onto a special tray, slid it under the microscope, and examined both sides.

Stanley straightened, never taking his eyes off the coin. "Where'd you get this coin?"

"I'm not at liberty to say at this time. Is it special or valuable?"

"Brogan, I think it's both. Let me check something in one of my books before I say more."

Stanley moved directly to a hardbound book on his shelf and thumbed through the pages before he stopped and laid the book on the counter, focusing on a picture with writing beneath it. He laid the coin on the book next to the picture, and a wide smile creased his face. He looked like a kid on his first trip to a candy store.

"What you have here is a Spanish coin dating back to the 1400s. I've never seen one like this before, and the book says there're only a few known to exist. This is a Spanish Reale; it's from the reign of Ferdinand and Isabella. It's part of the first mint, and there was a small error on the back of the coin. It was believed only a few got out of the Mint before the error was found, and all were recalled. Those recalled were melted down and re-minted. All the known coins like this are in museums in Spain or private collections, also in Spain. This coin is incredible and will be more so if it is professionally cleaned. It was minted from gold and silver. From the patina, I would say this coin has been in the water since the day it was lost. Even in this condition, I would value it in the thousands of dollars because it's so rare. A Spanish collector of coins may pay in the tens of thousands. What's it doing in Sandpiper?"

"I wish I knew Stanley. If I find out, I'll share the information with you for helping me today. The next thing I'll tell you will be hard to understand. You can't tell anybody about it. At least not now, and maybe never. Can you live with that?"

"I assume this is a police matter, and you have your reasons for secrecy, but I must confess that this find will be of National importance when and if you're able to share the information."

"I promise that when I can, you'll get the story first, and I may even be able to introduce you to the owner. That's the best I can do."

"I'm honored that you brought it to me. My lips are sealed, but when you leave here, please keep in mind if one was found, there may be more. If people find out where this coin was found, there'll be a rush of people to that location, hoping to find more. Fortunes have been made on less historical finds. Not everyone who looks for these sorts of relics is honest and trustworthy, so be guarded when sharing this information. Oh, and just so you know. I'm well aware I'm in Worcester County. I keep a gun in my special room and a small safe in my bedroom that houses a similar weapon. My wife and I practice with both, and we're pretty good."

"Stanley, you're talking to a second amendment advocate. I support a well-armed citizenry. I would've been disappointed if you had told me otherwise."

As Brogan climbed back in his car, he laid the property envelope on his front seat. *Now, I not only have a riddle but one that may bring more danger to Worcester County. I need to get with the Sheriff's Office Detective in charge of this case and interview Randy Long sooner rather than later.*

18

Solving the Problem

West Sandpiper ...

Two men sat huddled at a small table inside the deckhouse of the fishing trawler *Bloody Bucket.* The trawler was tied to the pier but rocked gently with the prevailing breeze, pulling insistently at the lines.

The owner and captain, Tony Plummer, said, "We still have a problem. Our attempt to protect our secret hasn't been conclusive. What do you suggest?"

The First mate, Donnie Blankenship, responded, "We both thought that Carl was the leak. He denied it over and over again despite what we put him through. It now appears he was telling the truth. No one would allow you to cut off their hands without changing their story. Even if he'd made up a lie, I could've understood it, but he insisted he'd told no one and didn't have the missing coin. Maybe he thought we were bluffing until it was too late. Fucking ocean even worked against us. He should've been swept out to sea, but no, he gets caught in a current that dumps him right on the beach."

"Donnie, there's only one other person who may've stolen our coin. He and Carl were tight, and Carl may've been trying to protect his friend. We ain't seen him since the discovery. Do you know where he is or why he stopped coming around looking for work?"

"Captain, I heard he got drunk, which is nothing new, but he got drunk and beat up his wife and set his own house on fire. The cops and fire department showed up, and the asshole got a rifle and shot one of the firefighters. A couple of cops snuck up and got the drop on him. He tried to shoot them, but they shot him first, and he's in critical but stable condition at the hospital. They operated on him, but he's in bad shape and may need another surgery."

"Jesus Christ, this is a disaster. Now we've got a guy who's all drugged up and could be saying anything to anybody. Even if he's not talking, he's definitely going to jail, and then he'll do anything to catch a break. Are the cops guarding him? Can you get in there to talk to him? Maybe tell him what happened to Carl and put the fear of God in him?"

"He's so fucked up they haven't even charged him with anything yet. No one's guarding him because he's not going anywhere unless he's carried out of there. The sheriff is probably figuring he'll save money by not having one of his people sitting around with a guy who can't even get out of bed. An old lady, who's a volunteer there, said he can't even talk to anyone because he is so drugged up."

"Donnie, maybe we should go talk to the wife and see what she has to say about this. Maybe he talked to her about the coin. He's always drunk or on his way to being drunk, so he may have confided in her."

"I'm way ahead of you on that, Captain. I went by his house

last night. There was no car or lights, so I jimmied the back door and took a look around. I found a note on the kitchen table addressed to Randy from Betty. It said she was leaving and taking their son with her and not coming back and asked him not to try to find her. There was some other bullshit in the note, but that was the gist of it. I turned the house upside down, but no coin or information about where she may've gone. No cell phone bills or anything that might help us find her. She's in the wind."

"All I know is we had eleven coins, and now we have ten. I know you, and I didn't take it, and it ain't lost. That fucking Randy is the only other person who was on this boat after we made the find. Donnie, go wake him up and talk to him."

"I'll take care of this. I just hope he wasn't stupid enough to have been carrying the coin in his pocket when he was arrested. Shit, for all we know, the police may have the coin and not know the significance of it. Let me deal with Randy first, then we'll plan our next step."

The captain nodded his agreement.

The First mate stood and exited the cabin, grabbing his floppy hat as he went. He pulled it down low. Once on the pier, he pulled his dark sunglasses from his pocket and covered his eyes. At sixty-five years old, his gait was a little unsteady after a lifetime of boats and hard work. His body was beginning to fail, but his thinking was clear and focused. *This is the biggest thing that ever happened in my life. I'm not gonna let a couple of assholes steal this chance away from me. I've never even thought of being rich, but now all that's about to change. Randy better have the right answers to my questions.*

19

OUR TURF

His cigarette smoke hung in the air, making it difficult for him to catch his breath. Sweat rolled down his chest and onto his washboard abs. Willy Spears had lost a half step over the last year, and he knew it. He'd turned thirty and was very aware that in his chosen career field, thirty was thought to be ancient.

He couldn't remember her name, but he couldn't forget how she had responded to his every need last night. Willy blamed it on the coke she had snorted before, during, and after.

The blonde-haired girl stirred as the sunlight coming through the bedroom window illuminated her face. Daylight made her look much younger than Willy remembered from the night before. That was the trouble with coke-whores. They were starting younger and younger. They also learned quickly how their body could be sold or traded for drugs.

She stretched without opening her eyes. Her nude body was magnificent. She possessed flawless skin, which belonged only to the young. This girl was definitely jailbait, but Willy never sweated the small shit. If she continued on her current journey, the drugs would soon take her youthful looks away.

Willy butted out his cigarette, "Hey girl, you gotta get your ass up and out of here. I got shit to do and don't have any more time for your nonsense."

She pouted her lips and seductively said, "Oh, come on, Willy, you know we had a good time last night. You were so hard. How about we just hang out today and get high? You know I'll do anything you like."

Willy thought to himself, *An hour from now, she'll be gone, and I'll never see her again.*

A perk of being the head of the Eastern Shore drug scene was a guaranteed endless supply of beautiful women who would do anything to be near him. Willy never sexually disappointed the ladies, but this little piece of trim had truly worn him out, and he was now sucking wind.

It was after 11:00 a.m. when Willy finally found himself showered and dressed for the new day. He'd given the girl a bag of dope and sent her on her way.

Willy was very comfortable in his current position in the drug community. Over the years, there had been a few skirmishes with other local boys who were looking to move up or move in. He'd made it a point to nip those attempts in the bud. People had died, and examples had been made.

Currently, things on the eastern shore were running smoothly, and both the product and the money were flowing. His organization was similar to a military operation. Each of the eight counties had a sergeant. Four of the sergeants reported to one lieutenant, and the other sergeants reported to the other second lieutenant. Both lieutenants reported directly to Willy.

Willy's personal protection was provided by Latasha Brinks, his driver, who had been with him from the beginning.

She was 5'10" and 140 lbs. of muscle and grit. She lived in a guest house on his property, so he could push a panic button to summon her if he needed her intervention.

Before coming to Willy, she had served two tours of duty in the Iraq war. She had seen death, and she had caused death. Willy paid her well, and she was worth every penny. During the few times she needed time off, one of Willy's lieutenants would fill in. Both of them were also very competent and trustworthy.

Willy had drug sources in Washington, Baltimore, Philadelphia, and even New York. Fentanyl, Heroin, and Cocaine had become the most sought-after drugs on the shore. Pharmaceuticals and Fentanyl-laced marijuana rounded out a very active and lucrative drug scene.

Nobody would fuck with Willy's turf. He was the big man in this small community. He picked up his cell phone and made a call, "Latisha, I need to get up out of here in about fifteen minutes."

"I'll be out front when you're ready to roll."

When Willy strolled out his door, his black Mercedes sedan sat idling at the curb. He wore gold chains, an oversized watch trimmed in diamonds, and was dressed to the T. He was the role model for many young men who wanted to be like him and have what he had.

As Latisha and Willy waited at a red light to get onto Route 50, a white van rolled through the intersection headed toward Sandpiper. Willy glimpsed a dark-haired beauty checking out his ride. Willy grinned to himself. *I'd like to get some of that ass!*

Looks like a fucking hustler to me, Ana thought as she turned her attention back toward her destination. *Maybe I'll see him again somewhere soon.*

20

MURDER UPDATE

Brogan hadn't gotten out of his coin expert's neighborhood before his cell phone rang. He answered, "Brogan."

"Brogan, this is Patty Ryan. I thought I'd catch you up on the body under the pier. Det. Carr developed two possible leads from his search for missing persons. Both were locals and had been reported by family members.

"The first guy was from the Tall Pines community, but we were able to discount him when we learned he was six foot six inches tall. Too tall for our John Doe.

"We're on our way to meet the family of the second guy. Their description over the phone is closer to what we have, but still too general to be sure of anything. His name is Carl Andrews. He's twenty-seven years old, white, dark hair, and has no known scars, marks, or tattoos. Their last contact with him is consistent with our timeline for the body being in the water.

"Here's the most promising part. He has no steady job but did some bartending and occasionally hired out on local fishing boats to earn money.

"His mother and uncle are waiting to meet us at his mother's house in Berlin. They say they have some recent photographs of him they'll give to us. I haven't shared our suspicions with them. No use getting them upset unnecessarily. Somebody told them about a body on the beach, so they're already thinking the worst. If we hit pay dirt, I'll give you a call."

"Thanks, Patty. Yeah, please let me know. If this is our guy, we should be able to get a pretty quick positive I.D. Have you asked them about a broken bone in his left arm?"

"No, I was holding that back and was going to ask them if he'd ever had any special dental work or broken bones and see what they say."

"Good idea. Let me know." Brogan disconnected the call. *This might be the opening we need to get this investigation started. If this is the victim, we'll start tracking all aspects of his life before he went missing. It'll be easier if he's a local boy.*

In another part of town, the stainless-steel doors slid soundlessly apart. A black cane was the first thing to exit the elevator, followed closely by an older gentleman shuffling forward with his head down and carefully watching his foot placement. A brown strap hung over his right shoulder, supporting the weight of the bag on his left hip. A single plastic tube providing oxygen snaked from the bag up the side of the old man's chest, separated at his neck, circled his ears, and met under his nose. A fuzzy gray beard and a floppy hat concealed the rest of his facial features.

His slow but steady pace drew no particular attention

from the busy nurses working at their station on the third floor. It was a common sight in a hospital.

He peeked from under the brim of his hat and read the progression of room numbers, seeking room 312. It was the number he'd been given when he had called and inquired about the location of his ailing cousin, Randy Long. When he drew up to room 312, the door was closed. Glancing around with his head still down, it appeared no one was paying him any attention. He turned the lever and quietly pushed the door open. The lights were turned down low. The devices hooked to the patient produced some illumination and sounds of their constant monitoring. An IV bag hung from a pole near the bed. It was half full. Randy Long was covered from foot to neck with bedding.

The old man studied his face, looking for signs that Randy was aware of his presence, but found none. He leaned close to his face and whispered his name, "Randy, it's Donnie, can you hear me? Wake up, Randy, we need to talk." Randy did not respond or react.

Donnie checked the room and saw a small dresser pushed against the wall. He pulled on a pair of surgical gloves and then opened the top drawer and saw a plastic bag containing clothing. It contained nothing but one pair of jockey underwear and a pair of jeans. He searched the jeans and found the pockets empty. He put the clothing back in the bag and put the bag back in the drawer before closing it.

Donnie quickly evaluated the situation and decided. He reached into his jacket pocket and pulled out a small wooden box. He removed the lid and slid it back into his pocket. Wrapped in a small white cloth was a syringe. He hastily removed the cap on the needle. Without hesitation, he injected the syringe into the seam of the IV bag just above the current fluid level. He pushed the plunger until the fentanyl emptied into the bag and mixed with the medication. The color in the bag did not change, and the slow drip continued.

Just as quickly, he withdrew the syringe from the bag and put it back in the box. He retrieved the lid and placed it back on the box before putting it back in his pocket. Randy still had not moved a muscle. Donnie took one last look at Randy and shook his head. *Sorry, pal. I've waited too long for something good to happen to me, and you're not going to stand in my way. Maybe you can hook up with your buddy Carl.*

Donnie reentered the empty hallway. He heard the voices of the medical staff from a nearby room. His slow but deliberate pace delivered him back to the elevator. No one paid any attention. He entered the elevator and pushed the button for the first floor. The doors were almost closed when Donnie heard the sound of an alarm coming from Randy Long's room.

Donnie drove two blocks to a 7-11 store. He pulled next to the dumpster in the back, wiped down the syringe, and tossed it, followed by the small box and his favorite hat, into the dumpster. He would miss his hat, but he had another one at home. *Different color, but the same comfortable style hat, all good.*

Donnie removed the cane and the oxygen machine from his backseat and tossed them both in the trunk. He'd thought himself very clever. *The props worked and made my job easy. The captain will be pleased; our last remaining problem has been taken care of. They still had ten coins and the potential for so much more.*

Donnie felt no remorse for what he had just done. Neither had he lost any sleep over swinging the huge fish cleaver into the wrists of Carl Andrews. Both men had made themselves obstacles that needed to be removed. Donnie was prepared to kill again. He and the Captain had already decided the two divers they hired would be expendable once their work was done. A secret shared with someone else is no longer a secret. The ocean is a dangerous place.

21

NO TURNING BACK

Brogan had left a message for the chief that he'd be working from home this Thursday morning to complete some reports before his new assignment. Trying to do reports in the P.D. was always a challenge, with the phones ringing and people popping in and out. A closed door was no barrier in a detective unit.

It was almost 11 a.m., and Brogan felt he had made good progress, having started at 6:30 a.m. With nearly all his paperwork caught up, a weight was off his shoulders. His cell phone sprang to life, reminding him being at home was also no barrier for a detective. He recognized the chief's phone number.

"Good morning, Chief. Something going on?"

"Actually, there is. I got a call last night from the State's Attorney, and he and I mutually agreed that your official start date will be this coming Monday. Do you think you'll need more time? If so, I guess you can finish up your reports on their dime."

"No. Monday will be great, and like you say, I'm only going upstairs."

"Brogan, I was notified yesterday afternoon that all the things you and I had talked about have been approved. The promotions for both Patty Ryan and Bob Carr have been made official. I'm bringing patrol officers David Quincy and Patrick Thurlow in as detectives. Both have had requests to be considered for the detective unit. They'll serve in a probationary status for six months to make sure it's a good fit.

"I just had all four of them in my office and gave them the news. Lieutenant Ryan and Sergeant Carr were informed that I'd made the final decision due to the high confidence and trust I have in each of them. They were told my decision was made easier by your recommendation and backing.

"Do you have any strong or negative feelings about Quincy and Thurlow?"

"No sir, both are excellent choices. I've watched both of them mature into fine officers. Both have written excellent reports and conducted thorough investigations on cases they've been assigned. They have the respect of their peers, and Patty and Bob will be happy to have them in the unit."

"Good to hear, Brogan. As you might imagine, all four left my office very excited about their new positions. I suspect you'll be hearing from Ryan and Carr very soon. I'm preparing an internal memorandum for everyone in our department, and the State's Attorney is preparing a written news release for everyone else in the county. We both thought that having a press conference for a photo opportunity was just making it a political matter rather than the good strategy move that it is. Sorry, I know how much you like to be in front of the cameras!"

"Yeah, right!"

"The police academy class is graduating in two weeks, and

we'll have four new officers, so manpower-wise, we'll be in good shape. Without you here, maybe things will calm down for a change. I've put a sealed envelope with two keys in it on your desk. One is your new office door upstairs, and the second opens a supply closet near your office should you need any stuff.

"Brogan, you know if you want anything at all, please call me. You've been a great help in professionalizing this operation, and I'll be forever grateful."

"Thanks, Chief. I caught a big break when you and the mayor offered me a job after I left Baltimore City. I'm glad it's worked out over the years. I'll be telling the mayor how much I appreciate him the next time I see him."

The two men disconnected the call. Brogan mused over the chief's comment about things calming down. *Maybe he's right. I do seem to attract a lot of bad circumstances. Nah, that's just a coincidence. Except I don't believe in coincidences. They've already backfilled my position, so I better not mess this up. No going back now.*

Brogan's phone was still in his hand when it rang again. He recognized the number. Patty Ryan.

22

HOW'S THAT POSSIBLE?

After fifteen minutes of high-energy conversation with Patty Ryan and Bob Carr, Brogan took the phone from his ear as the call ended with everyone being happy about everything. *First, they're sad because I'm leaving, and then they're happy for me because of my new job with the State's Attorney. Then they're elated about their promotions and new responsibilities, followed by self-doubt that they wouldn't be able to fill my shoes. Using the proper amount of congratulations and a touch of ego-building, I think I convinced them they were more than capable of their new assignments. Reminding them I would only be upstairs, I gave them a pep talk and my pledge to be there for both of them should they seek my counsel.*

Brogan chuckled to himself. *I'm suffering from the same self-doubts but have no one to seek counsel from. That's not true. My number one cheerleader, Kelly, is more than ready to boost my ego and encourage me through any difficulties. Yeah, and she also tells me when I fuck up. What more could I ask?*

For a third time, his phone rang. This time, he did not recognize the phone number. He answered with reservation. "Brogan."

"Hi, Brogan. This is Detective Mazzone from the sheriff's office."

"Hi, Frankie. How's it going?"

"Not too good at the moment. The sheriff suggested I give you a call. I just found out about your promotion to the state's attorney's office. Congratulations."

"Thank you, but I doubt the sheriff suggested you call me to congratulate me."

"You're right, he didn't. I'm the investigator handling the case of domestic abuse and the shooting of Randy Long. You were in charge that morning, and the sheriff thought I should bring you up to snuff on what's just happened."

"Okay. What's just happened?"

"Randy Long is dead. We just got a call from the hospital saying the monitoring devices in his room sounded the alarm, and they sent the crash cart to his room within a minute, but he was already dead when they got to his room. They tried to revive him, but he was non-responsive and coded. Dr. McCord was on the floor at the time and also responded to his room but was unable to resuscitate him.

"They don't know the cause of death. They said the surgery on his shoulder was considered a success, and he wasn't even in intensive care. All his vitals were checked just twenty minutes before the alarms went off. His chart noted no irregularities or signs of distress. He was resting comfortably. He never alerted the nurse's station that he needed help."

"How is that possible?" Brogan asked, mostly speaking to himself.

"They don't know. Maybe he had a heart attack or threw a blood clot to the brain or something along those lines, but according to his medical records, his heart was strong, and he was loaded up with blood thinners to prevent a clot. He was fine, but now he's dead. I'm on my way to the hospital. We're going to ask for a full autopsy and treat it as a suspicious death until we have some definitive answers. I tried to call his wife, but her phone is no longer active. We have a Deputy headed to her house to make a notification."

23

THE ARRIVAL

Julian asked Ana to drive the last ten miles of their journey. They were on Route 113, headed for a place called Snow Hill, MD. Julian pulled two folded papers from his pocket. He carefully unfolded both and studied them intensely.

Ana glanced over and could see one was a hand-drawn map, and the other sheet contained a hand-drawn picture of a house with the floorplan roughly drawn in. Ana had no idea what she was looking at and remained quiet, focusing on her driving.

Julian finally spoke, "Ana, help me look for a faded red mailbox on the right-hand side of the road, the number on it should be 13867, painted in white. It should be coming up pretty soon. When we find it, you'll turn into the driveway next to it."

Ana nodded and slowed the van just slightly while they searched the shoulder of the road. "There's nothing behind us, so I'm slowing down just a little so we don't miss it."

Sure enough, about a half-mile later, they both saw a red mailbox fixed to a wooden post coming up ahead. As they drew nearer, the numeral 13867 was listed on the side of the mailbox. Ana navigated a slow turn onto a gravel driveway. The driveway was straight and led them between fields of waist-high grass and weeds. Small clouds of dust followed the van's progress. After reaching a small growth of trees on either side of the driveway, it doglegged to the right and opened into more fields on either side. Ana slowed even more when the roof line of a one-story house appeared directly ahead of them. As they covered the distance, a ranch-style dwelling came into focus.

Very little grass grew around the dull brown house. The ground was just dirt and gravel. There was no attempt at landscaping. The front door was black and protected by an aluminum storm door that was weathered with age. Slightly to the left rear of the house was an outbuilding. It was large enough to store several vehicles but now held only a green lawn tractor.

Julian pointed out the windshield, "Pull over there between the house and the shed."

Ana did as she was told. Once she stopped, she put the van in park and sat there idling. Razor moved up between the seats and gazed through the windows at what might be her new home. She said nothing.

Ana's attention was drawn to another structure directly behind the dwelling. It was a large dog house with a rugged-looking chain lying in the dirt with one end bolted to the ground, and the other end, where the dog should be, was attached to nothing. A dog had created a well-worn path around the entire dog house, which was large and dark inside. It presented an eerie and somewhat threatening manifestation. Ana shuddered at the sight.

Julian used his phone to call Diego, who was somewhere behind them. "Hey Diego, we're here. Everything is as it's supposed to be. Use the map I gave you and look for the red mailbox. Come in very slowly so as not to raise the dust. I see no neighbors, but it doesn't mean they aren't near." Julian terminated the call.

Julian turned to Ana and Razor and said, "Diego and Tomas are about twenty minutes out. If you want to get out and stretch your legs, you may while we wait."

Razor and Ana exchanged glances between themselves and the dog house. Razor pulled the sliding side door open and stepped from the van. She stood perfectly still, listening for any sounds. She heard nothing and eased the straight edge from her hip pocket and advanced on the dog house. She felt the hair on the back of her neck tingle as she moved cautiously forward.

Ana cringed at the thought of a large dog leaping from the dog house and charging anyone armed with just a straight edge. She spoke to Razor through the open door, "Careful Chica, a large dog with sharp teeth is much more dangerous than a man full of bravado."

A slight grin came to Julian's face. He had been told the dog was no longer around, but he couldn't help but admire Razor's fearlessness in taking on a perceived threat. He had made a good choice in bringing her along.

When Razor cleared the dog house, she slid the weapon back in her pocket. She turned around and shrugged her shoulders at the van, and smiled. This prompted Ana to leave the van along with Julian. All three walked around near the van and waited.

Diego and Tomas came in slowly and parked next to

them. They gathered in a small circle, and Julian briefed them, "This'll be our home. No one knows where we are except the person who sent us. All arrangements have been made for us to stay here for at least a year or longer if needed. We're here to take over the local drug distribution and explore ways to get shipments directly from our suppliers. We'll learn about the local waterways and use them like highways. We'll face resistance from local drug dealers, and we'll have to gain the help of some local watermen, but we'll overcome all obstacles, as is the cartel way. I'll explain more as it becomes necessary. We need to take a few days to settle in and get the lay of the land. Do you have any questions? If not, remember you're to have no contact with anyone in Mexico. We're a team and only have each other. I can call for help if needed, but that's a last resort and will signal a lack of success on our part. This is our mission, and we must not fail."

Julian walked over to the dog house, reached down, and ran two fingers through the bolt drilled into the ground. He lifted the bolt straight up, and a small piece of plywood appeared out of the dirt. The bolt was just barely drilled into the wood. He placed it to the side and extracted a small metal box hidden in the ground. He returned the plywood and bolt to its original position and used his boot to cover it with loose dirt. He opened the unlocked box and pulled out a glassine baggie. It held five keys. All to the front door. He handed out four keys and kept one for himself. He laughed out loud as both women gave him the stink eye. "Welcome to America, let's get unloaded."

24

AT THE HOSPITAL

Brogan backed into a parking slot near the hospital's front doors. He had purposely avoided entering through the emergency room with its restricted parking. The two slots marked police parking, much closer to the front doors, remained empty. Brogan never sought the attention some officers felt was necessary.

Publicly advertising you're the police was not his thing. His gun was hidden under the left arm of his suit jacket, and his badge was clipped to his belt, hidden well to his side and away from the eyes of the casual observer. He always tried to have the edge by remaining anonymous.

When he entered the lobby, he noticed all was quiet and calm. He approached the reception counter and spoke to a gray-haired lady who saw beyond his anonymity, "Good morning, Brogan. How can I help you this morning?"

"Hi Brenda, I'm good. How about you?

"I'm fine, thanks."

"Brenda, have you been notified of the situation on the third floor?"

"Yes, but I was told to keep it on the Q-T. I was told that they had an incident and to direct any police to the third floor. Is that why you're here?"

"Brenda, did you see or hear anything unusual happening in the lobby since you've been on duty?"

"No, Brogan, I haven't. We always have people coming and going. Some stop here, and others just walk on by, already knowing where they're going."

"Did you have any inquiries this morning about the patient, Randy Long?"

"Yes, yes, I did. It was the first phone call I took this morning when I came on duty, around 9 a.m. His uncle called and wanted to know his room number so he could visit. I told him room 312, which is the number on our printout. He thanked me and then hung up. It was a little strange, he didn't ask about the patient's condition, our visiting hours, or if he had a phone. Is Mr. Long okay?"

"No, Brenda. He's not. He passed away unexpectedly, and the staff were unable to explain what occurred. We were notified, and we're going to investigate the circumstances. Michele Vickery and Detective Mazzone with the Sheriff's Office are on their way. I don't know her name, but a crime scene investigator from the Sheriff's Office should be here soon. Brenda, I know you well enough I can trust you to keep all of this information to yourself."

"Yes sir, of course. Oh, Vickery is already here. She went by a few minutes ago but didn't stop here at the counter."

"I'm going to stop in your security office and then go up to the third floor if anyone is looking for me."

"Yes, sir. Whatever you need."

Brogan left the lobby and traveled down a short hallway

to the security office. The door was closed. Brogan looked through the sidelight and saw Kevin Shaw seated in front of a panel of monitors showing different areas of the hospital. Brogan was grateful for the hospital's excellent surveillance system. Although the placement of cameras was to protect the hospital from liability claims, it also served as an excellent tool for conducting an investigation.

Brogan tapped on the heavy, solid wood door with one knuckle. Security Officer Shaw spun slowly on his office chair and saw Brogan at the door. Officer Shaw immediately went to the door, unlocked it, and admitted him into the small office.

"Hey, Kevin. I need your help this morning."

"I bet you do. Wendell Weston is the other security guy on duty today, and he's up on the third floor making sure it stays secure."

"Great, I'm going to need you to safeguard all the video recordings for today beginning around 7 a.m. I'll be back to review what you have for the lobby and the third-floor. To be safe, I'll eventually need everything from midnight on."

"No problem, I'll make arrangements so the video for the entire day is protected and a copy made. I'll get the hours and areas you're interested in right now segregated so it will expedite your review. I'll be here until 4 p.m. this afternoon if you need anything else. Our security log will alert the people coming on at 4 p.m. so they're on board with what to do."

Satisfied, Brogan proceeded back to the lobby and the bank of elevators. Already waiting for the elevator was Detective Mazzone.

"Frankie, can I catch a ride with you?"

Mazzone turned, smiled, and stuck out his hand. He and

Brogan shook and turned in unison as the bell pinged and the elevator doors opened.

"Brenda told me you were down at the security office, so I knew you had it handled. I was headed up to the third floor. Any problems at security?"

"No, Kevin Shaw is working the security desk and will get us everything we need. I told him I'd be back to view the videotapes after we were done on the third floor. Wendell is already helping to secure the patient's room."

"Good, our crime scene tech is about five minutes out."

The elevator stopped. The doors opened, giving access to the hallway. Both men could see Wendell Weston and a Berlin P.D. Officer conversing beyond the nurses' station. They further observed all the doors to the patients' rooms were closed. Four nurses were gathered at the nurses' station and engaged in quiet conversation.

Never a good thing when potential witnesses get together to discuss what they saw and did. Normally, the person with the strongest personality prevailed, and they all ended up agreeing they saw and did the same thing. Brogan and Mazzone would subsequently separate and interview each nurse in hopes of gaining independent observations and actions.

Brogan and Mazzone met with Weston and Officer Judy Stewart.

After everyone shook hands, Mazzone asked, "What's happened so far?"

Stewart answered first, "I was in the emergency room area with a car accident victim when my office called me. They said there'd been a suspicious death on the third floor, and I was to go secure the patient's room, station myself outside the door, and allow no one in or out except the police or the medical examiner.

"The nurses showed me the room. They said Dr. McCord had declared the patient deceased. The door was closed, and they said no one else was inside. I opened the door without entering the room. I verified the room was empty except for the deceased patient, closed the door, and I've been here ever since."

Brogan made a mental note. *No doctor was present at the nurse's station, so he'll have to be located and interviewed.*

Seeing that Stewart was done talking, Weston told the Detectives, "The nursing staff called the security office and said they had a situation concerning a deceased patient and asked one of us to come to the third floor to help secure the patient's room. They said the police were notified and were en route. When I got up here, I found Officer Stewart. I haven't looked in or entered the room."

Stewart spoke up. "Dr. Vickery is here, and I let her go inside the room. She's in there now."

Mazzone informed Stewart, "I have a Deputy coming to relieve you. Thanks for helping us today. Would you please write a report documenting what you've told us?"

"I'll standby until your deputy gets here and do a report as soon as I'm clear. I'll leave it with the duty officer at the P.D."

Mazzone and Brogan entered the room. Vickery turned and nodded her head, "About time you guys showed up."

Brogan replied, "What've we got, Doc?"

"Nothing obvious. I can't find any evidence of violence beyond his shoulder wound. His IV is still in his arm. It's possible someone injected something into his arm using the IV, but we won't know until the Medical Examiner's Office in

Baltimore has done toxicology on him. No signs he resisted whatever happened. With his pain medications working, he was probably asleep. He may never've known something was happening before he died. I'm sending the IV bag with him when he goes. I've been told he was completely covered up with his bedding when the nurses entered the room. They ripped everything off him to get to his body. They used the paddles on him in addition to CPR. Nothing happened. He flat-lined before they got in the room, and they couldn't get a response despite their best efforts. This could still be natural causes, but it's more than a little suspicious.

"I'm advising the crime tech to be extremely careful when securing the IV bag and any other fluids present. If he was poisoned in some way, the toxin used may still be present and dangerous."

Mazzone said, "Doctor, this'll be a Sheriff's Office investigation, so any information or evidence should be directed to our office. A deputy will guard the scene until the body is removed, and you release the scene in conjunction with the crime scene tech. If you need anything, just let me or the office know."

"I hear you're moving up in the world, Brogan," Michele remarked. "Congratulations. Have you already begun your new job?"

"Thanks, no, I officially start on Monday. Today, I'm sort of in training. Helping where I can without trying to butt in and take over. Detective Mazzone will make sure I stay in my lane," Brogan kidded.

Brogan and Mazzone retreated from the room after both took a couple of cell phone photos. They were greeted by Deputy Joan Briner, the crime scene tech, on her way in.

Mazzone told her, "This is my case; please give me a call if you find anything that might help us determine what happened here. See if the nurses will allow you to fingerprint them to eliminate their prints from any others you find in the room. Oh, yeah, there's a doctor who was helping try to resuscitate him, so his fingerprints may be present. They may've all been gloved up. You make the call."

Brogan turned to Mazzone. "Let's interview the nurses. One at a time. You take two, and I'll take the other two. Let's get them alone and see what they remember. We'll get together and compare notes after we're done. Then we'll run down the doctor and interview him together."

"Sounds like a plan," Mazzone said as he walked toward the nurse's station.

After all the interviews were done, it was pretty clear that no one knew what happened to Randy Long. All agreed protocols were followed in trying to revive him. Dr. McCord added no additional information. He was also at a loss.

One nurse, Kate Comer, said she recalled an older man in the hallway about the time the alarm sounded. After some thought, she said, "He was elderly, maybe a beard, used a cane and a portable oxygen machine on his hip. The only clothing I can remember is a khaki-colored floppy hat. I don't believe I'd be able to identify him. I never got a good look at his face."

Back in the Security Room with Kevin and Mazzone, and Brogan asked Kevin to bring up the video of the third-floor hallway. They began rolling it from 9 a.m. They fast-forwarded the video and watched as the nurses they interviewed came in and out of view as they made their rounds. They slowed the video at 9:45 a.m. when they saw Elaine Hughes, one of the nurses, enter room 312. She told Mazzone she found the patient asleep. He awoke as she checked his vitals; she found all were good and recorded the information on his chart. The patient was falling back asleep when she left the room seven minutes later. The time was 9:52 a.m.

The video rolled on until 10:15 a.m. when a man wearing a floppy hat came into view after exiting the elevator. He moved slowly away from the camera mounted over the elevator. He used a cane in his right hand to help support himself. The oxygen machine was clearly visible. He walked past the nurses' station without stopping. There was no indication he spoke or was spoken to during his passing. He stopped at room 312, kept his head down, but turned slightly and appeared to be checking his surroundings. When this action was paused, it revealed a light-colored beard. Rather than help, it obscured his facial features. Due to his suggested age and demeanor, both Brogan and Mazzone thought the beard was probably gray. He entered the room and closed the door.

At 10:20 a.m., the man in the floppy hat left room 312 and began a slow trek back to the elevator. Just as he disappeared into the elevator, the soundless video showed three nurses rushing toward and entering room 312. One was pushing a cart loaded with medical apparatus. One minute later, a male wearing a long white coat also rushed down the hallway and into room 312.

"Show us the video of the lobby starting at 10:20," Mazzone instructed.

Kevin pushed a few buttons, and the lobby appeared on the larger monitor on his desk. Just seconds into the video, the elevator doors opened, and the man in the floppy hat exited. He appeared to be in no rush but kept his head down even as he went out the front door.

"He's purposely avoiding the cameras!" Brogan exclaimed. "Show us the front of the hospital."

A few seconds later, the outside video came to life on the screen. The timing was perfect, and the man in the floppy hat was seen moving out the front doors and down the sidewalk towards the end of the parking lot and the main street running alongside the hospital. He disappeared from camera view after passing the entrance drive to the hospital.

"Show the clip again," Brogan ordered.

The video was replayed. "Look at the way he's walking. The cane is in his hand, but it's not touching the ground. He's carrying it rather than using it. His strides are longer, and he's more sure-footed. The cane is a prop. We need to get this description out to everyone. I think we're looking at a murderer making his escape," Brogan said.

Brogan glanced at this watch. *Shit, it's already 12:30 p.m. This guy has a two-hour head start on us. We're always playing catch-up, but maybe we'll get lucky.*

25

PERSON IN CUSTODY

The sheriff's office PCO put out the following broadcast for a person of interest. "Sheriff's office to all cars, all agencies. Be on the lookout for an older white male with a gray beard and a floppy-brimmed khaki hat. Last seen walking in the area of the county hospital. He's being sought for questioning in a suspicious death. You should approach with caution as he may be armed and dangerous. If subject is encountered, wait for backup and contact the sheriff's office."

Local media immediately picked up the story, and local radio stations were spreading the description to their listeners. Lynn Murphy from the local television media got the information from a reliable source, and it came with a still-frame picture taken in the hospital hallway, giving her viewers someone to look for.

At 1:30 p.m., a citizen called the Berlin Police Department. The recorded conversation came from a very excited woman. "I just saw him! He's got the hat on right now. He's walking on Old Sandpiper Road near Route 50. I didn't stop. I live on Old Sandpiper, so I'm going home and lock my doors. If I see him again, I'll call you. Oh, yeah, this is Barbara."

The woman had spoken quickly and disconnected the call before the police communications officer was able to ask for additional information. The cell phone number was captured, but return calls to the number went unanswered.

"Berlin to cars B-7 and B-9. We've just received a citizen call stating the wanted white male in the floppy hat has been sighted on Sandpiper Road near Route 50. Please investigate this sighting and report."

"B-7 to headquarters. I copy, and I'm en route."

"B-9 to headquarters. I'm responding."

"Car V-21 to Berlin Barrack. I just monitored two Berlin P.D. cars responding to the wanted person on Sandpiper Road. I'm in the area and will back them up."

Within minutes, car B-7, Officer Marty Wachter called by radio, "I've located a person meeting the description of the wanted person. He's on foot approximately half of a mile from Route 50 on Sandpiper Road. Car B-9 is with me now, and we'll be executing a felony stop."

Brogan and Mazzone were seated in Brogan's car. They sat on the parking lot of the hospital, planning the next steps in finding the suspect. They both sipped lukewarm coffee from a nearby Dunkin Donuts. Both heard the radio traffic relating to the suspect. Without a word, the contents of both coffee cups went out the side windows, and the empty cups were tossed on the rear floorboard.

Brogan said, "Maybe we just caught a break," as he pulled his car into gear. The tires chirped as they exited the hospital parking lot and headed to the location where the other police cars converged.

The man in the floppy hat looked at the approaching police cars with mild curiosity. He stepped from the roadway onto the grassy shoulder. The cars appeared to be going very fast as they approached. Suddenly, both vehicles braked with squealing tires. One car drove past the man and then cut sharply in front of him. The second car cut just as sharply on the other side of him. The man knew enough about the police to anticipate what was going to happen next. Both hands shot straight up over his head in the universal sign of surrender. Then he stood stock-still.

Both officers exited their vehicles and drew their firearms. Adrenaline was pumping.

Car B-9's Officer Jim Stone ordered, "Keep your hands where we can see them. Slowly get on your knees and then lay face down on the ground. Then don't move."

The floppy hat fell from the old man's head when he lay down. He said nothing.

The state trooper, driving V-21, arrived and joined the two Berlin officers. The trooper said, "I'll cover him while you hook him up."

Officer Stone moved in and quickly handcuffed the suspect to the rear. The two Berlin officers each took an arm, lifted the man to his feet, and pushed his upper body gently over the hood of the nearest police car. He was carefully patted down and found to be unarmed. Officer Marty Wachter called in and advised they had the person in custody.

Officer Jim Stone uttered, "I know this guy. This is stinky Ralph. He's usually homeless or living in one of the local shelters. His nickname comes from his infrequent bathing. I've never known him to cause any trouble. He had a tent in a small wooded area in the town, but we closed it down and moved him into a shelter. Haven't seen him since then, until now. I'm not sure, but I think he's about seventy years old."

Ralph, for the first time, spoke up, "Why you guys picking on me? I ain't done nothin' wrong. I was just walkin home. I ain't seventy. I'm seventy-five, and I ain't stinky!"

"Okay, Ralph, what's your last name?

"Strawbridge"

"Where're you living, Ralph?"

"About a mile up the road on the left. The little yellow house. They fixed up their shed behind their house, and that's where I live. I do chores, and they pay me and let me live there. I got my own out house and everything. Mr. and Mrs. Pieper will vouch for me. They're too old to do for themselves, so I helps them out."

Brogan and Mazzone arrived on the scene and took charge after speaking with Officer Stone.

"Hi, Ralph. I'm Brogan; I work for the state's attorney. This is Detective Mazzone. He works for the sheriff's office. We'd like to ask you a few questions. Do you know why you were stopped?"

"No sir, I don't. I didn't do nothin' wrong."

Mazzone said, "We're going to take your handcuffs off and then ask you a couple of questions. Is that okay with you?"

"Yes, sir, I'd appreciate you taking these cuffs off me, and I'll answer your questions."

Brogan said, "Ralph, you're not under arrest, and you don't have to talk with us if you don't want to. You're free to leave if you want."

"No, I don't mind talking to you. I have nowhere to go but home. Would you give me a ride home when we get done talking?"

"Sure, Ralph, we'll give you a ride home. Where've you been this morning?"

"I went to the 7-11 and got a hotdog and a soda. I go there most every day. They got the best hotdogs, and the sodas are good, too. Timmy, who works behind the counter, he'll tell you I was there, and I come in every day."

Brogan continued, "Ralph, did anything special happen this morning? Did you visit the hospital today?"

"Never visited no hospital, but something special did happen to me today."

"What was that, Ralph?"

"Well, after I ate my hotdog and drank my soda, I went to put my trash in the dumpster behind the store like I always do. Today, when I slid the side door open to dump my trash, I saw this hat just lying in there. It wasn't dirty or nothin. Just there, pretty as you please. I took it out, and it fit right on my head, so I kept it for myself. Pretty lucky, don't you think?"

"Instead of taking you home, how about we all go back to the 7-11 store? Think you could eat another hotdog, Ralph?"

"Oh yes, sir, I love hotdogs."

As Ralph was placed in the backseat of Brogan's car, Mazzone and Brogan came to appreciate why he had gotten his nickname. Both men rolled their windows down for the short trip to the 7-11. The floppy hat road in a glassine evidence bag on Detective Mazzone's lap.

While making the short drive, Brogan was thinking to himself. *As much as I'd like this to be our guy, I'm not feeling it. He looks a little taller and thinner than the guy in the video. The hat's right, but he says he just found it, and for some reason, I believe him. Gotta check it out, but I think we're still looking for a killer.*

Brogan glanced at Mazzone, and as their eyes met, he saw Mazzone give a slight shake of his head. Two cops, two gut feelings, and the same conclusion. *This ain't our guy.*

Ralph showed Brogan and Mazzone the dumpster and the side door he claimed to have opened. Brogan used a handkerchief and two fingers to slide the door open and peered in.

Ralph looked over Brogan's shoulder and said, "It was right there, right next to that empty cardboard box."

Brogan's eyes focused on the area being pointed out by Ralph and immediately saw it. A syringe was lying in plain sight just below the cardboard box. He turned to Mazzone, "You need to call your crime scene investigator and get her out here. I think we just found the murder weapon."

While Mazzone secured the dumpster, Brogan took Ralph inside the 7-11 and confirmed his story with Timmy Melford, the clerk behind the counter. "Yep, ole Ralph comes in here almost every day between noon and 1 p.m. He always gets the same thing. A hotdog and a soda. He usually sits on the brick window sill out front while he eats. Talks to people passing by but never causes any trouble, so we let him be. After he eats, he goes around back and throws his trash away."

The times jived with the video recording of the suspect as he left the hospital. The suspect could have easily left the hospital, deposited the hat and syringe in the dumpster, and been long gone before Ralph showed up for his hotdog. All the cameras at the 7 -11 were focused on the inside and the front of the store facing the gas pumps. A later review of the tapes showed Ralph but no other person resembling the suspect.

True to his word, Brogan rewarded Ralph with a hotdog and a soda for his help. Officer Stone had made the mistake of volunteering to tag along and was now rewarded. "Hey Jim, can you give Ralph a ride home? We're done with him for now." Mazzone asked. As Officer Stone left the parking lot with Ralph, his hotdog, and soda in the backseat, Brogan could see the driver's window being lowered. Ralph was happy and had already forgotten about his hat.

Brogan reflected, *Obviously, this case wasn't going to solve itself. Time to get back to work.*

26

A Lot Going On

The sheriff's office crime scene investigator showed up and began the disgusting job of searching the dumpster for possible evidence. She immediately removed the syringe and then examined every item in the dumpster while evaluating possible evidentiary value. The only other item she found that seemed out of place was a small wooden box containing a small, soft, white piece of cloth. It was found near the syringe, and when compared, it was a perfect compartment to house the syringe. The box was taken as potential evidence for further examination.

Brogan's phone vibrated in his pocket. "Brogan."

"Brogan, it's Patty. I just got off the phone with the medical examiner's office in Baltimore. We've got a positive identification on the body on the beach. They were able to confirm the victim is Carl Andrews, from the family in Berlin we'd already visited. Sergeant Carr and I are on our way to the mother's house to make notification."

"Okay. I know these notifications are tough, but you've been with me a few times when we did it together, so you'll be fine. At least now, the investigation can take a direction. Get everything you can get from the family about friends, enemies, love interests, or ongoing problems. You know the routine. Give me a call if you need any help or run into any problems. Good luck, Lieutenant."

"Thanks, Brogan. I'll make you proud."

"Already am Patty, already am." Brogan ended the call.

"Donnie, you dumb fuck. What were you thinking? I told you to go talk to the guy, find out about the coin, to scare him, not kill him. Now we've got real problems. The police are going to be all over this."

"Captain, I did it in a way they won't know I killed him. They'll think he just croaked of a heart attack or something."

"Donnie, they already know it's not kosher. The radio is saying the police are looking for a guy fitting your description. Right down to that stupid khaki hat you wear all the time."

Donnie paled when he heard what the captain said.

"Shit, man. Do you think I should get out of town for a while? I don't have a place to go! Everything I own and everyone I know is right here. I threw the hat and syringe away as soon as I left the hospital. No way they can make a positive I.D. I kept my head down just in case a camera picked me up.

There're a lot of people who look like me. They'll be looking for a guy who walks with a cane and uses oxygen. I was smart and left them false clues to follow."

"Donnie, what you're going to do is stay right on this boat. You ain't getting off for at least two weeks. You're going to shave that nasty-ass beard of yours and trim the hair on your head. You hear me, you're going to clean up your act. I'll bring you food and drink, and you just chill here with me.

Captain Plummer thought hard about what was going on. *Donnie is so goddamn stupid. He's gonna get us both locked up for murder if I'm not careful. If I keep him here with me, I'll have better control and keep him from making more mistakes. No way is he dragging me into a jail cell. He's been a good first mate, but if I have to, I'll leave him at the bottom of the ocean with those divers from Jersey. I just need to get that treasure on board and then clean up loose ends. I can always find another first mate!*

27

CONNECTING THE DOTS

An hour later, Brogan got another call. "Hey, what's up, Patty?"

"Brogan, you're not going to believe this shit. We just left the Andrews' house. The mom took it very hard but still wanted to talk to us and help find out what happened to her son. His Uncle was there and also wanted to help.

"While we were documenting all the normal stuff, his mom began to cry, saying, "I can't believe this is happening. First, Carl dies, and before we can bury him, his best friend passes away. They were so young. They'd been friends since elementary school and were like brothers. They even worked together from time to time on the boats. Randy never even knocked when he came over here. He was family. Now they're both gone."

I asked Mrs. Andrews for Randy's last name?" She replied, "Randy Long. I know he just got involved in some dispute involving his wife and the Sheriff's Office. News said he shot a fireman, but I can't see the Randy I know doing anything like that. He's always been a good boy. A state trooper shot him, and he was in the hospital. Last I heard, he was going to be okay, and now he's dead."

Patty gushed out, "Brogan, can you believe it? The dead guy on the beach and the dead guy in the hospital were best friends. You always say, 'There are no coincidences in police work.' These two cases are tied together. I'm not sure what's going on, but we definitely have solid links between two murders! They both worked the boats! We didn't share anything with the Andrews family. I just wanted to get out of there so I could call you."

Brogan felt his pulse race, "I agree, Patty. You and I need to meet with Detective Mazzone and start reviewing everything we have and where we need to go next. Can you meet in about an hour at the Sandpiper office? We can use the conference room and the big table to spread our stuff out. I'll have Mazzone meet us there. This thing is breaking wide open. We need to figure it out before anyone else dies."

28

WE NEED A PLAN

Brogan called State's Attorney Rudy Carol, "Rudy, it's Brogan. I know I don't start until Monday, but we have two homicide cases merging together. We've linked the murder of Carl Andrews, the body on the beach, with the murder of Randy Long at the county hospital. I've called all the investigators together for a meeting at Sandpiper P.D. Detective Mazzone, Patty Ryan, and Bob Carr are all going to be here so we can formulate an investigative plan. Not sure where this will go, but I thought you should know I'm already acting as your lead investigator."

"No shit Brogan," Rudy exclaimed, "this is great! I'm in Annapolis for an event, but I can leave and come back if you need me to be present."

"That's not necessary. I'll brief you tomorrow morning after we've come together on what we're going to do. I doubt we'll be moving on anything before tomorrow."

"Okay, makes sense, but I'm calling my guy working in Sandpiper, Assistant S.A. Jim Lyons. If he's available, I'm going to ask him to go to the P.D. and sit in on your meeting.

He's a good guy, Brogan. Got a good head on his shoulders. He'll help you with any legal issues you may be facing."

"Sure, the more people I have looking at our evidence, the better chance we'll have of coming up with a solid path forward."

Lyons was young and eager. After speaking with Rudy Carol, he'd left his wife and young son staring in disbelief as he abandoned his partially eaten dinner on the dining room table. "Love you guys," Lyons uttered as he kissed each. "I gotta go back to work. Don't wait up for me."

The harsh fluorescent lights of the conference room at the SPPD took a few moments to get used to. The investigators filed in with their box or bag of files. The mood was one of expectation and seriousness.

Detective Mazzone came to the meeting accompanied by another Sheriff's Office Detective, MJ Callanan. She was introduced around the table as his partner during their current investigation.

Patty Ryan and Bob Carr sat side by side. They opened their files and began spreading reports and photographs in front of them. Detective Mazzone performed a similar task in front of him and Detective Callanan.

Brogan opened the meeting, "Okay, folks. We have reasons to believe the two recent homicide investigations are linked by facts and circumstances developed during independent investigations being conducted by Sandpiper P.D. and the Sheriff's Office."

Brogan stepped to a large whiteboard at the end of the room. "Help me fill in the facts so we're all on the same page. I think we should start with a timeline. So many things have happened quickly I hope it'll help us put everything into perspective. Don't hesitate to speak up if you have something to add or if you think we're missing something important. We may have to massage this timeline as we go along."

A few minutes later, they had the beginnings of a timeline. Brogan reached into his suit pocket and produced a small coin envelope contained inside a clear evidence bag. He slid the coin out of the envelope and placed it in front of the investigators.

"Randy Long's wife, Betty, dropped this off at my office on the morning of Wednesday, May 22nd. With the coin was a note explaining she was leaving town. She was in fear of retaliation from her husband and was moving out of state to protect herself and her son.

"I wasn't there when she dropped this off, but she explained how she came into possession of the coin in the note. Randy had come home drunk one evening, saying he had found a way to end all their financial difficulties. He gave her the coin and told her to keep it a secret from everyone until he told her differently. She ended the note stating she was afraid this coin might be related to some criminal wrongdoing by Randy and some of his recent friends. She left it in my care so I could check it out. I know how to reach her, and she's willing to come back if we need her.

"I took it to a friend who's a coin collector. He had never seen this particular coin before but researched it while I was with him and found that it's very rare and quite valuable. He speculated that if there were more of these coins, their finding would be extremely important, and they'd be very sought after. My friend told me to use caution as once their existence became known, all types of treasure hunters would come forward hoping to find the motherlode. He concluded by saying numerous unscrupulous collectors would kill to possess such a rare coin. Fortunes have been made following such discoveries. He's unable to explain why it would be in the Sandpiper area but did believe, based on its condition, that the coin had spent a very long time in the water. Its existence does not leave this conference room. I believe we're staring at the motive for two murders".

Knowing its possible significance, not a single investigator moved to touch it.

Mazzone sat across from Patty Ryan and was looking at photographs she had spread in front of her. They were upside down to him, but he could see they were pictures of the scene of the body on the beach. "Patty, may I take a look at your photos?" he asked.

"Sure, help yourself, Frankie," as she pushed the photographs across the table.

Mazzone shuffled through the pictures and suddenly raised his head and asked Patty, "Have you seen the video pictures taken at the hospital after Long was murdered?"

"No, I haven't. Heard about it, but I've been on the road all day digging into possible witnesses or friends of the dead guy on the beach. Then, when a positive I.D. was made, I went to his mother's house and made notification. What do you see in my photographs?"

"Hey, Brogan, you better take a look at this," Mazzone said in an excited voice.

All the investigators gathered around Mazzone and

peered at the picture laid out before them. Brogan stood directly behind Mazzone and followed Mazzone's index finger to a person in one of Patty's pictures. The subject was walking away from the camera, and only a small portion of his face was visible. *Holy Shit!* "That's the same floppy bucket hat we saw in the hospital video," Brogan blurted.

Brogan snatched up the photo and held it close. Studying the image, a familiar fuzzy-looking beard was present.

"What the fuck. We got the same guy at both murder scenes. This is our guy, and there's no question he's most likely the doer in both cases. When we hit the streets tomorrow, be looking for this character. I think we need to keep these photos in-house. If we go public, the suspect could see them, and he's liable to bolt from the area or do some serious renovations to his appearance."

With eyes still fixed on the mystery coin and the newly revealed photographs, all the investigators began to come forward with suggestions for moving forward. Everyone contributed, and, in the end, a plan was agreed upon. Copies of both the beach and hospital pictures were made and distributed to each investigator.

Assistant States Attorney Jim Lyons gave it his stamp of approval and said, "I'll brief the state's attorney first thing tomorrow morning. Is that okay with you, Brogan?"

"Sure, Jim. Thanks for taking care of that for me. If Rudy has additional questions, I'll be available on my cell."

The first step in the plan was for everyone to go home and get some sleep. Tomorrow morning, there would be an all-out effort to find the killer. Papers and files were gathered, and one by one, they left the conference room. Brogan was the last to exit. Just before he turned out the conference room lights, he snapped a photo of the timeline.

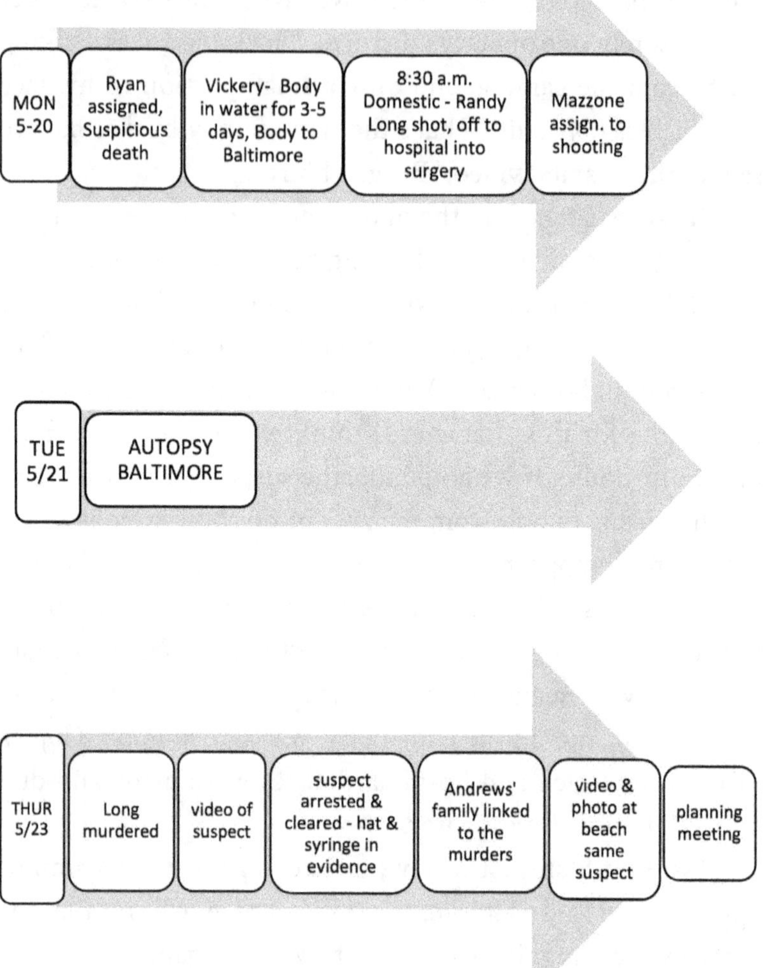

He turned off the lights and quietly closed the door.

He felt confident that this newly formed team of investigators would solve this case and send the bad guy to jail. *Sleep tonight might be elusive. This is a hell of a case to kick off my new assignment. But the men and women assigned to these investigations are good at what they do.*

Brogan went back to his place to find Kelly asleep on his couch. The television was playing some movie that was a period piece with a predictable formula involving a big-city woman who travels to a small town, preferably somewhere horses are involved. She finds a cowboy and inevitably falls in love. There is usually a wedding at the end, and they live happily ever after. Kelly says she loves these kinds of movies but rarely stays awake to see the end. Brogan smiled and turned the TV off. The silence awakened Kelly with a start.

"Hey, I was watching that!"

"Not through closed eyes, you weren't."

"Must have dozed off for just a couple of seconds."

"You can watch it again tomorrow."

"Brogan, fill me in on what's been going on at the cop shop."

After a thirty-minute briefing and sixty minutes of lovemaking, Brogan finally allowed himself to fall to sleep. Kelly was curled into him, snoring softly.

29

Under the Cover of Darkness

The cartel members had spent their first morning in Worcester County sprucing up their new home. While it would never make the cover of any Home Garden magazine, the two women had supervised the cleaning and placement of the sparse furniture available to them. To avoid the heavy lifting, Tomas had volunteered to take the grocery list to a nearby Food Lion and buy what they needed for the immediate future.

Tomas said, "My mama used to send me to the store with a list; I know what I'm doing."

"Yeah," said Diego, "you know what you're doing. You're avoiding working up a sweat. We've moved these couches and chairs around the room a bunch of times already. This shit is getting old."

"We gotta live with you three guys, but it doesn't mean we've got to live like pigs. Razor and I've done our fair share, and you wouldn't know the inside of a store past the beer cooler, so shut the fuck up and keep doing what I tell you to do!" Ana said with a look that made Diego look to Julian for support.

Julian rolled his eyes and said, "You heard the lady. Let's get this done so we can sit down and have a beer."

By noon, everything was pretty much in order. The food had been placed in the appropriate cabinets; the refrigerator was stocked with an abundance of beer, wine, soda, and even some bottles of water.

Julian told his team, "After lunch, we need to explore the area and find out what we're up against. Ana and I'll go into Sandpiper and check out the beach and the number of cops they have rolling around. If we can pick out a couple of drug dealers, we'll watch em and see if we can identify their supplier. I'm sure they'll be holding small amounts and need to be replenished frequently. We'll learn how they operate and who's running the show.

"Tomas will go with us, so he'll know his way around and perhaps hone in on local police communications to see how well they're protected. The more we know, the better off we'll be when we take over.

"Razor, you and Diego go to Salisbury. This is where I was told they have a small gang that runs the drug distribution in this county and several others. This is called the Eastern Shore, and it runs from the State of Delaware down into Virginia.

"We may have to spill a little blood to let the locals know their control is being challenged. We'll send the message it benefits them to work for us rather than against us. I want you two to do the same thing. Look for some street dealers and see if you can find their suppliers and their methods of operation. We won't be looking for a fight tonight, but if a problem arises, I expect you to deal with it quickly and violently. We are few, but we cannot be seen as weak."

By 2 p.m., the team had split up and went to the places designated by Julian.

Julian and Ana dropped Tomas near the police headquarters so he could observe and report back later. He had his fully charged laptop with him. It was loaded with several different software programs that would allow him to probe local police communications. They agreed to meet with him around 7 p.m. They had their burner phones, which were to be used as a last resort.

Tomas found a seat in a public bus stop shelter near police headquarters. He propped his laptop on his legs and began his work in plain sight. Buses came and went, but he remained unnoticed and undisturbed.

After parking their van, Julian and Ana entered the boardwalk portion of Sandpiper Beach. Julian thought, *This is where we were supposed to be. This'll soon be an area controlled by the Calupoh Cartel.*

It only took a couple of minutes to realize they were not dressed for the beach. They slipped into a boardwalk beach store, and fifteen minutes later, after a quick change of clothing, they emerged in shorts and tee shirts. Julian would not give up his rugged and worn work boots. Luckily, there were enough work-boot-loving beach visitors that Julian didn't draw any attention. They placed their jeans and long-sleeved shirts in the store's bag and joined the motley crew roaming the boardwalk. With their brown skin and dark hair, they fit in better than some of the lily-white bodies, fresh from the cities of Maryland, Pennsylvania, or Washington, D.C.

"Let's walk down to the water, suggested Ana. I've never had my feet in the Atlantic Ocean."

Julian wasn't so keen on the idea but acquiesced as he, too, had never set foot in the Atlantic.

Once they came to the wet sand, they plodded along, leaving footprints to mark their progress. Ana moved to the dry sand and removed her sandals. She ventured into the water. She remained there a total of ten seconds before retreating with a shrill mantra, "Oh, that's so fucking cold. How can people get in there?"

Julian laughed, "I don't know, but I'll take your word for it. I'm not trying to prove anything. I've seen it, and that's enough for me. From the looks of those waves, we won't be bringing any product ashore on this beach. I hope the rivers and inland waterways are calmer and will meet our needs. We'll explore them another day."

At 7 p.m., they picked Tomas up as planned.

"This police department doesn't protect their radio transmissions. Anyone can listen to them. They probably have a black channel, but given a little time, I'm sure I'll be able to hack it. Their phones are easily tapped. Given enough time, I can access their investigation files and personnel records if we need them." Tomas reported.

Julian said, "You did good, Tomas, I'm glad you came with us. Your skills will be valuable and make our job far easier."

Ana remained silent. *We shouldn't underestimate these Gringos. They're not corrupt like in Mexico, and they're not stupid. I hope Julian realizes this.*

By 10 p.m., they had found two different street dealers working near the boardwalk. Buyers seemed to know who they were because they would walk right up to them, exchange a few words, and then move off the boardwalk onto a side street where an exchange of money for product would take place. Around 11 p.m., a dark vehicle with tinted windows drove down the side street, and the dealer would leave the boardwalk and come to the passenger side of the vehicle, where another exchange would take place. This was either done by a schedule or a text message letting the dealer know when to leave the boardwalk.

Julian saw the cameras covering the boardwalk but also observed the darker side streets' absence of cameras. *Made sense. Someone had done some advance thinking and planning.*

"Follow the car," Ana said. "Let's see where it takes us."

Forty minutes later, the car had been up five different side streets leading to the boardwalk and four different parking lots near busy bars and nightclubs. Business was good. At least nine different street dealers working an area that is only about ten miles long and less than two miles wide.

Julian smiled, "We've found an excellent location to move our product. Once we've taken over, we'll flood the streets with whatever the people are looking for. With our connections, we'll have no problem ordering product of any kind. Now, we must identify some safe water passages to use for deliveries and remove the gang leaders in Salisbury. I believe it'll be far easier than the bosses at home thought. I'll wait until we're sure before I report back."

Again, Ana remained silent. *Julian is fooling himself, thinking this'll be easy.*

Tomas had no comment. *All that street shit, violence, and danger aren't my problem.* His world consisted of a computer screen and the internet. Dropping the computer on his foot would be his only danger.

By midnight, the clientele had vanished from the boardwalk, and the dealers had vanished as well. Even the parking lots were nearly empty, and those dealers had also disappeared into the darkness.

The trio followed the supply vehicle out of Sandpiper, over the bridge, and onto Route 50, heading towards Salisbury. Traffic was light, so they gave the vehicle plenty of room, following at a healthy distance. About five miles out of Sandpiper, the vehicle made a right-hand turn and drove onto a dark two-lane road.

Julian slowed until the taillights disappeared before making the righthand turn. He then sped up just enough that he thought he should be able to see the taillights again, but that didn't happen.

"Damn, I've lost him. Where the hell did he go?"

Ana, riding shotgun, was checking the driveways as they rode by. "There, there," she said. "The last driveway we passed. The car is up there, and I saw two people getting out. Turn around and go back slowly so we can check and be sure."

Julian found another driveway, which allowed him to back up and go back the way they had come.

"Go slow, but don't stop, and don't look up the driveway in case they're looking. I'll be able to see without making it look obvious."

Julian drove as directed, and they passed by the driveway at about twenty miles an hour.

"Yes. That's the car," Ana confirmed. "There're lights on in the house that weren't on when we passed before. This may be where they live or a stash house for drugs and money. These guys are either stupid or very confident or maybe a little of both."

They found a small place to pull over and watched the darkened driveway using their rearview mirror. An hour later, with no visual activity at the house, they decided to go home. They had done very well considering what they had accomplished in a single day.

"I wonder how Razor and Diego are doing in Salisbury?" Julian said to no one in particular.

Ana responded, "Razor and Diego will do fine. They can be a very scary pair."

30 SALISBURY

Diego and Razor spent the entire afternoon exploring the Salisbury area. The downtown area was clean and busy, with people coming and going. Diego noticed the difference, "There're many police here; very different from where we came from. In Mexico, there's poverty and despair. The people fear the cartels."

Razor responded, "Can you blame them? Even the cartels fear each other. Every day, there's killing. We're slaughtering our people just to have control to make more money. Our drugs bring even more death. Even the tourist resorts and hotels along the coast are now targeted. The Government is corrupt. That's why there's no hope for a future in Mexico. Our people are fleeing Mexico to go to the U.S. The cartels have turned it into a money-making venture ripe with rape, assaults and murder. No one knows how many bodies are buried in the deserts approaching the border."

"In Mexico, we'd be seeing cartel soldiers on the streets. Where're the gang members?" Diego asked.

Razor answered his question, "Things are different here

in the United States, especially in small cities. The dealers stay hidden during the daylight hours, but after it gets dark, we'll find them. They can't hide from us."

By 9 p.m., the scene had changed in Salisbury. Groups of young people cruised the streets with no obvious destination. Suspicious gatherings were happening near the mall and outside of bars and public parks. The dealers were out, but obviously, making their presence hard to detect. In Mexico, everything is brazen and out in the open. Just daring the police to act at their peril.

"Diego, pull over in that parking lot across the street from that strip shopping center."

"What'd you see, Razor?"

"Pull next to that closed business with the car pointing out. I'll show you."

Diego positioned their vehicle. He turned off the headlights and engine. Turning to Razor, he said, "Show me what you see."

Razor slid down in her seat to eliminate her profile and indicated Diego to do the same. "See that laundromat at the end of the strip? Watch it closely because someone is hiding in the shadow of the building."

Sure enough, Diego saw movement, and a tall, thin male materialized out of the shadows. His appearance coincided with an older model BMW entering the parking lot and moving directly toward the end of the building housing the laundromat. The driver turned so the passenger side of his vehicle was facing the shadowy figure. The vehicle passenger lowered his window and passed something out the window. A moment later, the vehicle pulled away and drove to the other end of the strip mall. Another black male stepped out from the side of the building as the BMW slowed to a stop. The window had remained down, and the man on foot passed something to the passenger before the car drove away.

"Razor, did you see that? The first guy collected the money, and the second guy delivered the product. These guys are pretty slick. Did you notice the three kids on bicycles near the road? I think they're the watchers. They're watching for the police."

"Yes, they've been doing this for a long time. I bet the guy with the product has a stash location nearby, so he's not holding more than what he's delivering at any given time."

Diego and Razor watched the same procedure over and over again for the next two hours.

"I doubt they use this same location every night. Somehow, they're communicating with the buyers so they know where to go. By the time the police get information or a complaint about what's going on, the gang has changed locations, leaving the police one step behind."

"Diego, Julian is expecting us to return with some good information on how this gang operates and who's their leader. We can't do that simply by watching drug deals go down. We must isolate one of these customers and find out what they know."

"What if they won't talk to us?"

"We'll convince them to talk to us or pay a serious price for their silence. I'm sure you and I'll get the information we seek."

Diego nodded his head slowly. He thought to himself, *I'll get the information.*

The next car that pulled into the parking lot was a small Chevrolet sedan. The single occupant was a middle-aged male. He apparently knew the routine as he pulled up to the right spot, passenger window down. The shadowy figure approached the car, and an exchange was made. He drove to the far end of the lot, slowed almost to a stop, and another exchange took place.

"Follow him," said Razor. "When he stops somewhere, we'll take him and find out what we need. No more guessing. Julian expects answers, not questions."

Surprising both Razor and Diego, the car only traveled about two blocks before pulling off into a darkened area beside a closed deli. Diego quickly pulled off the road in a dark area just past the deli and threw their car into park. Both exited and jogged back to where the Chevrolet sat, motor running, headlights extinguished.

Diego held a blued 9 mm semi-automatic down by his right leg and a small tactical flashlight clenched in his left. Razor moved to the passenger side while Diego slid silently up to the driver's door. She looked across the roof to Diego and nodded.

Without a word being spoken, Diego turned on the flashlight and blinded the man sitting inside the car. The dark-haired man had been preoccupied cooking up the heroin he had just purchased, preparing to inject the milky solution into his arm. Rubber tubing was tied off just above his elbow, and the syringe lay on the center console, ready to draw the drug from the cooking spoon.

Vacant eyes stared into the bright light. Panic came to his facial expression, and he reached for the syringe. His only concern was to get his fix. Diego was prepared to smash the side window, but when he jerked on the door handle, it swung open.

"Move, and I'll blow your brains out."

The driver's right hand held the syringe but did not attempt to move. If he heard the passenger door open, he did not react. Razor placed her gun to the side of his head.

"Do as you're told, and you might go home tonight."

"Okay, I give up. I just need my fix. Are you cops?"

Razor lowered her voice to a whisper, "No, we're far worse than the cops. Keep both hands where we can see them."

"Hey, I'm not going to give you any problems. I only have twenty dollars in my pocket, but you can have it. If you want the car, you can have that too. Just don't kill me."

The man opened his hand, leaving the syringe on the console next to a burnt spoon still holding a little wad of cotton and a milky solution.

Diego pulled the man roughly from the vehicle and pushed him up against the side of the car. He patted him down but found no weapons. He removed a flimsy wallet from his rear pocket and tossed it to Razor, who was now standing next to him. She quickly went through it, removing a twenty-dollar bill and putting it in her pocket. She found a Maryland Driver's License and was able to read it by the ambient light of the moon.

"This says you're Joseph P. Strand. Is that right?"

"Yeah, that's me. Everybody calls me Joey."

"Joey, do you live at this address in Salisbury?"

"That's my mother's address, but she's letting me live in her basement. I'm trying to find a job so I can help her out. I'm trying to get clean. It's hard. You know what I mean?"

"No, Joey, I don't know what you mean, but you need to understand what I mean. I'm going to ask you some questions, and you're going to answer them quickly and truthfully, or I'm going to hurt you really bad." To emphasize her directions, Razor drew her razor from her hip pocket. She opened it and let the moonlight glint off the blade.

"Do you understand me, Joey?"

"Yes, ma'am, what do you want to know?"

"Who sold you that heroin?"

"Skinny. I don't know his real name, but that's his street name. I buy from him all the time. He's always holding good shit."

"Okay, Joey, how did you know Skinny would be at the shopping center tonight?"

"He sends me a text every afternoon. Today, it said laundromat. Sometimes, it says carwash, tennis courts, park, or Mall. It changes all the time, but he's always there until midnight. If it gets past midnight, I have to wait until the next day. Those are hard days for me."

"Who does Skinny work for?"

"I'm not sure, but I've seen Slick Melvin around sometimes when I cop from him. Slick Melvin is a street name, too. I don't know his real name."

"Joey, tell me who everyone works for."

"Willy Spears. That's the guy. He grew up here in Salisbury, and he knows everybody. He was a few years ahead of me in school, but everybody knew if you were looking to get high, he was the man to see. I never see him on the street anymore, so I guess he's just running things now."

"Where does Willy live?"

"Not sure, but rumor has it he has a real nice place somewhere just outside of town. He's got nice cars and nice women around him all the time. I don't ask too many questions about

Willy. He's dangerous and paranoid. If he found out I was asking questions, they'd stop selling me my stuff."

"Joey, is Willie black or White, what does he look like?"

"He may be black, maybe mixed. I'm 5'10, and he's a little taller than me, maybe 6 feet. The last time I saw him, he was in good shape. Looked like he was working out. Always dressed sharp. Kind of like a pimp. A lot of bling and tailored clothes. He don't wear no hat or nothing like that. Keeps his hair in dreadlocks. He's got cold eyes. Not somebody you'd wanna fuck with, for sure. That's all I know. Can I go now?"

"Okay, Joey, this is how it's going to work. I just took a picture of your driver's license, so I know where your mom lives. If you tell anyone about this little meet-up, I'll find out about it, and I'll pay you a visit. I'd hate to have to hurt your mom, but I will if I hear you've been running your mouth. I want you to write your cell number on a piece of paper and give it to my partner. If I call you, I expect you to answer in case I have more questions. Do we understand each other?"

Joey scribbled his cell number on a piece of a McDonald's bag he pulled from his floorboards and handed it to Diego. He remained pressed against his car even though Diego was no longer pinning him in that position.

"Joey, I think you've earned that fix, so we're going to leave now so you can do your thing. Any questions?"

"No, no, I understand. I won't say shit to nobody, I promise."

"Alright, Joey. Just pretend this never happened, and you'll be fine. If you think Willy is dangerous, you haven't seen my skills yet. Are we clear?"

"Ab—so—lutely," he stuttered.

Diego and Razor disappeared into the darkness, got in

their car, and drove away without illuminating their headlights until they were a hundred yards down the road. Neither thought Joey would try to get their tag number, but no use taking chances.

Julian would be pleased. Willy Spears, not so much.

31 ALONE

Julian's eyes popped open. His cell phone was ringing on the small nightstand next to his bed. Behind his phone was a plastic clock; the glowing numerals announced the time was 3:00 a.m.

Who'd be calling at this hour? Diego and Razor had come home around midnight and reported their progress. Everyone was in the house! No one had this number except Rafael. If he's calling, there is a serious problem!

Julian reluctantly hit the receive button on his phone. "Hello."

"Julian, it is Rafael. Listen to me because I don't have much time."

Julian had the phone pressed tight against his ear but was having trouble hearing. There were loud noises in the background. He heard the distinctive sound of gunshots. People were screaming inaudibly nearby.

"Rafael, what is it? What's going on?"

"Just listen, Julian. We're dead. We're all dead! There was a meeting today, but it was a trap, an ambush. The Sinaloa Cartel has declared war on us. They're killing our people, our families. Soon, I'll be dead. You must never come back. They'll kill you too. I've destroyed all the information about your assignment, and I'll destroy this cell phone as soon as I hang up. No one knows where you are or who's with you. None of you can come back here. Never associate yourself with our cartel, or they'll come for you. Do you understand?"

"No Rafael. This can't be true. Can you get away and hide? I'll come for you."

"No, Julian. I'm lost, but I'll kill as many of these motherfuckers as I can before they take me. Take the money and drugs we sent with you and just disappear. There's no longer a record of you here. There's no longer a Calupoh Cartel."

Gunfire and screaming became louder. Julian heard in the background, "Help me, Rafael. I'm hit!" And then silence.

Julian pressed the phone even harder to his head and whispered, "Rafael, are you still there?" Nothing but silence. The phone was dead or crushed. Rafael's final act of defiance.

It was only then that Julian realized he was no longer by himself. His phone ringing and his elevated voice while talking to Rafael had awakened the entire team, who now stood in his doorway.

After a moment, Ana was the first to speak, "Julian, what's going on? What's happened?"

"It was Rafael. Our cartel is under attack. Everyone is dead. The Sinaloa Cartel has taken over. Rafael is by now dead, too. His message was for us to hide ourselves and never come back to Mexico, or we'd be killed. He said they know nothing of us or our assignment and have no way of knowing unless we go back. There were gunshots and screaming, and then the phone went dead. Rafael said he would destroy it to prevent them from finding us."

The looks on the faces of Julian's team were all the same. One of stark disbelief and terror.

One singular thought. *We are alone!*

32 CHOICES

Sleep was not an option. Everyone was awake and in a state of shock. Julian was the only one who knew what was supposed to happen. The phone call removed whatever plan had been in place.

Julian directed everyone to sit at the chipped Formica top table that served as their dining table and gathering place. There were only four chairs, so Tomas turned a plastic bucket upside down and used it as his seat.

"You all know what's happened. We're alone and have no backup or support. We can't go home because we have no home. Everyone we know is either dead or in hiding. Our cartel no longer exists. We're on our own, and we have to make some very difficult decisions.

"We were sent here with a large sum of money and drugs. It's hidden in the van, and I can retrieve it. The question is simple. Do we continue together or go our separate ways?

"I can offer each of you ten thousand dollars, and you go out on your own, or you can stay, and we'll continue with our plan to take over this gang of drug dealers. You'll share in the profits we'll make from controlling the distribution of drugs on the Eastern Shore.

"I wish I could offer you a lot of time to consider your decision, but we don't have time. I was told we were safe here for up to a year, and the rent had already been paid, but I can assure you of nothing. We'll have to adjust as events require. Questions?"

Diego spoke first. "What're you going to do, Julian? Do you wish to go your separate way and get lost in America?"

"No, Diego. I'll stay here. I was given an assignment, and I still believe there's a chance we'll succeed."

"I've no place to go. I'll stay with you."

Ana weighed in, "I came here because I trusted you to complete our mission. Nothing has changed for me. I'll also stay."

Razor looked into the eyes of her companions, "Okay, what the fuck, I'm in."

"How about you, Tomas?" Julian asked.

"Well, this is definitely not what I signed up for, but it's the only game in town. Let's keep going. I want to make some money, and you guys are the only ones I know who can make that happen. Who do we have to kill to make me money?"

Julian nodded, a smile crossed his lips, "From what I know so far, we need to kill some fucking guy named Willy, and the sooner the better.

"Okay, everybody, try and get some rest. Tomorrow, we find Willy and do what we have to do."

Julian slapped his hand on the center of the table. One by one, his team stacked their hands upon his. Their decision was made, and fate would be the judge of their choices.

33

THE MID ATLANTIC

A week before, Carl Andrews' body washed up on the beach, approximately fifty miles directly out to sea from Sandpiper.

The fishing trawler, *Bloody Bucket,* chugged slowly through the gently rolling waves. The boat itself could no longer live up to its name; it was more of a rust bucket than a bloody bucket. The proud days of this fishing trawler were far behind. Its daily use in the salty Atlantic had taken a toll on the ole girl. However, neglect had played a far larger role. Rust had taken hold of most of the exposed metal of the boat, but no one seemed to care. What paint remained was dull and peeling. The engine had needed to be overhauled a long time ago, but as long as it was running, there was no attempt to ensure its continued life. The metal mesh was being dragged behind the boat on the sea floor, followed by the nets. They were key to capturing the precious scallops that lay deep and waiting to be harvested.

This was how Captain Plummer and First Mate Blankenship made their living. The scallops were only available for a short time, so they were working hard to harvest enough to cover their expenses and put a little extra money in their pocket.

The fact the scallops were here was a secret, mostly kept by the locals. The scallops they were bringing aboard were wild and natural and, to the connoisseur, far more tasty. Directly off the coast of Sandpiper was a natural resource in a place that few knew of. Sandpiper, the beach resort known for its crabs and boardwalk, is also known for its sweet wild scallops.

This location is called Elephant's Trunk, a natural depression running from north to south approximately fifty miles offshore at a depth of about two hundred feet. When viewed on a navigation chart, it resembles an Elephant's Trunk with its mouth open.

This ***is not*** the Baltimore Canyon, which has a depth of upwards of eleven thousand feet and is about seventy miles offshore.

It was 4 a.m. Captain Plummer and the First Mate had consumed nearly a fifth of Captain Morgan between them.

"Donnie, I'm going below to catch a few winks before sunup. You in any shape to steer this thing?"

"Yeah, I got it, Cap. If anything happens, I'll wake you up. I'm getting ready to bring up the net soon, and I got our two helpers here to do the hard work. Get some rest."

Donnie yelled over to the two crewmembers they had hired to make this run. "You two start getting ready. We'll be bringing the net up in about thirty minutes, and that's when your work will really start."

During the next half hour, Donnie nodded, trying to stay awake. It had been a long day. A few more hours and they'd be heading back to shore. He nodded again.

Carl Andrews looked at his friend, Randy Long. "Jesus, Randy, those guys are all fucked up. They've been drinking since we left the dock. I don't know how they do it."

Randy chuckled, "Practice, my man, practice. I've been out with these guys a half dozen times, and it's always the same. If they didn't have the coordinates already written down, we'd never find the place where the scallops are."

Thirty minutes went by quickly. Donnie yelled to the guys, "Okay, I'm going to start bringing up the net."

The net slowly coiled onto its roller, being propelled by the wench, when suddenly, the boat shifted severely to the starboard side.

"What the fuck just happened?"

Captain Plummer emerged from down below. "Donnie, what the hell is going on?" he said as he pushed Donnie out of the captain's seat and took control of the boat.

"I don't know, Cap. The boat just went to the starboard side. Maybe one of the thrusters failed."

"Donnie, you asshole. We're not in the channel. The net and rigging have been dragging along the wall of the depression. The net is now dragging along the ledge."

The Captain came to a full stop. "Randy and Carl stand next to the net as I slowly bring it onboard. Check for damage to the rigging or tears in the net."

"Damn it, Donnie, you may've just put us out of business, you dumb fuck!"

Randy and Carl kept their eyes fixed on the net as it came aboard.

"Captain, I think we might be okay. I'm not seein' any damage, but there's not many scallops. Maybe they got knocked out of the net when we hit the wall." Randy exclaimed.

No sooner were the words out of his mouth when both Randy and Carl saw pieces of debris clinging to the net. Carl yelled first, "Captain, we got somethin' in the net. Looks like pieces of wood, and there's a metal can stuck in the net, too."

The captain stopped the winch. "Take all that shit out of the net and throw it overboard. Once the net is clean, let me know, and I'll start it rolling again."

The two young men cleared the net, and Randy grabbed what he thought was an old crushed beer can. He realized it was an old tin or metal box that was badly dented but still intact. He shook it, and it rattled, so he took it to the captain. "Look what we caught."

The captain grabbed the box from Randy and heard a sound as he turned it over and examined it. "Looks old. Not very big. It might be weights or hooks lost by some ancient fisherman. Get me a flathead screwdriver so I can open it up."

Donnie produced a knife and said, "Try this Cap."

"I'll end up stabbing myself with that. Give me the screwdriver."

Randy found a screwdriver in the boat's toolbox and handed it to the captain. A small crack allowed the captain to insert the screwdriver to pry the lid up. Water and muck drained from the small box first but were then followed by metal disks. The captain quickly put his hand under the box and caught the coins before they fell to the deck. He laid the coins on the dash area of the boat and spread them out. There were eleven in all.

Donnie reached for a coin, but the captain slapped his hand away. "Donnie, just hold on. You've done enough already. Let me take a look first. Maybe we just found us a treasure or at least some beer money once we get back to shore."

Plummer had been to sea all his adult life and had seen a lot of stuff pulled from the water. He had been shown old coins and artifacts recovered from shipwrecks along the east coast. He was now staring at some very old coins. Nothing like he had ever seen before. A smile crossed his lips.

"Donnie, if you weren't so fucking ugly, I'd probably kiss you right now. I think we done found us some treasure."

Thinking quickly, he recorded their exact coordinates and slipped the paper into his pocket. "Get me a small pot of ocean water. These coins may need to stay in seawater."

Carl retrieved a pot of seawater and watched the coins being placed carefully inside. Now, the four men circled the pot and gazed at what had been found.

The captain was the first to break the spell. "Gentleman, we're done looking for scallops today. It's time to celebrate our little treasure find. I think we all need a drink. Get a couple of bottles up here, Donnie, it's party time!"

Speaking to Carl and Randy, the Captain said, "You guys keep bringing in the net and removing any trash. Keep a sharp eye out for any other containers that might contain coins or valuables."

When the helpers were out of earshot, Plummer pulled Donnie aside. "Donnie, keep your mouth shut and listen to me. I think we've just dragged the net across an old sunken ship. That accounts for the pieces of wood. I'll bet these coins are worth thousands, and there just might be a hell of a lot more stuff sittin' down there waiting for us to pull it up. You might be a fuck up most of the time, but you're my fuck up, and you've been loyal all these years. We're gonna be rich and retired fishermen. I know two guys from Jersey who run a dive shop. I'm gonna call them and see if I can get them to come down and dive on our site. We gotta keep this a secret, do you understand?"

"I do, Captain, and I won't say a word. What about those two kids we got working with us today?"

"I have the coordinates, and no way they'd find this place in a million years. We'll hide the coins until I can get them checked out. We'll tell the boys to keep their mouths shut and to return to the boat in a couple of days. Just play along with whatever I say. I'll tell them if the coins are worth anything, we'll be cutting them in for a percentage. Of course, that's not gonna happen, but that should keep them quiet for a couple of days."

"Aye, aye, Cap." *He's going to call me a fuck up one too many times, and I'm gonna rip his head off. I'll bite my tongue until I have my fair share of this treasure, and I'll be the one deciding what my fair share will be.*

After reeling in the net, the four men continued to drink as they took a slow ride back to Sandpiper. The captain pulled one of the coins from the pot and wiped it dry with a soft cloth. It had a dull shine to it, and there was writing on it, but it appeared to be in a foreign language. Ten minutes later, all the coins were pulled from the water and wiped carefully dry.

"You guys watch over these while I go get something out of my cabin," Plummer said.

A few moments later, he returned with a soft leather pouch with a drawstring. He inserted his fingers inside the opening and pried the pouch wide open. "Hey Randy, gather them up and drop them in this pouch. I'll put it in my safe for the time being."

Randy did as he was told. He gathered the coins. *My family and I need a treasure as much as these guys, and I don't trust either of them to be straight with me. He carefully palmed one coin into his other hand and withheld it from the gaping pouch. For now, I'll keep this one coin to myself. What Carl doesn't know can't hurt him. Maybe we'll all be rich.*

The sun had risen by the time they tied off at the pier. They all swore to keep the secret. Time will tell.

34

Beat the Streets

At 8:00 a.m., you could feel the enthusiasm in the PD conference room as the investigators gathered again. This time, they had a target: no name, but pictures of a figure present at both crime scenes. More than a person of interest, a prime suspect. The mutual feeling in the room was to find this guy, slap the cuffs on him, and then find out why he killed two young Sandpiper residents.

Frankie and Patty huddled together at the end of the conference table. "How do you want to work this, Frankie? Can you and Callanan gather the names of all of Randy's and Carl's friends and begin interviewing them? We need to know when they last had contact and with whom. Also, any information about where they may've been working, especially the boats and any local bars. Did either of them talk about having a problem with someone? Did these guys gamble or bet on the horses? Did they get themselves in trouble with people they owed money to? We need to establish a motive if we can."

"Yeah, we can do that. I already have a few names that've never been contacted. The list of friends will grow from what we learn. If we get a strong lead or the name of a suspect, I'll call you right away, and we can revise our plan as we go."

"Bob Carr and I'll hit the marinas and see what we can find out. There're so many damn boats in this town we'll have our work cut out for us. Brogan is here and willing to help. I'll ask him if he wants to go with me and Bob to the marinas. We've already searched where they both lived and found no check stubs for employment. Most of these guys work for cash paid under the table."

Frankie nodded in agreement and went to speak with his investigator.

The two teams were formed and went their separate ways, trying to run down more facts, more leads, and more information. Everyone was pretty much convinced by the end of the day, a name would be connected to the photographs, and the investigation would turn into a manhunt. The majority of cops would think in the back of their minds, *Let it be me. Let me be the one who finds this guy. This is why I became a cop and why I wanted to be a detective. Let me be the one on the six o'clock news standing next to the Chief/Sheriff, humbly accepting the gratitude of a grateful community.* If a cop is not into this ego-building mindset, he probably isn't a very good cop. Everyone says it's a team effort, but everybody wants to lead the team and score the winning point. Patty said, "Okay, boys, let's beat the streets. We'll meet back here at 6 p.m. unless something breaks before then."

Brogan tagged along with Patty Ryan and Bob Carr, visiting the local marinas in an attempt to identify which boat captain hired these victims.

Brogan reminded Patty and Bob, "They may've worked on more than one boat, and it doesn't necessarily mean it was a commercial boat. The privately-owned charter boats frequently hire deck hands to help the tourists with their tackle and baiting their lines."

West Sandpiper had two major marinas that fit this description.

Bob Carr went to the marina with a large number of private charters for fishing trips near Finnegan Jacks, a local haunt. Twenty or more charter boats were tied to the piers next to a large parking lot. Charters went out daily loaded with hopeful fishermen, with only a few actually knowing what they were doing. Was it the lure of the sea, the opportunity to catch the big one, or perhaps just a boat ride with beer? All in all, it was a fun experience.

Patty and Brogan went to mostly commercial areas between Sunset Boulevard and Harbor Drive. The channel leading into a public boat launch was lined with fishing trawlers. It was a direct shot from there to the inlet leading to the Atlantic Ocean. Each Captain had his plan and itinerary for catching fish, scallops, clams, or crabs. Theirs was not a nine-to-five job. They left and returned at all hours of the day and night. The Harbormaster was going to be Patty and Brogan's first location. Maybe they would find their answers in one stop. Maybe not.

Brogan rode with Patty. "If we strike out here, we've still got the marina at 12th Street on the bay, and there're charter boats tied up at different piers from Inlet North. Even some of the larger pleasure boat Captains hire deckhands when they take their friends out for a cruise. This'll be like looking for the preverbal needle in a haystack. Luckily for us, most of the captains know each other. Keep your fingers crossed because even though the deckhands move around, the Captains usually know where to find them."

While on Harbor Street interviewing a trawler captain, Brogan noticed an empty length of pier large enough to hold a boat. "Captain, is there a boat normally tied up across from you?"

"Yeah, the *Bloody Bucket,* it went out very early this morning. Probably headed out to look for scallops. It's that time of year, and I know Captain Plummer relies on the money he makes from scallops each year."

"The *Bloody Bucket*? Sounds a little extreme."

"Yeah, go figure. I've never known why it's called that, and I don't think I want to. It's a piece of shit. Rust everywhere, and the paint peeling off. The captain doesn't seem to care. I'd hate to be on board if a real storm was to blow up while they're out there."

"Do you know Plummer's first name?"

"It's Tony. He's an older guy. Been around here longer than I have, and I've been tying up here for fifteen years. He and his first mate drink like a fish, no pun intended, but they still go out every day, usually leaving before the sun comes up or coming in shortly after the sun comes up. Crazy hours, but he makes it work."

"Does he hire deckhands?"

"He does. Usually, young guys help them with the nets. Mostly college-age or locals looking for some extra bucks. I know he pays them in cash, and they come and they go. He had two extra guys on his boat this morning when they left. He waved, but I didn't pay much attention. Oh, I did see his first mate, Donnie. He's a piece of work. Not sure I've ever seen him sober."

Patty chimed in, "Is that their car, the blue SUV, parked over there near the pier?"

"No, unless they just got it. Plummer lives on his boat, and Donnie drives an old pickup truck. I don't see Donnie's truck, but it's always in and out of the shop. He either Ubers or gets someone to drop him off. I think sometimes he just bunks out on the boat while his truck's in the shop. Those two guys have been together as long as I've known them. Donnie hauls Plummer around if he needs to go somewhere."

"Thanks, Captain. May I have your cell number in case we have further questions?"

"Sure, I even have a card." The man dug into his wallet and produced a dinghy card that may have been white at one time. It said Captain George Howlett, Fishing Services, LLC, with a local cell number. That explained the boat's name, *The Howlett.*

Brogan thought, *If I had the time, I'd love to hear the story. I'm sure this name is attached to a family of seafaring sailors. Maybe fishermen, maybe Vets who served their country at sea. Always stories behind the naming of these boats. I'll remember to come back when this is all settled and hear* The Howlett's *story.*

Patty and Brogan continued to work on both sides of the channel, speaking with boat captains, deckhands, the harbormaster, and even the Coast Guard, which had a small office on the channel. No one was able to help. In some cases, the pictures of the two boys looked familiar, but no one was sure, and no one remembered specifically seeing them on any of the boats.

At 5:30 p.m., they decided to look for Detective Carr and see if he'd had any luck. As they drove out on Harbor Road, Patty noticed the blue SUV with a New Jersey tag still sitting at the pier. Not all that unusual for Sandpiper. People came from far and wide. Some lived in the area for years before changing their tags to Maryland. Only then did so because some aggressive and attentive police officer jerked them up and told them to get Maryland tags on their car or it would be towed the next time the officer saw it on the road. Patty slowed, pulled over, and jotted the tag number down, intending to run it when they got back to the station.

Carr, Mazzone, and Callanan had also struck out with no solid leads that would begin the manhunt. This was police work. Hours and days of footwork, interviews, and wrong turns. The investigators, if nothing else, were persistent and knew they must continue the routine work to get the break in the case. Everyone agreed to meet back up the next day at the same time to begin again.

Patty was walking out the door with Brogan when she stopped dead in her tracks and said, "You go on. I forgot something. I'll see you in the morning."

"Something I can help you with?" Brogan asked.

"Nah, I got it. It'll only take me a minute, and then I'm headed home to get some rest."

"Okay. See you in the a.m."

Patty returned to the Communications Room of the P.D. and handed the P.C.O. a scrap of paper with a New Jersey tag number. It only took a couple of minutes, and the P.C.O. handed Patty a printout of the results of the tag search.

The tag came back to Dark Sea Adventures at a street address in Cape May, New Jersey. It was listed to a 2019 Chevrolet SUV. The tag was current, and there were no warrants or wants for the tag number.

Patty took the printout and returned to her desk. She sat down at her computer and Googled Dark Sea Adventures in Cape May. Google spit back a finding. It was a dive shop offering lessons and diving equipment. It also offered diving expeditions on sunken ships in the Cape May area. *Okay, what was this vehicle doing in Maryland? Why was it sitting at the empty pier all day long? Should've checked it out more closely. At least looked inside for anything unusual or interesting. I'll tell Brogan first thing tomorrow, and we'll check it out. Shit, it might be gone. I'll ride by on my way home, and if it's still there, I'll check it out myself. I won't be able to sleep until I do.*

35

TREASURE HUNT

Before the police even began their day, the crew of the *Bloody Bucket* was meeting with two scuba divers who had driven through the night to arrive pier side in West Sandpiper at 5 a.m. It was part of the hiring agreement they entered into with Captain Tony Plummer. He had insisted his trawler must cast off by 6 a.m. Plummer had agreed to meet the diver's demand for two thousand dollars a day. Plummer and Blankenship briefed the divers on what to expect.

Plummer explained, "This trip is highly secretive but'll be well worth your time. I'm gonna take you to a place where we believe a treasure of great value is ours for the taking. In addition to the two thousand dollars, I'm offering you five percent of anything you bring up." To convince them, he pulled a coin from his pocket.

"I took this to a dealer in Washington DC; he confirmed I had something rare. He offered me fifteen hundred dollars right off the bat. I said no way; I'll come back with more shit, and then we'll talk about a deal. I told him to professionally clean it, and the bastard hesitated, so I picked up the coin and started to leave. I guess seeing a potential fortune walk out the door was enough to change his fucking mind. I stayed and watched him clean it, and before I left, I gave him the number to my burner phone. We can go back to him or find other dealers to see who's willing to pay the most with no questions asked. The damn guy was so quick to offer me the fifteen hundred dollars for one coin before it was cleaned, I think he was probably lowballing me. I believe our treasure may be worth far more than we're hoping for."

The divers, Wayne Pettit and Lester McCarthy, were impressed.

Wayne said, "We've explored a lot of wrecks and found some old coins, but nothing like this. If they're more, we're definitely into something good. You've got yourself a deal. We've got a lot of gear we need to unload onto the boat, so let's get started."

Wayne and Lester exchanged a look when they saw the condition of Plummer's boat. Lester thought, *We ought to be getting hazardous duty pay for just going out on this rusty relic.*

Captain Plummer glanced at the coordinates and slipped the piece of paper back into his front pocket.

Donnie saw this move and smiled to himself. *His front pocket is securing our fortune, and he calls me a stupid fuck!*

Plummer charted a circuitous route to the correct coordinates. To protect this location, he had already demanded the divers leave their GPS-equipped cell phones locked in their vehicle along with their Apple watches. He permitted only their dive watches to be taken on his boat. Once at sea, the eye can only see about three miles in any direction due to the curvature of the Earth. The Atlantic Ocean is a very big place, and even if someone knew the treasure was close to the

Elephant Trunk, it would be of little help. The depression ran from New Jersey to Virginia. Hundreds of miles with a target that may be as small as a one-hundred-yard debris field. They had stumbled on the location, and without the coordinates, they would never find it again.

This was not going to be an archeological search. The captain had no interest in knowing the name of the ship or the age of historical things like wine jugs or storage bottles. This was a search-and-destroy mission. If it wasn't gold, silver, or something else of value, then it stays on the sea floor.

A normally two-hour trip had taken them a little over three hours to arrive at the wreck site. The entire time, the divers were setting up and checking all their equipment. The captain told Wayne and Lester, "Depth finder places the wreck at between forty and fifty feet down."

Based on that information, Wayne said, "We have two sets of tanks. We can make two dives today. We can stay down for thirty to forty-five minutes for each dive. The largest problem facing us is relocating the site. Even with your coordinates, the time it took you to realize what you had found and actually note the coordinates, you probably traveled some distance. Our greatest advantage is that you said it's right on the edge of the ledge. That will narrow our area of focus significantly. Hopefully, when you dragged your net along this area, it stirred up enough debris to make it more visible. The sky is mostly clear, so we should have sufficient sunlight to easily see the surface along the edge. If any part of the ship or treasure fell over the ledge, it would be scattered along the wall and the floor of the depression two hundred feet below and well out of our reach."

Lester articulated, "The cameras mounted on top of our

diving masks will allow you to see everything we're seeing. The monitor set up in the deck house will have a split screen for your viewing. We'll be able to talk back and forth on our radio system. Just hope the currents aren't too crazy down there. It may be tricky being close to the sudden drop-off, but we'll see. We'll follow the anchor line down to the sea floor. To avoid getting the bends, we'll stop at the thirty-foot level, both going down and coming up. We'll be working on a buddy system and within sight of each other during the entire dive. When we find the wreckage, adjust the coordinates accordingly, so when we come back, we'll be able to sit right on top of the site. Any questions?"

Donnie shook his head. Plummer looked at the divers and said, "No, we're good."

And with that, both men entered the water, cleared their masks, put their regulators in their mouths, and disappeared below the waves.

Plummer turned to Donnie. "Take that fucking flag off the rear of our boat."

"They said they needed that flag up to show they're divers in the water."

"I know what they said, Donnie. Take it down. We're fishermen, and if someone should get within sight, I don't want them to know what we're doing today. Are you following me, Donnie? When they say they're coming up, you can put the flag back up."

The first twenty minutes were intense with anticipation. The divers moved slowly north along the edge of the ledge. They knew if the coordinates were off, the wreck might lay a little north.

A dark spot appeared in Wayne's video, small but definitely

out of place for the otherwise barren and sandy bottom. As he grew closer, the shadow began to take form. It was a piece of wood sticking out of the sand at an awkward angle. Both divers stopped and viewed the area before them. Numerous sticks and debris appeared in front of them.

"You guys seeing this?" Lester said with obvious excitement in his voice.

Donnie reached for the mike to answer the question, but Plummer snatched it from his hand and glared at him as if he were a bug under his shoe.

"Yes, we can see it," Plummer responded while turning his back on Donnie so he could record the new coordinates. He used the same piece of paper from his pocket, scratching out the old and entering the new.

Donnie's eyes bored into Plummer's back. *So, this is how it's going to be now that we're about to be rich! I should've known he'd never change. His days of belittling me are growing short. Once I get my share, I'm done with this asshole.*

The divers' began a tight grid search among the debris and almost immediately held up a handful of old coins clustered together just below the surface. A few feet further and again, they held up what appeared to be an old necklace. The gems in the necklace were dull with age and exposure, but they were gems nonetheless. Each find was placed in bags attached to the diver's belts.

On the ocean's surface, Donnie and Plummer looked around to make sure their hooting and hollering weren't drawing any unwanted attention. They were alone. Not another boat in sight.

A few minutes later, the divers advised they were coming up. Donnie looked around and saw nothing on the horizon before he placed the diver-down flag back up. Ten minutes later, both divers were back on the boat. Very happy but obviously tired from their swim and search.

Plummer pulled out a card table and set it up on the deck, allowing the divers to empty the contents of their dive bags. Coins, jewelry, and a small statue of an unidentified figure covered the table. A small fortune had been recovered, and no one knew what else was down there waiting to be found.

Everyone was laughing, high-fiving each other, and generally out of control.

Donnie saw it first. A small dot on the horizon. Another boat appeared to be coming their way.

Plummer reacted immediately. "Pull down the diving flag and raise the anchor. Whoever this is can't know what we've been up to. Cover up all the diving equipment with the tarps in that cabinet on the port side. Put the treasure in this empty ice chest. You two go below deck and get out of that diving gear, then get back up here and be quick. As soon as the anchor is up, I'm going to start the engine and head towards that boat. I'll do all the talking. Break out a few beers and pretend to be having a good time.

A short time later, they drew near another fishing trawler. Both killed their engines, and the Captain of the other boat yelled across a twenty-foot gap. "Hey, you guys, okay? I thought at first you were dead in the water. I tried to hail you on the radio but got no answer, so I thought I'd better check on you."

"Yeah, we're good." Plummer said "We were having a little trouble with the engine, but I figured it out. I'm afraid it may be a temporary fix, so we're going to head in and have my mechanic give it a look—my fault about the radio. I turned everything off to save on the batteries in case we needed them to get this damn thing started again. I really appreciate you coming to our aid. You guys want a couple of beers for your effort? We got no scallops, but we got beer."

The crew of the other trawler laughed but declined the offer of beer. "You keep your beer. You may need a few if that mechanic finds anything really wrong with your engine. Thanks for leaving your scallops down there for us. Call us on the radio if you can't make it in. We gotta hang together out here. Don't want to have to call the Coasties to bail us out. Once they're on your boat, they're into everything."

Plummer laughed, started his engine, waved, and pulled slowly away, headed back to Sandpiper.

Plummer said, "Okay, this is what's going to happen. We're going back to Sandpiper. Tomorrow morning, we leave at 5 a.m. Can you guys get your depleted tanks refilled once we get back?"

"Yeah, no problem. There's a small dive shop in Berlin. They should be able to help us. Didn't you want to try another dive today?"

"Not with that other boat in the area. We may be diving on that wreck for a few days, so I don't want to draw any attention to our being there. That other trawler will drag the center area of the depression and move to another area if they come out tomorrow. I'm going to lock up our treasure in the ship's safe for tonight. I live on the boat, so it'll be safe. Buy anything else you need at that dive shop, and I'll pay for it. We need to move quickly."

"Good for us," Wayne said, "we'll fill our empty tanks and find a motel for the night. We'll be back at 4:30 a.m., so we can head out at 5. We got nothing on our calendars that's more important than this, so you've got us as long as it takes."

The ride home was uneventful. The divers left right away to get to the dive shop before it closed. Donnie helped Plummer carry the ice chest down below and stow the treasure in the safe in the Captain's cabin.

Plummer told Donnie, "You gas up the boat for tomorrow's trip."

Plummer sat in his Captain's chair up in the deckhouse, drinking directly from a bottle of Captain Morgan while watching Donnie do the work. Plummer was lost in his thoughts. *One more day of diving should be enough to set me up for life. How am I gonna spend all my money? Especially since I've decided I won't be sharing it with anybody else. After the dive tomorrow, I'll eliminate the two divers and then get rid of Donnie on the way back in. I know that stupid fucker can't keep a secret. Once he's drunk, there's no telling what he might do or say. Better not to have to worry. At least better for me.*

Donnie finished topping off the gas tanks and came to where the Captain was still enjoying his Captain Morgan. "Hey Cap, how about we catch something to eat? You buying tonight?"

"Donnie, I'm thinking about going ashore and eating at the restaurant down the street. I'll bring you something back in an hour or two."

"Why can't I go with you?"

"Just look in the mirror, Donnie. You're filthy, dirty, and not fit to go into a restaurant. You stink of gas and oil. I thought cutting all your hair off and shaving that beard would be a good start for you cleaning yourself up a little. You just don't get it." Plummer said as he slid off his seat and turned to get his baseball cap off a nearby peg.

"Never mind Cap. You don't have to bring me anything."

Plummer turned to face Donnie, "Why? You don't —

Donnie didn't hear the rest as he plunged a nine-inch fillet knife into Plummer's belly.

"Guess you won't be going either, will you, you dumb fucker!" Donnie said calmly while holding the knife in place with both hands.

Plummer reached down with both hands, placing them on top of Donnie's and pushing toward Donnie to remove the knife. Donnie was far too strong and simply walked forward, pushing Plummer into the bulkhead and bearing down on the knife deeply in the stomach wall. Plummer was going into shock, and his legs could no longer support his weight.

"Donnie, what're you doing?" Plummer whispered. "What've you done? Help me, we're partners. We're gonna be rich." Donnie felt nothing as he watched the blood leak out of his belly.

"No, Captain. We're not partners, and you're not going to be rich. You've treated me like shit, bossed me around, humiliated me in front of other people, and had me do all your dirty work for years. I'm going to be rich, and you're going to be dead."

Disbelief filled Plummer's face as he looked more disappointed than angry or hurt. "Donnie, I'm sorry. Please help me."

"Here, I'll help you," Donnie said as he pulled the knife out and then plunged it deep into Plummer's heart. "Need any more help?"

Donnie released the handle of the knife, knelt, slipped his fingers into the captain's right pocket, and removed a small slip of paper that had two sets of coordinates with one circled. Clear directions to his future. "Thanks, Cap."

36

ONLY TAKE A MINUTE

Donnie quickly searched the body and removed the cap's wallet, cash, keys, and a small knife. "You don't have much in the way of worldly belongings, do you?" he said to Plummer. Grabbing a blue tarp from the deck locker, he rolled the captain up like a mummy and wrapped an excessive amount of silver duct tape around the body. Then, drug it carelessly down the steps to the lower cabins.

"How about I put you in your cabin so you can rest until we go for your last boat ride? It'll be fitting for you to be buried at sea." Donnie kinda liked havin' a one-sided conversation without insults being thrown in his face.

He glanced at the safe containing the treasure. Long ago, he'd learned the combination by watching a very drunk Plummer opening it. He locked the cabin door and put the key in his pocket. Returning topside, he grabbed a hose to begin the chore of washing down the decks. Captain Plummer's blood, mixed with dried fish blood, ran through the scuppers and disappeared over the side of the boat. The sun would be going down soon, so he grabbed the remains of a cold-cut sub he'd stashed in the refrigerator yesterday. He ate wholeheartedly without remorse for any of his actions over the past few weeks.

Headlights swept the boat as a car pulled up to the dock directly next to the boat. *Have the divers come back? Nah, that's not an SUV. Damn, looks like a cop car!*

Patty Ryan was disappointed when she arrived at the marina and found the SUV from New Jersey gone from where it had been parked. She swung her unmarked patrol car up near the channel. Disappointment turned to anticipation. The fishing trawler, *Bloody Bucket*, was tied to the dock, and there were lights showing through the cabin windows. Her headlights illuminated a man on the back deck hanging up a hose on a nearby piling.

Well, look what I have here. One more quick interview and then home to get some rest. This should only take a minute.

Patty put her car in park and turned it off. The headlights stayed lit for a few more seconds before they turned themselves off. She grabbed her notepad and pen and then exited her vehicle. She walked the few steps to the side of the trawler.

"Evening, ma'am, can I help you?"

A bald, clean-shaven man dressed in dirty jeans and an even dirtier tee shirt looked up at her from the deck. He appeared to be in his sixties with a stocky build.

"Hi, I hope so. I'm Detective Ryan from Sandpiper P.D. Are you the Captain of this boat?"

"No, ma'am, I'm the First Mate. My name's Donnie. Captain Plummer is ashore picking up some supplies."

"Donnie, do you have a minute to answer some questions?"

"Yeah, don't see why not. You want to come on board so we can talk?"

"That would be great," Patty said. She easily stepped across the twelve-inch gap from the pier to the small ladder in the boat. There was no railing on the ladder, so Donnie stepped forward quickly and offered his hand to steady her as she backed down onto the deck.

Patty reluctantly took his hand, knowing she would need to take a moist towelette to her hands as soon as she returned to her car. Everything about this boat was dirty. Still, taking his hand was far wiser than falling and taking a full-body slide across the wet decking.

"We can talk in here," Donnie said as he turned to the open door of the deck house.

She followed him into the well-lighted cabin and watched as he nimbly climbed up into what was the Captain's chair behind the wheel. He pointed to another elevated seat directly across the aisle from him. Dressed in slacks, Patty had no problem taking the offered seat. *Now, my slacks will need a trip to the dry cleaners.*

"Donnie, may I ask your last name just for my records?"

"Sure, it's Davenport."

"Where do you live, Mr. Davenport?"

"Right here on this boat most of the time. Sometimes, when I feel like a change, I'll get a room at a nearby motel. They've known me for a long time and gave me a special rate. They've got real nice showers in their rooms, and I like to sleep on a real bed once in a while."

"I'm here trying to run down some information we have on two young men who worked on the boats part-time. Do you know Randy Long or Carl Andrews?" She passed him the photographs. He accepted them and looked closely at each picture.

While he examined photos, Ryan examined him. There was something about him that tweaked her as being wrong.

What am I missing? Do I know this guy from a previous case or meeting?

The realization came slowly. *This guy works on a boat, and his arms are deeply tanned, but he doesn't have a tan on his face or the top of his head. Where's his tan? I guess he might protect his face and head with a hat and sunglasses covering his eyes.*

Her thoughts were interrupted when Donnie answered, "These guys look familiar, but they've never worked on this boat. I've been on this bucket for twenty years, and a lot of kids have worked on her, but not these two. Maybe I saw them in one of the local bars. What'd they do?"

While Donnie was talking, Patty glanced over his shoulder and saw a dark blue hat partially hidden, stuffed between a cabinet and the bulkhead behind him. Patty recognized the bucket hat immediately. Her brain and gut reached a simultaneous conclusion. *This might be our guy. He could've cut his hair and shaved his beard to change his appearance. It explains the pale skin. Umm, not sure enough to make an immediate arrest, but we'll need to look hard at this guy. I'll call Brogan as soon as I get back in my car and run this by him. I'll need to do a full background and workup. See if he's in the system.*

Donnie studied Ryan as he handed back the photographs. She hadn't answered his question about what the two had done. He knew both were dead. *Why didn't she answer my question? What's she lookin at behind me?*

"Sorry, I couldn't help. If you give me a card, I'll talk to the Captain about these two. Can I keep the pictures?"

"Ah, yes, yes you can, Mr. Davenport. That'd be great. I have extras in my car, so you can keep these." She handed a card and the pictures back to Davenport. His eyes bored into hers.

"Guess we're done then?" he said.

"Yep, we're done. Please ask the Captain to call me if he recognizes either one of these young men and thank you for your time."

Patty slid from her seat, extended her hand, took his grimy hand, and gave it a shake. She turned towards the steps to the main deck that would take her back to her car.

She heard the squeak of the seat behind her as Donnie shifted his weight. Suddenly, she was struck in the back of the head and knocked unconscious. *Damn, I thought Plummer was out of his mind when he bought this old belaying pin at the antique store years ago. He said it reminded him of sailors of long ago. Still works, so I guess he was right.*

"Sorry, Missy. You're trouble. I could tell you were gettin suspicious. I can't risk lettin you get off this boat. Hope you don't get seasick because tomorrow you'll be goin' out with me and the boys. Sorry, it's gonna be a one-way trip."

Donnie turned off the cabin lights and removed Patty's gun, handcuffs, and cell phone from her limp body. He placed her car keys in his pocket and walked up to the main deck to look around. Nobody is paying any attention. He went to the railing, flanking the channel, and quietly dropped Patty's stuff in the water.

He grabbed the roll of duct tape, returned to Patty, and checked her neck for a pulse. It was strong, so he commenced to bind her wrists and ankles before lifting her on his shoulder and moving towards the captain's cabin.

Donnie tossed Patty Ryan on the bed, lifted her head, and wrapped several turns of duct tape over her mouth. He was careful not to cover her nose, allowing her to breathe. Seeing Patty lying there so vulnerable stirred something in Donnie. He had never considered himself a pervert. His sexual appetite was normally sated with a skin magazine and a quick right hand. His age, appearance, and lack of social skills had pretty much denied him any sexual relationships. He had been keeping a vow he'd made to himself years ago. Never going to pay for something that might give me a disease. That would be stupid.

Maybe before tossing her overboard, she might be willing to negotiate to stay alive. Wouldn't hurt to try. If she resisted, she'd immediately join the other passengers on their journey to the bottom of the sea. It would only take a minute!

37

LOOKING FOR WILLY

Tomas watched from the front door as his cohorts drove away. He was not invited to go with them, and for that, he was glad. They were driving off to certain danger. *What'll I do if they never come back? No one knows where I am. I'm a stranger in this country. Can I make it on my own?* He shook off the bad thoughts. *They will return. They must.*

It was 7 p.m., the sun would set soon, and nature would deliver what they sought. Their plan, as loose as it was, depended upon the cover of darkness to succeed.

Julian and Ana rode up front, and Razor and Diego sat behind them, observing the passing scenery from the back seat. They decided the van offered them the best options for what they intended to do.

"Do you remember how to get back to the house?" Ana asked Julian.

"I think so, but I'm sure you'll correct me if I'm wrong."

She smiled, "Count on it."

Diego said, "Tell me more about this house we're going to. Does it sit by itself, or are the neighbors close?"

Ana told Diego and Razor, "There's some distance between houses, and there're no street lights. It's a very dark area at night. We'll hide the van somewhere nearby, cut across some fields, and come in behind the house. There're trees and shrubbery, so our approach should go unnoticed. When we were there the other night, I didn't hear any dogs barking, and there were no outside spotlights or even porch lights. There'll be no one there when we arrive. The last time they got home just before midnight."

Razor said, "So we break in and wait inside for them to arrive?"

Julian responded, "Yes, it'll be the best way to take control of the situation. If we wait until they're inside and then come in, we'll probably be met with resistance in the form of a hail of bullets. This way, we'll have the drop on them before they know what happened. They're cocky and not cautious, but when we surprise them, they may go for their guns. Our guns are silenced, so we'll be shooting first if we have to. Try not to kill them. We need to talk to them. Then we can kill them."

Diego nodded his head. *I like this plan. It's time for us to make a move, and hitting a possible stash house is a great start. Finding out where this guy Willy lives shouldn't be hard if someone is still alive to talk to us.*

An hour later, the van was stashed on a farm road, and their small group had made their way to the backyard of the house that was their target. The house was totally dark, and there were no vehicles in the driveway.

Julian told everyone, "Glove up. Diego, you go find a place near the front of the house where you can stop anyone trying to flee through the front door. No one must get away to sound an alarm or warn the rest of the gang what's coming their way. Make sure your spot hides you from anyone pulling into the driveway. When they come, just let them enter. We'll be ready for them. Don't come in until you see Razor wave for you to do so." Diego broke off and began circling the house. It was 9 p.m., so he knew the wait may be long.

Julian and the two women crept up to the rear of the house. The windows were curtained. No light appeared behind any of them. The rear door's upper portion was glass. There was no overhead light, and no spotlights had sprung to life. Ana placed her ear near the glass and listened. Nothing, not a sound.

She gave her two companions a thumbs up. Julian turned the door handle. Locked. He produced a lockpick set, knelt at the door, and began to probe. It was an old lock, and it took only about two minutes before he heard the tumblers fall into place. The door opened silently into a kitchen area.

Ana and Razor produced two small flashlights and waited to see if an alarm would sound or if someone would come to investigate. Nothing happened. All three held guns in their free hands and began to move deeper into the house. Fifteen minutes later, the house had been cleared. One blink of a flashlight from Razor told Diego they were in.

The backdoor was relocked, and Ana and Julian found comfortable positions just off the living room where they could conceal themselves and wait to spring their trap. They laid a roll of duct tape near their feet.

Razor moved through the two bedrooms and found a couple pounds of pot in one of the closets, hidden only by some dirty laundry thrown over it. She decided further searching with her flashlight might give them away, so she retreated to the kitchen, where she found a shotgun propped against the side of the refrigerator. It was loaded and ready to go, but dismissed it as being too noisy. She ejected the shells, tossed them in the trash can, and put it back where she found it. She took a kitchen chair, moved it into a small hallway, and joined in the wait.

At 11:40 p.m., Diego saw a set of headlights approaching. He had a good hiding place but lowered himself even further in anticipation. Without signaling, the vehicle slowed and turned into the driveway. The headlights swept over his hiding place and then across the front of the darkened house. The driver's door opened, and a sturdy-built black male stepped from the car. The passenger door opened, and a younger version of the same guy joined him on the driveway. They were laughing over some joke or story. The passenger had a dark bag slung over his shoulder. The driver jingled his keys as they made their way up the short sidewalk to the front door. The driver paused, turned, and pointed the keys towards the car. Headlights flashed once, and the horn tooted, verifying the car was now locked and the alarm was set.

"Damn, I always forget to turn on the porch light before we leave. Darker than a well-digger's ass out here. I can't even see where to stick the key. Oh there, I got it," the driver said as he pushed the door open with his left shoulder. The passenger followed closely behind him as they entered. A moment later, the living room was bathed in light as a switch had been thrown.

Diego heard loud but undistinguishable voices coming from the house. He moved quickly towards the front door. Sure enough, the front door flew open as the passenger attempted to escape the interior of the house. Diego met him with a devastating punch to the midsection, and when he involuntarily bent forward, Diego followed up by placing his hands on the man's shoulders and pushing him forcefully back through the door. "Where do you think you're going?" Diego said. He stopped at the entryway and observed the scene before him.

The driver was on the floor with three guns pointed at him. The passenger was now on the floor near him. The dark leather messenger bag lay close by.

Julian ordered. "Hands behind your head, or you die! Razor, frisk them. Ana get two chairs from the kitchen. Diego, stay right where you are."

Everyone complied, and very quickly, the two drug dealers were seated and duct-taped to the chairs, their ankles to the legs, their arms behind their backs, and to the back of the chair. A couple of wraps around their chests and a short strip over their mouths made sure they weren't going anywhere.

Julian examined the two guns that had been removed from the duo and placed them on a nearby coffee table. They were semi-automatics loaded with one in the chamber. *We were wise to set up this ambush. This could've become loud and ugly fast.*

The leather bag had been opened and dumped on a couch. Several thousand dollars in small bills rubber banded together created a small mountain of cash. Impressive for one night's work in the beach town of Sandpiper. There were no drugs in the pouch or on either man.

"Diego, go out to the car and search for product. I doubt these guys sold out."

Diego returned about ten minutes later carrying a green garbage bag. The garbage bag held a small pharmacy of various drugs proportioned and bagged for sale. Inside were at least five pounds of pot in glassine bags of varying sizes and weights. Small wax envelopes were banded together by rubber bands. They housed white powder. Other envelopes and small bags contained pills and tablets of various colors and sizes.

With both men contained and quiet, a thorough search of the house was done. It soon began to look like a drug warehouse as more and more drugs and money were found throughout and then piled in the living room.

Julian fronted the two men. "I'm going to ask some questions, and you're going to answer me if you want to live to see tomorrow. Understood?

The older one looked defiantly at Julian and did not move. The younger guy glanced at his partner and followed his lead, and sat frozen.

"Okay, I guess you want to play tough guys. As you can tell, we're all Hispanic. We've come from Mexico on the orders of our cartel. They've sent us to take over your operation. You have two choices. You can work for us, or you can die tonight. We already know about Willy, and tonight, Willy can't save you. He's probably laid up in bed with some coke whore while you're facing our guns. We just want to know where Willy lives so we can negotiate with him for a peaceful takeover. Doesn't that make sense to you? If you die, he'll just replace you. We won't tell him who told us where he lives. You'll have new bosses, but life will go on, and you'll continue to do what you do.

"Razor, remove the tape on his mouth," Julian instructed, pointing his gun at the older one.

"What do you say, hombre? Can we do business?"

"Who are you fucking people? Do you know who you're going up against? He'll kill you, and then he'll kill us for having talked to you. This is my kid brother. He knows nothing. Let him go, and maybe we can talk."

"First of all, I'm asking the questions, and nobody is going anywhere until I have answers to our questions. The only people in danger of dying tonight are you and your little brother. Razor put the tape back on his mouth.

"Now, Razor, take the tape off the brother."

She ripped the tape from his lips. Beads of sweat stood out on his forehead. His eyes had welled up, but he fought to remain brave in the face of danger he had never experienced before.

"Okay, little man. Your turn. You heard the questions. You got some answers?"

"I don't know nothing. I was just riding along with my brother tonight. I'm not part of this. I don't even know Willy or where he lives."

"Why you carrying a gun if you're not involved?"

The kid shook his head and remained silent.

"Too bad, I guess we don't need you anymore."

Julian moved forward and placed the silencer against the young kid's head. The older brother reacted violently, almost turning his chair over before Diego held him in place. He shook his head, and his eyes grew wide, knowing what was about to happen.

Julian hesitated and then told Razor, "Put the tape back on the kid and take it off his brother." Julian bent over the brother.

"What? You got something to say now?"

"He's telling the truth. He don't know nothing. I was just showing him how I get my money. Kind of showing off for my younger brother. I gave him the gun in case we got jacked. Please let him go."

"Re-tape him and turn the TV on." Razor did as instructed.

Julian went to the kid, placed the tip of the gun on his right knee, and pulled the trigger.

The tape couldn't completely silence the scream that followed the shot. Blood immediately soaked the jeans around his knee, and he thrashed wildly about. Tears ran down his cheeks, and the terror showed in his eyes.

Julian moved back to the older brother. "Now, see what you've made me do? The kid will probably walk with a limp or with a cane for the rest of his life. If you still wish to remain silent, I'll shoot him in his other knee, and he'll be in a wheelchair for the rest of his life."

The older brother slumped as much as he could in his current position and bowed his head in submission.

Things moved quickly after that. They learned the older brother was Martin and the kid was Michael. They both lived in Salisbury, and Martin was a lieutenant in Willy's organization.

He said, "I've known Willy my entire life and worked for him even before I got out of high school. This is one of Willy's stash houses. Tomorrow, a guy named Slick Melvin will come around and collect the money for the last two days and resupply us with whatever drugs we need. I've never been in Willy's new house."

Martin continued, "The new house is a two-story white colonial-looking place with big columns on the front porch. It's on Route 12 on the righthand side of the road, about two miles outside the Salisbury town limits. It's gated and surrounded by a tall iron fence. At least two dogs patrol the grounds at night. There're cameras and alarms. Slick Melvin told me there's a swimming pool in the back and a small guest house on the property. He also told me that no drugs or drug money is kept in Willy's house. There's another stash house where all the money and drugs are kept. I don't know where that is. Willy is paranoid and very dangerous."

"Okay. Sorry about the kid, but it didn't have to be that way. What we're going to do is place pillowcases over your head. We won't tie them so you can breathe. We're taking all the money, drugs, your guns, and cell phones with us. Slick Melvin can cut you free in the morning."

The pillowcases were put in place. The van was brought to the house and loaded with the fruits of their efforts. Julian stood at the open door of the van until everyone else got in. "One more thing," Julian said, "and we'll be gone." He walked back into the house, approached the men from behind, and shot both of them in the head. The silenced gun made very little noise. The TV played on. There was a plume of blood on the fronts of the pillowcases.

Once they pulled out of the driveway, Julian said, "We're going home. We need a plan to take Willy out. If we try to crash into his home, we may not succeed. We have no room for failure. To Willy, it'll look like a simple robbery and removal of witnesses. He'll reach out to his friends and enemies to find out who ripped him and killed two of his people. The police will be all over that stash house, so he's going to lay low. We'll be patient and come up with a better plan to deal with him. Let's see if the dealers appear on the streets tomorrow night in Sandpiper. We did good. You guys split the money among yourselves."

Ana thought to herself, *Willy is going to really be pissed. He'll want blood for what happened tonight and take this as a personal affront to his power. He'll be super cautious. We need to show caution ourselves. I hope Julian comes up with a smart plan.*

38

RETURN TO ELEPHANT'S TRUNK

It was semi-dark when Patty awoke with a throbbing headache. It took a few minutes to realize her current situation. With the tips of her fingers, she could feel the duct tape that bound her wrists. She was unable to move her feet or legs, so she assumed they were also bound. But most alarming was the tape over her mouth.

What happened? Where am I? Her memory rushed back. *I was on the* Bloody Bucket. *Oh shit, he's our guy. He figured out I was on to him. I was leaving to call Brogan, and that's the last thing I remember. Donnie must have a reason for keeping me alive. I need to calm down and take slow, steady breaths. As long as I'm alive, I still have a chance. Okay, start working on this tape; maybe I can get myself loose. Jeez, I've got to pee of all times.*

Above deck, Donnie prepared the boat for departure. *The divers should be here in a few minutes, and I want to be out to sea before the rest of this marina wakes up.*

At 4:30 a.m., the divers returned. Anxious to get back on the wreck, they quickly loaded their re-filled air tanks onto the boat along with some other supplies they had purchased.

"Captain still asleep?" Wayne asked.

Donnie responded. "No, he got a call last night from his brother's wife in Florida. His brother had a heart attack and is in the hospital. Doesn't look good, so the cap got a flight out of Salisbury to Florida so he can be with his brother. He said to take you guys out to the site and continue our search. I can handle the boat okay if you guys are still willing to go."

With no hesitation, Lester said, "Yeah, let's go. We don't want to lose a good day just sitting around waiting for Plummer to come back. Maybe we'll be lucky and bring up a lot of stuff to make the captain happy when he comes back. We'll help you dock the boat when we return. Do you have the coordinates we need?"

"I do, and we can pull out in about ten minutes. Should put us going through the Inlet around 5 a.m. just like we planned."

Exhausted from trying to loosen the tape, Patty lay still. She felt the boat move slightly and then heard muted conversation. She couldn't understand the words but felt the boat to rock intermittently as if people were walking about.

Patty struggled to get a look at her surroundings. It must be daylight because she was now able to see she was in a cabin and lying on a small bed. She peeked over the edge of the bed and was startled by a human form wrapped tightly in a tarp lying on the floor next to her.

This may be my chance. If I start kicking and moving around, maybe whoever is on the boat will hear me and come to investigate.

For the first time, Patty saw a white piece of paper taped on the wall she was facing. In large block letters, it said, YOU MAKE NOISE AND I WILL CUT YOUR THROAT! She had no doubt Donnie would carry out his threat, so she remained quiet and went back to working on her taped wrists.

A couple of minutes later, the engine came to life, and she felt the boat begin to move under its power. She doubled her efforts to get free. *The tape on my wrists is loosening. Gotta get free. No one knows where I am. Living or dying depends on me.* She fought back the tears and panic growing inside her chest. *To survive, I need to stay calm.*

The boat began to pick up speed. *Where're they taking me, and what's going to happen when we get there?* The panic subsided, but reality didn't. She continued to work on the tape as she peed herself.

39

WHERE'S PATTY RYAN?

Brogan sat quietly in the conference room. He reviewed the notes he'd made during yesterday's interviews to be sure he hadn't missed anything.

Bob Carr, Frankie Mazzone, M.J. Callanan, and Assistant State's Attorney Jim Lyons were all present and comparing notes before returning to the streets.

Where's Patty Ryan? Brogan had never known her to be late for anything, and if she was running behind, she would be blowing up his phone with the reason why.

"Hey, Bob, where's Patty this morning? Did she get stuck picking up coffee and donuts?"

"I don't know where she is. I haven't heard from her since yesterday. I tried to call her just in case she overslept, but it went right to voice mail. Want me to try again?"

"Yes, please. Not like her to be running late."

A minute later, Carr said, "Brogan, it's still going to voicemail."

Brogan scrolled through his contacts and said, "Let me call her boyfriend, Terry, and see if she's home or if he knows why her phone is turned off."

Terry picked up on the first ring. "Hey Brogan, you guys make an arrest last night in those murders?"

"No, Terry, I was looking for Patty. Is she there?"

"No, she's not. She never came home last night. I thought you guys had found the killer, and she was working an all-nighter. She never called me, but I assumed it'd gotten so late she was afraid of waking me up. Has something happened? Where is she?"

"Not sure, Terry, but let me go, so I'll find out. I'll call you or have her call you as soon as I know something. Please call me if you hear from her." Brogan ended the call.

"Listen up, everybody. Patty Ryan didn't get home last night, and her boyfriend hasn't heard from her. Do any of you know if she was working on something after we secured yesterday?"

No one spoke up, and a look of worry was shared among the investigators.

Brogan remembered. *Patty said she had something to take care of just as we were leaving. She went back into the P.D.*

It took only a minute for Brogan to wake up yesterday's late-shift duty officer. Sergeant Blake said, "I remember Patty coming into the duty officer's area and then talking with the PCO. Something about running a tag number. Patty went back to the detective's office for a few minutes and then left without saying where she was going. I assumed she was done for the day. I never heard from her again. Why, is something going on with Patty?"

"Yeah, she didn't go home last night, and she's not answering her phone this morning. I'm getting worried. I'm going to call PCO Scott and see what she knows."

"Okay, Brogan. Look, if we need to go looking for her,

have someone call me, and I'll come in right away to help. Good luck."

Brogan called PCO Maggie Scott. "Sorry, Maggie, for waking you up, but we can't find Patty Ryan this morning, and I understand she had you run a tag number last night before she left the P.D."

"Yeah, no problem, Brogan I was already up. Patty asked me to run a New Jersey tag number and then took the printout back to her office. She left a few minutes later, and I assumed she was heading home like the rest of you. Now that you mention it, I don't remember her going 10-7 home before I went off duty at 11:00 p.m. Do you think she ran into trouble? Do you need me to come back in to help look for her?"

"Okay, don't panic, Maggie. She wouldn't be the first person to fall asleep in their patrol car. She's been running this murder case pretty hard and probably hasn't had much rest. Did you log the tag number on the radio log when you ran it last night?"

"Yep, it's on there. Came back to a vehicle from Cape May, New Jersey. No warrants or wants on the vehicle. I think it was a Chevy SUV. Can't remember any more details. Run it again to find out what I can't remember."

Brogan quickly walked from the conference room to the communications room. Without a word, he picked up the clipboard holding the radio logs and scanned them for about the time he and Patty were leaving last night. It was right there.

He spun the clipboard around so it faced Bonnie, the P.C.O. currently on duty. "Run this tag again for me, please," Brogan said, pointing to the New Jersey tag number.

Bonnie ran the tag number without question, printed out

the results, and handed it to Brogan. One glance at the information and Brogan did a Google search on the company. His finding had him sprinting back to the conference room.

"Saddle up, everybody. We're all headed to the marina between Sunset and Harbor. There was an SUV parked there yesterday with New Jersey tags. Patty apparently ran the tag. It comes back to a dive shop in Cape May. They list diving on shipwrecks as one of their specialties. It may tie in with the coin we have. I think Patty went back there last night, and after that, I don't know what happened, but I need all of you to help me find her. Let's roll."

Brogan was out the door, not waiting for the rest to join him. The group jammed their paperwork into their carrying cases with little regard for order. One of their own may be in danger. Searching for a killer is dangerous work, and all of them were aware of how quickly things can go downhill with likely fatal results.

Assistant S.A. Jim Lyons was calling Rudy Carol as he left the P.D. to brief him on what was occurring. He jumped in the vehicle with Detective Carr, and they sped out of the P.D. parking lot.

Brogan was the first to arrive and immediately saw the same blue SUV sitting parked near the channel. The tag number confirmed his observation. Yesterday, it had been parked facing the channel. Today, it was parked facing out, suggesting something may have been loaded or unloaded through the back hatch. He stopped just feet from its front bumper, blocking it from leaving. He came out of his car with his gun in hand and down by his side. The back windows were heavily tinted, so he quickly peered through the front windshield and driver's side window. Rubber diving gear was in plain view through the separation between the front seats; this evidence corroborated that the SUV was affiliated with a dive shop. A chrome dive tank lay on its side, along with additional dive gear. Most of the rear area was still obscured from view. Brogan banged on the side of the vehicle and yelled, "Patty, are you in there? Patty, if you can hear me kick the wall or back hatch." Nothing!

Other police cars started pulling up. Brogan ordered, "Carr and Callanan, ride around this neighborhood and see if you can locate an old pickup truck or Patty's patrol vehicle. It's a dark green Ford. I don't know about the pickup. If you find any trucks, run the tags. We're looking for anything listed to a guy named Donnie Davenport. Mazzone, go to the other side of this channel and see if anyone is on the boats over there. Find out if the *Bloody Bucket* was here this morning, and if it was, try and find out what time it pulled out and where it might be headed."

Brogan retreated to his car and pulled a six-cell steel flashlight from where it was wedged under the headrest of the passenger seat. He walked back to the SUV, and with a single swing, the passenger side window turned into fragments falling both inside and outside the door. Using the flashlight, Brogan swept glass fragments from the bottom of what once was a window. He reached in and unlocked the door. Moments later, all the doors were open, and he searched for any evidence that Detective Ryan had ever been in this vehicle. He found nothing and slammed all the doors closed. Exigent circumstances would support his actions, but either he or the town would probably be on the hook for a new window. Tough shit. At least he knew Patty wasn't being held in this vehicle.

Frankie Mazzone came quickly onto the lot, slamming his car into park. "Brogan, I talked to Captain Howlett across the way. He says the *Bloody Bucket* was here this morning but pulled out around 5:00 a.m. He says the First Mate was driving the boat when it left. There were at least two other passengers, but he didn't see Captain Plummer. Best guess is they're headed out to get scallops, and that would mean they're headed to the Elephant's Trunk. It's a deep depression known for its scallop fishing, about fifty miles out. The problem is it's extremely long, running north to south. Captain Howlett believes, based on the condition of the boat, Plummer would probably be in an area straight out from Sandpiper. He emphasized that was only his best guess."

While Brogan digested the information he had just received and briefly pondered his next move, he heard the deep-throated sound of a very large boat motor. It sounded like an Angel sent to help. Brogan saw a slick black cigarette boat ease its way down the channel heading out towards the ocean. The deep drum of the engine left little to the imagination. This boat was thunder, just waiting to be released. The man behind the wheel was young and tanned, with thick blonde hair. He was almost model-pretty. He confidently wheeled his powerful boat towards the open sea.

Brogan ran to the channel and yelled to be heard above the engine noise. "Police emergency! I need you to pull over here." He pulled his badge from his belt and waved it above his head.

The boat eased to dockside, and the operator looked up at Brogan with a look that said, "What? I didn't do anything wrong." The young man put the boat in neutral, which reduced the engine noise by only a few decibels.

Brogan repeated his situation. "I have a police emergency, and life is in danger. I need you and your boat to take me out into the Ocean to rescue a police officer in trouble."

The blonde-haired man answered Brogan's comments with, "I'll help in any way I can. Come aboard. By the way, I'm Buck Savage."

"One minute, please," Brogan said and retreated to the trunk of his car, where he pulled out two ballistics vests, an AR15, and a pair of binoculars and shoved them in a duffel bag. Three full magazines were also jammed into the bag. He jogged back to the waiting boat.

Before boarding, he turned to a bewildered Frankie Mazzone, who was making a move to join Brogan. "No, Frankie, I need you to contact the Coast Guard and tell them what's going on. If Patty isn't already dead, I think she's on that boat, and I doubt she'll be coming back unless I go get her. See if you can get their helicopter up and out to Elephant's Trunk. Tell them the boat is the *Bloody Bucket* and our suspect is Donnie Davenport, just in case things go bad for me and my young friend."

Fortunately, the driver of the cigarette boat didn't hear that part as Brogan turned from Mazzone and dropped a couple of feet over the side of the channel into the waiting boat. Mazzone nodded and headed back to his patrol car.

"Where're we going?" Buck said.

"Do you know Elephant's Trunk?"

"I do. I've fished it for shark. Not in this boat, of course."

"How fast can you get out there? I was told it's about fifty miles out."

"That's correct. How fast can I go, officer?"

"As fast as you can. This is a life or death situation."

A small grin came to the face of Buck Savage. "I've never had the police tell me I can go as fast I can. Get in that chair next to me, and don't try to stand up." Savage reached into a small cabinet, plugged a couple of wires into the dash, and handed Brogan a set of earmuffs while placing a pair on his head.

"We can talk to each other through these. Otherwise, the noise is too loud."

Brogan quickly slid the earmuffs over his head, covering his ears. The sounds of the engine died away, and he heard Buck Savage say, "Can you hear me, okay?"

"I can, how about me."

Buck gave him a thumbs-up and moved to the center of the channel. He moved slowly towards the exit into the bay. "I can't go too fast until we get out of this channel. Our wake would damage all these other boats."

Brogan nodded in understanding. Two minutes later, they exited the channel. Buck turned to Brogan and said, "Hang the fuck on! I'll get us there in under an hour."

Buck slammed the throttle forward, and the boat jumped up on the plane, and they roared across a short expanse of the bay and out through the inlet into the Atlantic Ocean. The ocean and weather were working in their favor. The water was nearly flat, and the sun was dazzling.

Hang on, Patty, I'm coming to get you.

40

ON TOP OF THE WRECK

The route and speed of the *Bloody Bucket* under the command of Donnie Davenport took about three hours before reaching the correct coordinates a little after 8 a.m. Donnie was convinced his indirect route would keep its location a secret from the two divers. He killed the engine and dropped anchor immediately.

"The prize should be right below us. If you follow the anchor chain down to the seabed, you should be able to begin loading treasure right away." Donnie said, full of confidence and enthusiasm.

The weather was calm, and the sun was blindingly bright off the flat surface of the water. The divers made last-minute adjustments to their equipment before entering the water. Wasting no time, they descended into the depths. It was 9:40 a.m.

Donnie thought, *this is a good time to check my female passenger,* as he went down the short but steep steps into the galley area and along the narrow passageway to the captain's cabin.

He unlocked the door and entered cautiously in case she had freed herself. As best as he could tell, she hadn't moved since he put her on the bed. He smelled a faint odor of urine. *I guess I should've checked on her sooner. Poor thing probably held out as long as she could. Maybe she's concussed and won't ever wake up. That would be a real shame.*

He placed two fingers to her neck and felt her pulse. It sounded strong to him, but he was no expert. He pulled the tape from her mouth so she could breathe easier. She was still facing his note on the bulkhead, so he was confident she would keep her mouth shut. *If not, I'll come down and cut her throat!* He touched her hair, turned, and left the cabin, locking the door as he went back up to the deck.

Patty waited a full five minutes before she opened her eyes. She had been awake during the entire ordeal. Allowing that creep to touch her without showing revulsion had taken every bit of willpower she had. He hadn't even checked the duct tape, the stupid S.O.B. The loose tape around her wrists had gone undiscovered. She renewed her efforts to free herself. *Time is running out.*

The divers were on their way up. So was the diver-down flag. Donnie waited patiently for both divers to re-enter the boat. They were laden with treasure from the seafloor. Coins, statues, and a couple of goblets embedded with stones and gems. Everything was dumped into the empty ice chest. There was little care or regard for maintaining the pristine condition of their recoveries. It was almost a foregone conclusion that these pillaged items would be sold on the black market and, in some instances, melted down for their gold or silver content. Gems and stones would be removed to be placed in settings worth far less than the originals. Whatever it took to hide the truth of recovery from the authorities.

Donnie eyed the contents of the ice chest closely. *There lays my future. A future of luxury and comfort. No more dirty boats and stinking fish in my life. Clean showers, beds, and clothing will be mine forever. How quickly life has changed. This is a special occasion. Everybody on this boat is taking their last boat ride. I'll do a little sanitizing and head back alone. The bank of Elephant's Trunk will be closed. I wonder what I can get for these coordinates. I bet Plummer never thought about that. Small minded man. He should've been nicer to me.*

Lester said, "We need about an hour's rest before going back down. It'll be our last dive for today. There's a lot of stuff down there, so we could be doing this for a week or more. When does Plummer intend to take some of these things to get them evaluated?"

"Not sure. When he sees all this, he may want to do it sooner than later. You guys getting anxious to start getting your share?"

"Yeah, I guess we are. All those old things are fucking interesting, but it'll look better to us when they turn into green Benjamins, if you know what I mean." Wayne responded with a wide smile.

Donnie kept his thoughts to himself. *You were right about one thing. This'll be your last dive. Not just for today but forever.*

Once the divers returned to the water, Donnie took the diver-down flag off the back of the boat and threw it in a corner of the deck. *Won't need that anymore.* He then went to a locker in the wheelhouse and removed a sawed-off twelve-gauge shotgun, and loaded it with double 00 buck. He also procured for himself the Captain's 45 Caliber, 30 shot, MAC-10. *Damn, this is a sweet machine gun.* He brought both up to the deck, made sure the safeties were off and laid them near the railing where they would be handy. He covered them with a piece of tarp. It was 10:15 a.m., and cleanup was about to begin.

41

GET THE SUN AT OUR BACK

Brogan had ridden in and even driven a few speed boats in his time of living in Sandpiper, but nothing like this. The cigarette boat felt more like he was flying just above the water. The ocean was nearly as flat as a pond. The sun was now up and blazing across the surface of the water.

Buck Savage was young but very confident in his handling of the boat that had become a rescue vessel. If Patty was still alive, this thing would definitely take them to her faster than anything short of a plane or helicopter. Brogan mulled over in his mind how to handle things if they encountered the *Bloody Bucket* at sea. *This boat is fast but noisy. It's going to be hard to sneak up on them, but a speeding cigarette boat on the Atlantic Ocean was certainly not an unusual event and might not even be considered suspicious. If we can get close enough, we'll still have the element of surprise.* Brogan rechecked his sidearm and found it was fully loaded with one in the pipe and the safety in the off position. If it became a shootout, Brogan was ready but couldn't help but wonder. *I'll be shooting from a moving boat, aiming at targets on another moving boat that'll probably be shooting back.* That was plan A. Plan B was the same.

Savage spoke to Brogan through the headsets. "Detective Brogan, at our speed, we may arrive at Elephant's Trunk before the trawler. I'm going to take us south about five miles. If we haven't overtaken the *Bloody Bucket,* it's pretty safe to assume it's north of us. When we hit the Trunk, I'll follow it north."

Brogan saw the wisdom in this strategy and asked Savage. "Can you do that and keep the sun at our back?"

"Yes. I was thinking the same thing. I can even slow down a little and reduce the decibels this engine is putting out so we can get pretty close before we're seen or heard."

"Buck, do you have a gun on this boat?"

"Yes, I've got a 40 caliber Glock here in the glove box."

"Do you know how to use it?"

"Yes, sir, I do. I never shot a person, but I can hit a target even when this boat is moving. I practice all the time."

"Okay. This might be the day you've got to shoot at a person. Do you think you can do that if our lives are in danger? And stop calling me sir and detective. Just Brogan!"

"If I think we're in danger, I'll be shooting right alongside you, Brogan."

"Good enough. At least one guy on the boat we're after is responsible for two murders that we're aware of, and I believe he's kidnapped a female police officer and has no intention of returning her to shore. I'm authorizing you to shoot to kill."

Wide-eyed, Buck answered, "Got it. Shoot to kill. This is fucking crazy, but I'm in."

The cigarette boat turned slightly south and maintained its gut-wrenching speed.

42

We Need to Make This Right

While Brogan was speeding south on the Atlantic, Willy Spear's cell phone rang on his kitchen table.

Willy checked it. Not many people had this number. Of course, it was a burner phone, but its existence was known to but a few. He relaxed when he saw the number calling was one he recognized. It belonged to Slick Melvin.

"Hey, what's up?"

"Willy, we got a fucking problem. A serious fucking problem. You alone? Can you talk?"

"Yeah, what's wrong?"

"Willy, I came by the storage house this morning to pick up the proceeds and re-stock the supply. It's Martin and his little brother, Michael. They're both here tied up and sitting in chairs. They're both fucking dead with pillowcases over their heads. They've been shot in the back of the head. Executed! All our shit and cash are gone. The place has been turned upside down, and everything gone. Even took the guns and ammo I know they had here. No sign of who did this. What you want me to do?"

"Anybody with you, Melvin?"

"Just Freddie. You know he's always with me. He saw what happened here. He fucking freaked out, but I calmed him down. Nobody else knows. That's why I called you."

"Okay, Melvin. No police. You hear me, no goddamn police?"

"I hear you, Willy."

"Okay. Wrap up the bodies and put 'em in your car. Wipe it down, wipe the whole place down so there's no fingerprints or stuff that'll tie that house to us. It's rented under a false name, and the guy who owns it has never met any of our people. He just gets a cash envelope every month in the mail. I doubt he even reports the rental as income. He lives in New Jersey, so he don't come down to check on it or nothing."

We've had that house for three years. Never had a problem there. Yard is kept neat, and there's never been a call for police.

"Melvin, just sanitize the house. Wipe up the blood and make it look normal. Tonight, take the bodies somewhere isolated and bury em deep so the animals won't be digging them up."

I'll keep paying the rent for a few more months, and then I'll send a note in the last cash envelope that our rental period is over. No explanation. Just ended.

"Leave a couple of windows cracked open an inch or two to allow ventilation. If some small critters get in there and tear it up a little, that's not going to hurt us. When you leave, never go back there. Can you handle all this, Melvin?"

"I can, Willy. Me and Freddie, we'll get right on it. When it's done, I'll text you that it's done. Freddie can keep the secret, so don't worry about him. He knows what would happen to him if you hear about this from anybody else."

"Melvin, I don't know the motherfuckers who did this,

but I promise you I'm going to make them pay. Listen for any street talk. I'll call certain people who should know what happened. Shift your operation to the other storage house and keep going as normal. Replace Martin and Michael. If anybody asks, they left town. Someone'll get nervous and start asking questions. When they do, I'll know about it, and we'll make an example out of them. Are we clear, Melvin?"

"Yes, Willy, I'm clear. I'll send you a text."

Willy remained calm and focused while talking to Slick Melvin, but inside, he was seething. *Who is dumb enough to be fucking with me? This feels a little too slick to be some junkies just ripping off a stash house. I need to make it right, and I need to do it quick. I need to keep my shit tight.*

He shoved his piece into his belt and covered it with a light jacket. He called Latisha, and it was picked up on the first ring.

"Yes?"

"Latisha. We've got a big problem. We need to talk away from this house. Have you gone over the car this morning?"

"I have. It's clean. I'll be out front in just a couple of minutes."

"Latisha, we need to be careful. Someone is trying to hurt me. I'll tell you once we're away from the house. This is not the cops. Keep your eyes open."

Willy shut the front door behind him, signaled for Latisha to stay behind the wheel, and he dropped into the front passenger seat. This is something he never did. Latisha tensed up slightly. Willy nodded, and they pulled away, blending into normal traffic.

Two blocks away, another vehicle eased into traffic going in the same direction. Razor picked up her cell phone.

43

BLOOD IN THE WATER

Buck turned to Brogan and shook his head. "We should've caught up to the trawler by now if it went south. I think we should turn north, stay in the Elephant's Trunk, putting the sun at our back."

"Do it, Buck."

The boat turned, and the engine roared to full power. The water remained calm, giving Brogan a chance to use an expensive pair of binoculars Buck had on the boat to scan the route North. The smell of the salt air invaded his nose. His hair rippled as the boat cut through the water. The sky remained clear and very blue. Only a couple of cotton ball clouds were visible in the far-distant sky.

At the wreck site, the divers had signaled their intention to surface. Donnie prepared to meet them at the side of the boat. Wayne's head broke the surface first. A couple of moments later, Lester surfaced. They both clung to the ladder hanging on the side of the boat. Wayne looked up. "Donnie, we did real good today. The stuff we found is the best so far. We're all going to be rich." Lester nodded his head in enthusiastic agreement.

"Those bags must be heavy. Hand them up to me, and it'll be easier for you to climb on board."

Wayne complied immediately, glad to have the weight removed from his body. Lester followed suit and handed his bag up to Donnie, who lifted it over the side and lowered it to the deck right next to the tarp hiding his guns.

In one smooth motion, Donnie lifted the tarp away and grabbed the shotgun. Lester's upper body had just cleared the side railing when Donnie stood straight and fired directly into his chest. The blast was so powerful it blew Lester off the ladder backward into the sea. A devasting wound was clear to see. He was dead before he hit the water.

Donnie quickly leaned over the rail and locked eyes with a stunned Wayne, who appeared to be unable to comprehend what had just happened. The sight of the shotgun in Donnie's hands answered the question. Wayne pushed away from the ladder and struggled to position himself to dive. Too late. The shotgun spoke again, removing his face and killing him instantly. Both men's weight belts hung over a rung of the ladder, so they floated temporarily on the surface. A large ring of blood was forming around the bodies.

With no hesitation, Donnie lowered the shotgun to the deck, went to the wheelhouse, and then down the steps to the captain's cabin. He fumbled, getting the key in the lock. He swung the door open and hesitated before entering. The woman lay still on the bed, apparently still unconscious.

"Hey, Captain. How about going for a swim today? I want

you to join Wayne and Lester." Donnie chuckled at his own joke before snatching the captain by his feet and dragging him out of the cabin, down the passageway, and then up the short flight of steps. With each step, the captain's head banged against the steps. "Oops, sorry about that! I'll have you in the water in a minute."

Once on the deck, Donnie propped the body against the railing where the other bodies floated nearby. He removed a large knife from its sheath on his belt and plunged it through the mummy-like wrapping before pushing it overboard. *Now your blood can mix with the divers. You'll have company soon enough.* Donnie leaned over the rail and plunged his knife into the water, washing away the blood.

Patty squirmed for all she was worth trying to break her bonds, but she didn't have the leverage and strength to break or remove the multiple wraps of duct tape. She had heard the two blasts from the shotgun and recognized them for what they were. When Donnie had dragged the captain out of the cabin, she knew something terrible was taking place. She heard his comments and thought she knew what they meant. Donnie left the cabin door open, and she knew why. She could hear him coming back.

He's coming to get me. He's coming to kill me. Her thoughts turned to her boyfriend and what might have been. She had never felt fear like what engulfed her in this moment. She conjured up the last of her resolve. *I won't surrender. I'll fight, kick, bite. Resist as long as I can. Fuck this crazy asshole!*

Donnie man-handled Patty up onto his shoulder, carried her up to the wheelhouse, and put her in a seated position in the captain's chair. He heard her grunt while being carried, so he knew she was conscious.

"Hey sweetie. Welcome back to the world of the living. At least some of us are living." Donnie was giggling, so pleased with himself. He placed a single wrap of duct tape around Patty and the chair holding her upright. He then spun the chair around so it was facing the rear of the boat. "Take a look, Detective."

Patty opened her eyes and saw two bodies dressed in diving suits floating near the boat. Both were in a dark pool of blood. And obviously dead based on the wounds she could see. *No sign of the Captain!*

As if reading her mind, Donnie said, "Sorry, the Captain couldn't wait. He decided to check out the seabed."

Patty's eyes grew wide when she saw several dark shapes moving in the water, approaching the bodies. *Sharks! They've smelled the blood and are coming to feed.*

There was a thrashing in the water as the bodies began moving rapidly around. The sharks had attacked, and it was becoming a feeding frenzy. More dark fins appeared. Patty closed her eyes, not bearing to watch anymore.

"Don't worry, Detective. I won't let them get to you. You and I're going to move away from here, and then I'll explain my plan." Donnie leaned past Patty and started the engine. They didn't sound as loud as normal, but Donnie realized the two shotgun blasts had made him temporarily deaf. Nothing serious or permanent. He turned the boat west towards Sandpiper. He busied himself, loading all the treasure into the ice chest. It was heavy, but it all fit. The large ice chest smelled of dead fish, but it also reeked of wealth.

44

WE MAY BE TOO LATE

Brogan lowered the binoculars. "Buck, I see it. It's a fishing trawler. Too far away to see any details, but it's in the right place. It's gotta be the *Bloody Bucket.* I saw two flashes of light, but not sure what it was. I thought at first it was a flash from gunfire, but it was awfully bright, and I didn't hear any report. Did you see or hear anything?"

"I thought I saw some flashes, too, but there was no sound over these engines. If we can't hear them, maybe they can't hear us. With the sun behind us, they surely can't see us. I've marked the direction and will head towards them. Any other suggestions?"

"No, we've got to take a chance and get close to them. Detective Ryan may be in grave danger right now, so we don't have the luxury of waiting."

Brogan watched through the binoculars as the outline of the trawler grew slowly larger and more distinct. Something changed while he watched. White water was visible at the rear of the boat. Someone had started the engine, and the boat appeared to be moving to the left, which would take it back towards Sandpiper.

"Buck, the boat is moving and turning towards Sandpiper. Hold our course. We need to check that area to be sure they didn't throw Ryan overboard and leave her to drown after she's exhausted. We're fifty miles out, and it would take an Olympic swimmer to make it to shore. I know Patty can swim, but she'd never make that distance. Keep a close eye for anything in the water."

Ten minutes later, the cigarette boat reached the area where the trawler had first been spotted. Buck slowed the boat down to help find anything in the water. The water was still calm, but the sun was causing a lot of reflection. There was suddenly a disturbance in the water off to their port side. Brogan pointed to the location where he could now see violent movement.

"Oh, Jesus Christ. It's sharks. They're tearing something apart. Move closer." Brogan's stomach rolled over at the thought. *If these bastards have thrown Patty to the sharks, I'll hunt them 'em down no matter how long it takes. When I find them 'em, I'll kill 'em, every fucking one of them 'em!*

The sight was horrific. The torso of a human being bobbed in the water. Arms had been ripped off. Large bite marks and missing flesh showed attacks on the upper legs.

Brogan thought he was going to throw up, and then something registered. The body was encased in black rubber. A diver's suit. A shark nudged the corpse, and it turned enough to see the face of a man. A white man with short hair. Eyes are staring into nothingness. *Not Patty, thank God. Nothing I can do for this poor soul other than go after his killers.* Brogan snapped out of his momentary trance and turned to Buck. Buck was watching with his mouth agape, his deep tan now pale.

"Buck, you okay? We need to move. I need you to level up right now! We may be too late."

Buck turned his focus to the dash and wheel in front of him. "Brogan, what do you want me to do?"

"Go get that fucking trawler and get your gun where you can grab it. I'll tell you what to do when we get close."

The cigarette boat jumped out of the water and began closing on the trawler, which was now about three miles away. Brogan ripped his suit jacket off, making access to his shoulder holstered weapon easier. He gritted his teeth and prepared for confrontation.

On the *Bloody Bucket,* Donnie had been busy. He switched off the bilge pump that normally removed excess water from the hull of the boat. He opened several seacocks attached to the aging hull, allowing ocean water to begin flooding the lower areas of the trawler. It would take a few hours, but with ocean water coming in and no bilge pump to get it out, the *Bloody Bucket* would slowly fill with water and slip quietly into the sea. He dragged the hard rubber dinghy off the roof of the deck house. While the dinghy sat on the deck, the ice chest loaded with treasure was tied in place, and a small 20 hp motor was lashed in the center, ready to be placed on the stern bracket. A five-gallon can of marine gas was roped securely inside the craft. A first aid kit and two life vests were always stowed on the dinghy. His guns, including a flare pistol, had been placed in a waterproof bag and remained on the deck near where Donnie worked. His knife had a compass embedded in its handle, which would be enough for him to navigate back to shore. A couple of bottles of water and some snacks were thrown in with the guns. He was good to go.

He reviewed his plan in his head. *See if the young police lady would be willing to trade her virtue for an extended life. I'd sure like to have a taste of her. If not, no problem. Let her stay taped to her seat. Scuttle the boat, jump in the dinghy, and go home to report the sinking of the* Bloody Bucket. *The Captain, in this case, would've gone down with his ship. Grieve and share my story with the Coast Guard about how I begged the captain to give up his attempts to repair a broken seacock and come with me on the dinghy. Provide them with false coordinates for the sinking location. Cooperate and act devastated. If asked, admit being interviewed by a woman detective who drove off after the interview. Let things play out. Eventually, tell everybody that I'm too many bad memories here and you are moving to Florida to be close to family members. DISAPPEAR!*

"Hey, Detective. I guess you've seen enough to know I'm leaving this boat very soon. You've got to make a choice. I don't want to kill you, so if you're willing to party with me for a little while, I'll take you with me and dump you on a stretch of Assateague Island. You can make your way back to civilization. I'll be long gone by the time you can tell your story. You can leave out the part about giving me a blow job just to stay alive. That'll always be our little secret. Whatta' ya say?"

"I say go fuck yourself, you miserable prick!"

"Well, I guess that about says it all. That's a stupid decision, but I respect your courage. Hell, I bet you blow your boyfriend or husband, and all he gives you is a night out to dinner. I'm offering your life. Last chance?"

"Fuck you."

"Okay then. I'll be leaving now, and if you see the Captain, say hi. Since you're in his chair, I guess that makes you the Captain. Very nautical of you to want to go down with the ship," he laughed.

With that, Donnie tugged and pushed until the dinghy slid over the side. He tied the dinghy to the *Bloody Bucket* and noticed the boat was already sitting much lower in the water. *I bet this ole tub'll hit bottom faster than I thought. That's a good thing. Pretty soon, I'll be alone on my way headed home. The sole survivor. A terrible tragedy at sea. I had warned him to make repairs to that hull. Everyone who knew the boat also knew it was a piece of shit.*

Donnie heard a buzzing noise. Sounded like a motor. The bilge pump was off, and the engine had been shut off. He looked towards where he thought the sound was coming from and immediately had to shade his eyes from the sun. The noise was growing louder. Donnie reached for his gun bag.

Buck and Brogan were right on target. The trawler sat perfectly still in the water. No immediate signs of life, but they were still a couple hundred yards out.

Then Brogan saw her through the binoculars and yelled to Buck. "There she is. She's sitting in the wheelhouse. She looks okay, but she's not moving." Then he saw why. "She's fucking duct taped to the chair. She can't move. Shit, the boat is sinking. See how low she is in the water. Pull up next to the Bucket, and I'll jump over and cut her loose."

Buck maneuvered the cigarette boat on a course and speed that would allow him to pull alongside the *Bloody Bucket.* With only about six feet separating the boats, Brogan got ready for his jump.

Donnie had been hiding on the other side of the deck house and rose with the MAC-10 in his hands. Patty screamed, "Brogan, he's got a gun!"

Brogan saw him and yelled to Buck. "Pull away he's got a gun. Turn away!"

Donnie let loose with the MAC-10. Fortunately for

Brogan, the first shot missed him by inches, and the rest of the rounds flew harmlessly over his head. The kick of the MAC-10 surprised Donnie, and the barrel climbed steadily upward with each subsequent round fired.

Brogan pulled his handgun, had a clear shot, and fired at Donnie. The bullet flew nearly true as it caught Donnie in his right shoulder. The MAC-10 spun out of his grip and skittered across the deck. Brogan began his leap, but simultaneously, Buck had spun the wheel of the cigarette boat to turn away. Brogan's launching platform moved about four feet away as he pushed off the cigarette boat, resulting in a landing in the water about three feet short of his goal.

Buck recognized what happened, grabbed his gun, and fired two or three shots in the general direction of the trawler. He purposely aimed high, not wanting to hit the Detective in the deckhouse. He hoped to keep the guy with the machine gun from sticking his head up while Brogan was in the water.

Brogan surfaced and swam quickly to the rear of the boat and sought cover. His shoes felt like lead weights, and he kicked them off his feet, letting them sink beneath him. In the water, he'd now lost sight of Donnie and the MAC-10. *If Donnie recovered the MAC-10, he'll make short work of me if I try to come over the railing.* Brogan's mind whirled. *I can't help Patty from down here, and there's a lot of sharks still in this area. All this thrashing around is probably ringing their dinner bell.*

Even though his landing in the sea had been unexpected, his training had taught him to retain his grip on his gun. He had swum to the boat using the gun as an extension of his hand. He now held it above the water, waiting for the shooter to peek his head over the side. *I'll blow the fucker's head off.* Brogan waited. Nothing happened.

Donnie was hurt, but not too bad. He was bleeding, but he didn't feel too much pain. *Maybe he just nicked me. I gotta get off this boat.*

He peeked cautiously around the corner of the deck house and saw the cigarette boat about fifty yards away. The guy who was going to jump on the *Bloody Bucket* was gone. *Guess I got him. The sharks will finish him off. Stick with the plan.* He grabbed the MAC-10, threw it in the bag, and he and the bag went over the side into the dinghy. He untied the rope, and the dinghy drifted away from the trawler. Donnie bent to the task of mounting the small engine to the back of his boat. Time to head for shore. *I'll keep the* Bloody Bucket *between me and that cigarette boat for as long as I can. He'll be busy trying to help his friend in the water. In thirty minutes, the* Bloody Bucket *will be on the way to the bottom. I might have to tell the cops we were attacked by pirates in a cigarette boat. Fuck it. When I get to land, I'll find some wheels and be gone before they can get their shit together.*

"Brogan, are you there? Brogan, are you okay? He's gone, Brogan. He took a dinghy and is getting away."

When Brogan heard Patty's weak voice, he grabbed the stern and pulled himself onto the sinking boat. No injuries other than his pride for making a failed jump. He made his way towards the deckhouse, where Patty remained lashed to a chair. His ever-available flick knife appeared in his right hand, and he slashed the tape holding her to the chair. "Come on, Patty, we've got to get off this thing. It's about to go under, and we don't want to get dragged down with her. Can you swim? We need to head for the cigarette boat." Patty gained her feet and answered Brogan by hurling herself over the rail and swimming towards the cigarette boat that was now circling back towards the trawler. Brogan jammed his gun back into his shoulder holster and dove overboard a few strokes behind her.

Buck Savage eased the cigarette boat up to them and cut the engine. He tossed them a couple of life preservers and began lowering a rope ladder over the side of the boat. "You guys all right?" Buck asked as he helped Ryan onboard with a butt push from Brogan.

Brogan, with Buck's help, reeled himself on board and fell to the deck, where he lay trying to catch his breath. Coughing up water, Brogan asked, "Patty, are you hurt? Did that guy hurt you?"

"No, Brogan, he didn't. I'm fine. He was going to let me die, but he never laid a hand on me. The guy's fucking nuts. They found a sunken ship and've been looting it for the treasure. He killed the captain and two scuba divers who were helping them. He fed them to the sharks and was going to let me go down with the ship. He's got some of the treasure in an ice chest on that dinghy. He's headed to shore." She kept Donnie's last offer to herself.

Brogan began to speak, but his voice was drowned out by engine noise and downdraft from a helicopter hovering directly above them. Brogan looked up expecting to see the colors of the U.S. Coast Guard, but to his surprise, the helicopter was pitch black and very sleek looking. It looked like a corporate chopper of some kind. The side door slid open, and a smiling Frankie Mazzone stared down at the two wet cops huddled on the deck of the cigarette boat. Mazzone gave them a questioning thumbs up, and Brogan immediately gave it back to him and pointed in the direction of the dinghy that was slowly but surely pulling away from them.

The loud noise of compressed air escaping and a hot engine meeting the cold water of the Atlantic were the last sounds of the *Bloody Bucket* as she disappeared below the surface.

Mazzone pulled his head back in the helicopter, and a moment later, it rose steadily in the air, dipped its nose down, and sprinted towards the escaping dinghy.

Donnie couldn't figure out what was going on, but he knew it wasn't good. The *Bloody Bucket* was gone, but now the cigarette boat and a helicopter were together. Suddenly, the helicopter was coming right for him. He reached into the bag and, produced the shotgun, and pointed it at the approaching helicopter. When he thought it was close enough, he fired at the helicopter. The pilot never flinched but came straight at the dinghy. Some guy with an AR-15 hung partially out the door and opened fire on Donnie and his dinghy. The bullets chewed right through the dinghy, and the engine stalled. Donnie miraculously had not been hit. He immediately grabbed and pulled on a life jacket. He took the ice chest and roped it to his body. *No one is gonna take my treasure away from me.* The dinghy sunk slowly beneath him, leaving him bobbing in the water. *Damn, shoulder is stinging bad,* he thought as he awaited rescue. He glanced at his shoulder and saw it was now heavily bloodied. *Shit, I got hit.*

As the cigarette boat approached, the people on board were waving frantically and pointing towards him. He wanted to waive back, but his right shoulder hurt really bad now, and he wouldn't release his grip on the ice chest with his left hand.

The blackfin moved silently through the water. The shark had its target in sight. The smell of blood had drawn the shark to this meeting. The shark rose slowly, its mouth opened, exposing lines of razor-sharp teeth.

Donnie never knew what hit him. The shark clamped onto his bloody shoulder and pulled him into the depths. The violent shaking loosened the ice chest that flew open, dumping its precious cargo back into the sea.

The helicopter remained on the scene for approximately twenty minutes, searching for the victim of the shark attack. Running low on fuel, it signaled the cigarette boat they were leaving and banked sharply towards the Sandpiper airport nearly fifty miles away. The crew of the cigarette boat gave it an additional half-hour with no sightings before turning towards home.

As he and Patty sat together on the ride back, Brogan stared off at the horizon. *Six people died, and a lost treasure remained lost. They died because of the greed of Captain Tony Plummer and his First Mate, Donnie Blankenship. This was my first week working as the lead investigator for the state's attorney's office. Hoorah!*

As the adrenaline rush retreated, Brogan breathed a sigh of relief. Patty Ryan sat quietly, knowing how close she had come to death. Buck Savage piloted the cigarette boat towards home, still feeling the tremendous rush that would probably last a lifetime. Boy, did he have some stories to tell his buds.

45

Welcome Home

About halfway back to Sandpiper, Buck spoke in disbelief. "I can't believe what I didn't do!"

Brogan and Patty looked at him, puzzled by the admission and what it meant.

"I didn't record the coordinates where the *Bloody Bucket* sank or the location where the dinghy sunk along with the shark attack. How're we going to go back and find the treasure?"

Brogan answered, "I don't know Buck. Maybe that treasure doesn't want to be found. I'm not superstitious, but I know bad karma when I see it. Six people have already lost their lives because of that treasure. Maybe it's for the best that we can't find our way back to it."

Patty Ryan nodded her head in agreement and acceptance. Buck, however, made a face that revealed conflicted thoughts. *Maybe I can figure it out, somehow reconstruct the trip, and get close enough to find the sunken ship.* Realistically, he knew otherwise. Without coordinates or visible markers, it's a big ocean that has hidden secrets for many years. *Shit!*

When they got close enough to land to have a cell signal,

Brogan called the state's attorney and briefed him on everything that had happened. Rudy Carol was elated that his office had played a major role in solving both the sheriff's office and Sandpiper P.D.'s homicides. The four deaths that occurred at sea were complicated, but with no suspects, he was sure he'd be able to put the entire matter to rest.

"Thanks, Brogan. You did a hell of a job and worked well with Detective Mazzone and Ryan to resolve this situation. I hope you're not going to bring this level of crime and violence into my office too often. I'll brief the sheriff and the chief. I'll leave out the use of a private helicopter during this operation, but when you know more, I'd like to know how that came about." Brogan ended the call and then placed a call to Kelly Hart.

"Kelly, it's Brogan. I'll be home in about an hour, where're you going to be?"

"I'll be wherever you tell me to be. Have you had dinner already?"

"No, I missed lunch and haven't had time for dinner yet. Meet me at my place. I need to change my clothes."

"No lunch, no dinner, and now you have to change your clothes. Sounds like there's a story to be told."

"Yeah, I'll fill you in on the nitty-gritty when I see you. We'll go grab a bite somewhere if you want to wait for me."

"Of course, I'll wait. You know I love story time!"

Twenty minutes later, the cigarette boat eased up to the dock area where Brogan's car was parked. Frankie Mazzone sat on a piling, smiling like a Cheshire cat.

"How was your boat ride?" he asked jokingly.

Brogan responded, "Oh, it was good. How about your helicopter ride?"

"Actually, was very exciting. My Navy Seal buddy, who happens to be a pilot, borrowed the company's chopper for a few hours. His boss, a retired Marine Corps Colonel, approved the trip. The Coast Guard was busy further down south, and I didn't think I should wait. I hope we didn't interfere with the party you had going on when we got there."

"No, we were glad to see you and your pal. I'd like to meet this guy and personally thank him over a beer. It looked like he may've seen some action while serving in the Navy."

"I can arrange the meet, and he did see some action, but he won't talk about it. You know, the Navy Seals. All very hush-hush. Oh, thanks for calling the S.A. and briefing him. He got on the horn with the sheriff and made me look like a hero. If I keep following you around, Brogan, I just might get promoted if I don't get killed first. Need anything from me now?"

"No, not any more today. Go home and get some rest. You and your buddy are heroes, and a promotion would be a good idea. Thanks for everything. Before I forget, was there any damage to the helicopter when Donnie fired his shotgun at you guys?"

"Not a scratch. Don't know where he was aiming, but I wasn't about to give him a chance to adjust his aim. Son of a bitch got what he deserved, but that's a hell of a way to go."

Mazzone gave Brogan and Patty Ryan a two-finger salute and walked away.

Patty's hair and clothing were destroyed by her swim in the ocean. She looked like the preverbal drowned rat. She glanced up at the spot that had been vacated by Mazzone, and there stood her boyfriend, Terry, hands on hips with a small smile on his face.

"Terry," she exclaimed. "How'd you know I'd be here?"

"Got a text from Brogan saying where you'd be and that you might want to see me." With a furrowed brow as he got a good look at Patty and Brogan's saturated clothing, Terry asked, "What the hell happened?"

"It's a long story. Please take me home, and I'll tell you all about it."

Brogan helped her off the boat and said, "I'll talk to you tomorrow. Your police car is back at the office. Get Carr to give you a lift into work tomorrow. Big paperwork day is facing you. You're a solid cop, Patty. A little unconventional in the way you solved your first homicide assignment, but they'll get easier in the future. Glad you're okay."

Finally, Brogan was left alone with Buck Savage.

"Couldn't have done it without you and your very speedy boat. Thank you is not enough, but it's all I got. I'm going to write you up for a citizen's award for your bravery and help today. Send me a bill for the gas we burned up, and if you find any bullet holes in your boat, we'll take care of that, too."

"Thanks, Brogan. I admit, at times, I was a little shaky, but I was confident you wouldn't let anything bad happen to me. It was like being a cop in a cop movie. I thought all that shit was just for television. It's pretty exciting stuff if you ask me. Nobody's going to believe me when I tell them this story. I already checked the boat. No bullet holes. The gas is on me. You know the old saying, 'If you have to ask how much it costs to fill it up, you can't afford the boat.'"

Brogan got his full name, address, and cell number and climbed out of the boat.

"I hope to see you around, Buck."

"You're welcome aboard this boat any time. Maybe we can take a ride without bullets flying." Buck laughed, slowly pulled away, and headed for his dock up the channel.

Brogan got a towel from his trunk, covered the driver's seat, and drove home, hoping he could sneak into his place unseen by his neighbors, who already thought he was a wild man when they read or heard about some of his recent adventures. *I can hear the neighbors now, "Not again!" They probably aren't sure they want to still live next to me. Hell, I wouldn't want to live next to me.*

46

MISSING

Kelly was sitting on the couch when Brogan came home. Casually dressed in dress pants and a ribbed sweater, her blonde hair lay on her shoulders and shone in the overhead light. The smile on her face dissolved when she saw Brogan.

She leaped from the couch and hurried to meet him.

"Are you okay? What happened? You're soaking wet. Where're your shoes?"

"Took a little swim in the ocean. I'm fine. Let me get out of these wet clothes, take a hot shower, and I'll tell you what happened. It's been a hell of a day."

"I can see that. Go hit the shower while I get you some dry clothes."

A few minutes later, Kelly tapped on the bathroom door before entering the steam-filled space. Brogan stood under the shower, allowing the hot water to douse his body. He looked okay; actually, he looked very good. Kelly felt a warmth in her core but dismissed it, knowing Brogan needed to unwind. She laid his underwear on the bathroom counter, spun on her heels, and left the bathroom. In the bedroom, she set aside some clothes, a warm sweatshirt and a pair of L.L. Bean sweat pants. Her man needed to get comfortable more than he needed a night out at a restaurant.

"Brogan, I laid out clothes for you. We're going to eat in tonight. I'm going to make your favorite supper."

"Are you sure? I can take you someplace to eat."

"Raincheck. Tonight, we get dry and warm."

Kelly went to the kitchen and began putting together a man-sized breakfast for Brogan's dinner. Two eggs over easy, sausage patties, three strips of bacon, hash brown potatoes, and toasted English muffins, with jelly, of course. A small glass of orange juice topped off the presentation. Kelly had learned how to make a good breakfast during her teenage years working at Jack's Diner in Sandpiper. She knew it was his favorite. Kelly grinned while making his eggs. *He doesn't know it's my favorite, too.*

After wolfing down his feast, he told his story to Kelly while she ate at a slower and more civilized speed. She listened carefully to his rendition of events, knowing full well that he was downplaying any dangers to himself.

"I'm so glad Patty is alright. Sounds like she was in mortal danger, but kept her head about her. She knew you'd come and rescue her."

Brogan smirked at that comment. "I feel very lucky to have gotten to her in time. I hope she can bounce back from this. Sometimes, these kinds of things can make you take a hard look at your career choices. She's a good cop, and I told her so. Not sure how he got the drop on her, but I bet it never happens again."

Wanting to change the subject, Brogan asked. "I haven't seen you in two days. What've you been up to? Any interesting stuff going on?"

"Maybe. Marie Barnette called me into her office and had me meet this very nice older woman named Linda Hamilton. Mrs. Hamilton knew Marie had a private detective working in her law office. She has a problem and thought Marie and I could help her. She lives alone in an apartment in Salisbury.

"Linda told me, 'I have two sons, and they've both gone missing. My oldest son, Martin, lives in a house outside of Sandpiper, and he religiously calls every day to check on me. I haven't heard from him for three days, and he's not picking up his cell phone. The last time I saw my youngest son, Michael, he said he was going to meet up with Martin. He's also not picking up his cell calls or responding to text messages. This is so out of character for them, and I'm frightened out of my mind something bad has happened.'

"I dug a little deeper into her story, and Linda said Martin was working for a man named Willy Spears. Martin was vague about exactly what he did for Mr. Spears, but over the last year, Martin had been able to buy a car and rent a house. Martin had even offered to help his mother with any expenses she might be incurring. She said she had declined his offer. He seemed happy and was independent for the first time, so she said she didn't push him for more information.

"Marie and I said we'd help her and try and locate her missing sons. I also learned Mrs. Hamilton hadn't filed a formal missing person's report because she thought they'd be upset with her if they were just off having a few days of fun together. She was distraught and unsure of what to do. I asked her if she'd gone to the house where her son lives. She said she'd never been there but knew it was on Sixty Foot Road off of Route 50. I suggested we take a ride and see if we could find the house."

Brogan broke into Kelly's narrative and asked. "Did you find the house?"

"Yes, we did. I took Linda with me, and we drove along Sixty Foot Road until she pointed out a car she believed belonged to Martin. I made her stay in my car while I checked out the house. No one answered the door, and the house was quiet. Both front and back doors were locked, but I found three different windows that were open about two or three inches. A little unusual because there were no screens on the windows, making it a haven for insects to call home. I yelled through the openings to see if I could get a response, but it was dead quiet. The car in the driveway was also locked, and nothing was showing that would confirm it was Martin's car. I checked the neighbors, but no one was home. The whole thing kind of freaked me out. My gut was telling me something was wrong, but I didn't see anything that yelled crime scene. I peeked through the open windows, and everything looked to be in order. I did a sniff test but couldn't smell anything unusual.

"When I was a cop, I would've probably pushed the live and well-check aspect and gone in through a window, but with nothing other than cracked open windows, I didn't think I wanted to get my ass sued off for an unlawful entry. Especially with a law-abiding citizen witness sitting in my car. I gave Mrs. Hamilton the tag number of the car in the driveway and told her to go to the Sheriff's Office tomorrow and report both her sons missing and give the Deputies the tag number so they can confirm it belongs to Martin.

She's going to call me when that's been done, and I'll follow up with the Sheriff's Office. She gave me the name and phone number of one of Martin's friends. She also gave me photographs of both her sons. I called Martin's friend and got a voicemail and left a message for him to call me. No call yet."

Brogan pondered what he had been told, "Could be something, could be nothing. Strange, but not crazy strange. I think you made all the right moves. If you get any pushback from the sheriff's office about sharing information with a P.I., let me know. Detective Frankie Mazzone is one of my new best friends. I'll whisper in his ear if you want me to. That name, Willy Spears, rings a bell, but I'm not sure where I know it from. It'll come to me."

This was part of what Kelly loved about Brogan. When he asked her what she had been doing, he listened to her and was interested in what she had to say. Kelly had been around a lot of men, and most would ask her questions and then only half listen to her responses or seem uninterested. Brogan would help but wouldn't insert himself or over-critique her actions. He showed her respect as a medically retired police officer who knew what she was doing.

"I think I'll be okay, but it's good to know I have backup if I need it. You looked exhausted. Do you want to make it any early night?"

"Yeah, I do. Thanks. The bed will feel real good tonight."

"I promise to leave you alone so you can get some sleep."

"Don't make promises I can't keep. I'm tired, but I'm not dead. Come to bed with me. Just be easy on this old man."

Kelly rolled her eyes and grabbed his hand. *The dishes can wait til the morning.*

Kelly's dog, Duncan, followed them down the hall, hoping to be invited to join them. No invitation was forthcoming, so he curled up on his bed and guarded them against possible intruders.

47
FOLLOW UP

Brogan and Kelly were up early the next day, going their separate ways. Brogan went to his new office at the P.D. to begin the task of documenting all the actions he'd taken yesterday. Kelly was in search of the missing brothers. Both promised to check in with each other later in the afternoon.

It was 8 a.m. when Kelly returned to the house on Sixty Foot Road. Everything at the house appeared to be unchanged. She checked both the front and back doors. She had placed a Tell on each door before leaving at her last visit. The very small sticks placed leaning against the hinge corner of each door remained in the upright position. Neither door had been opened. A check of the car revealed nothing had changed, and it remained locked.

At the house next door, a pickup truck was tucked in close to the house. Kelly walked across the side yard and knocked on the neighbor's driveway-facing door. While waiting for someone to respond, she noticed a camera doorbell installed in the door frame.

The door was answered by a middle-aged woman dressed

in jeans and a baggy sweatshirt bearing the logo of the Baltimore Orioles. Her short dark hair was neatly combed. She smiled warmly at Kelly and said, "Hello, can I help you?"

"Hi, my name is Kelly Hart. This is my business card. I'm a private detective who's been hired by a family member to find two missing men whom we believe are living next door to you." Kelly pointed to the house in question.

"Oh, my name's Susie. I didn't know two guys were living there. I've only seen one guy, and he drives that car in the driveway. I don't even know his name, but he always says hi when I see him coming and going. He keeps to himself. I think we both work some crazy shifts because I've seen him come and go at all hours of the day and night. Somebody stops by occasionally because I've seen another car in the driveway, but I've never seen the driver."

"His name is Martin. He and his younger brother Michael both went missing about three days ago. Anything unusual happen around that time?"

"Not that I'm aware of. My boyfriend lives with me, but he's a member of the National Guard and has been on his yearly two-week summer camp, so he's been away. I'm usually so tired from work when I get home; I grab something to eat and crash in my bedroom and watch TV to wind down before going to sleep. My bedroom is on the other side of my house, so I don't see anything going on over on this side. Never been any problems over there, and that guy has been there at least a year. Do you think something bad happened to them? I'm always a little scared when I'm here alone, but there's never been anything to support my fears. I guess I just don't do well alone. I do have a gun, and I know how to use it, so that gives me some comfort."

"Susie, I noticed you have one of those doorbell cameras. Does it work?"

"Yeah, it does. It works really well, but I never take the time to review the tapes. I think the only time anyone rings the doorbell is when a delivery guy rings it to let me know he's dropped a package."

"Do you know how to review the tapes? I'd like to look at them for the last few days?"

"Sure, why not. Today's my day off, and I've got nothing else to do. If something's going on next door, I'd like to know about it. Come on in, and we'll check it out together."

An hour later, Kelly had a really bad feeling and far more questions than answers. She and Susie had begun their review of the tapes starting four days ago. Luckily, the pickup truck was always parked past the side door, allowing the camera to view the front of the neighbor's house and driveway.

At 9 p.m., four days earlier, the silhouette of a man crossed the view of the camera. With no exterior lights on, his figure was very grainy on the tape. Identification would be doubtful. He had come from the rear of the subject house, moving into an area of the front yard not covered by the camera. At 11:40 p.m., car headlights turned into the driveway, and the car parked where Martin's car was currently parked. The interior light of the vehicle came on when the driver and passenger car doors opened. The car doors closed, and the interior lights went out, but the headlights remained on, illuminating both men as they made their way to the front door. The headlights went off before they got to the door, but a moment later, the door opened, and an interior light turned on, flooding the area in front of the door. One of the two men still stood at the threshold, waiting to enter.

"That's Michael," Kelly said to Susie, "he's the younger brother. It was hard to see, but I think the first guy was Martin."

A few seconds later, the tape revealed the silhouette man as he crossed the front yard, moving directly to the front door. Michael or Martin attempted to exit the front door, but the man pushed him back inside and stepped in behind him just before the door was closed, you could see on the tape the image of the silhouette man was wearing a bandana on his head.

Susie turned to Kelly, "What's going on? That guy just pushed someone back into the house. He looked Hispanic and was wearing a bandana on his head; he seemed to be pretty tall. Do you know who he is?"

"No, I don't, but I have a bad feeling about what we just saw. We need to keep watching and see what happens."

About five minutes later, the front door opened, and the man with the bandana went to the car parked in the driveway. It was obvious he was searching it and placing whatever he found in a large garbage bag. He used the remote to lock the car and returned to the house.

Twenty minutes later, a white or cream-colored van backed into the driveway, and the back doors were opened by the bandana man and a smallish-looking woman with short dark hair. Her features also looked Hispanic. For about ten minutes, there was a steady flow of stuff being carried out of the house and placed in the van. The bandana man and the small Hispanic woman were soon joined by two other people who had not been seen before. One was a woman with dark hair hanging just below her shoulders, and a man who also had dark features. Everyone was getting in the van, but it didn't move. The new guy walked from the driver's side of the van and went back into the house. As he reappeared exiting the house, he was jamming something in his waistband. He returned to the driver's side of the van. The van turned left out of the driveway without braking or turning on the headlights. And disappeared into the night.

"Holy shit," said Susie." What happened to Martin and Michael? I think those people were waiting for them and then ambushed them when they came home. Do you think they hurt them or tied them up and left them in the house?"

"I don't know, Susie, but I'm going to find out right now."

Kelly pulled back her light jacket and pulled her handgun from its holster. She checked to be sure there was a round in the chamber and removed the magazine to be sure it was topped off. Satisfied, she moved to Susie's side door.

"Susie, lock the door behind me and keep an eye on the house. I'm going in through a window. If I'm not back in ten minutes or less, call the police and tell them there's a possible "Officer down" and give them the address for next door. Don't come out yourself until after the police have secured the house. Check your watch. Ten minutes, Susie. Not a minute more."

"Don't go. I'm afraid for you."

"Just do what I told you to do, Susie. I'll be back in less than ten minutes, and we'll go from there." Kelly was out the door and heard the latch fall into place as she moved cautiously toward the side of the house.

Exactly eight minutes later, Susie saw Kelly walking back towards her house. Kelly no longer held her gun in her hand and gave Susie a little wave as she crossed the yard. Susie unlocked and threw the door open. "What'd you find? Are they in there? Are they dead?"

"Calm down, Susie. The house is empty. Everything is in order, and there's no evidence the house was searched, or there was a crime. I made sure not to touch anything so a police crime scene unit could go over it with a fine-tooth comb. Just because I didn't see anything doesn't mean something bad didn't happen in there. To me, it looked like someone had gone out of their way to make it look normal. It was too clean and orderly. At least we know they're not in there hog-tied requiring help. We need to watch the rest of the tapes. I'm sorry for taking up your whole day off."

Susie was into it now. "Fuck it. This is the most exciting thing I've ever been involved in. I work at the fucking chicken factory doing the same boring shit day after day. Scottie is off playing with his gun for the National Guard. It's about time I had some excitement in my life. Please stay and let me watch the tapes with you. You want a beer?"

"Raincheck on the beer, but a bottle of water would be great."

"Water for you and a beer for me. Let's get started."

They fast-forwarded through the tapes, looking for any kind of movement. Nothing happened until 1:15 p.m. the next day when a car pulled into the driveway and parked behind Martin's car.

Two men exited the car and went to the front door. One guy was a large, fat guy with a shaved head and lots of bling hanging around his neck. The other guy was on the other end of the spectrum. Thin as a reed with a simple tee shirt and jeans. They stood at the front door for a few minutes, apparently trying to get someone to answer the door.

The big guy appeared to be agitated. He waved his hands and spoke with the skinny guy. The skinny guy took off around the other side of the house. Two minutes later, skinny opened the front door, stuck his head out, looked around, and allowed the big guy to enter.

At 4:30 p.m., the big guy came out the front door and got in his car, backed out onto Sixty Foot Road, turned around, and backed into the driveway. This time, he backed onto the grass and proceeded by Martin's car and disappeared on the other side of the house, going towards the back door. Fifteen minutes later, the big guy drove around Martin's car and turned left on Sixty Foot Road. Skinny was riding shotgun.

"Kelly, what'd you think that was all about?"

"I think we just saw the cleanup crew take care of business. Did you notice both the front and back tags of the car had those dark plastic covers on them, so we couldn't read the tag number?"

"No shit. I didn't notice that. Now what?"

"We'll keep watching until we get to where I pulled in the driveway today."

They saw no one come or go from the house until yesterday when Kelly and Mrs. Hamilton showed up, and then nothing again until this morning when Kelly returned.

It took a couple of phone calls and some tech help to figure out how to download the tapes to Kelly's laptop, which she had brought into the house. A couple more calls by Susie to the vendor assured her the tapes would not be deleted or destroyed as they may be evidence in a crime. Names of people were obtained and threatened with consequences if they didn't protect these tapes.

During all of this, Kelly had received a call from Mrs. Hamilton.

"Kelly, I went to the sheriff's office, and they took a missing person report on Martin and Michael. Deputy Becky

Ramsway is handling the case. I gave her your name and asked her to share anything she found out with you. She said she knew who you were and would work with you."

Kelly kept her efforts and findings to herself. *I still don't have any concrete evidence that anything untold had happened to Linda's sons; I won't upset this mother with my gut feelings. I'll keep looking.* She jotted down Deputy Ramsway's name in her investigative journal and would give the Deputy twenty-four hours before bringing her into the fold. So far, everything was circumstantial but extremely suspicious. She wondered if the Deputy would reach out to her.

Kelly told Susie, "If the police show up asking questions, tell them everything that's happened and give them my business card. Don't tell anyone else. Only the police.

"Susie, whoever these guys are, they have no idea that your video exists, and it's better to keep it that way. I don't think you're in any danger after four days, but stay alert and wary. Call me if anything suspicious happens. Call the police if you feel threatened in any way."

"I got my gun, and my boyfriend should be home the day after tomorrow. He'll keep our secret, and he's handy with a gun. We'll be fine. Please try and find my neighbor and let me know how this turns out."

"I will. Thank you for your help. You're a good neighbor."

"Fucking A. Now, I'll be a nosey neighbor. If I see anything, I'll write it down and make sure you see the video. Good luck, Kelly. Never met a Private Detective before. You've got a really cool job. Too dangerous for me, but I envy you."

Kelly left with a little spring in her step. *I'm on this now! I'm going to find these guys. I'm sure of that, maybe alive, but maybe not.*

48

CIRCLING FOR THE KILL

Without taking her eyes off the road, Razor hit the speed dial, and a moment later, it was answered by Ana.

"Yes, Razor, what's going on?"

"I think Willy Spears is on the move. His car just left the house with at least two people in it. Windows are tinted, so I can't be positive. I'm two cars behind him, and we're headed out of Salisbury on Route 12 headed towards Snow Hill."

Ana quickly responded, "We're near the college. We'll try and catch up. Try not to lose him, but be careful not to alert them that you're following them."

Razor shook her head in frustration. *I've never done a moving surveillance before. Now, I'm doing one by myself. Get close, but not too close. Don't lose him, but don't let him know you're following him. How the fuck am I supposed to do that?*

"Willy, we may have company. Don't turn around, but there's a cream-colored car behind us. It pulled out from a parking place right after we pulled out of the driveway. It's two cars back with one person in the car. It keeps pulling over to the center line like it's going to pass; then, it slides back into its lane. I think the driver is peeking to make sure we're still here. What ya want me to do?" Latisha asked while checking her side and rearview mirrors for the umpteenth time.

"Keep driving normal. I'll get my boys on the horn and run a little surveillance of our own. We need to know who this is and if there's any possibility that they're involved in what happened to Martin and his brother." Willy pulled his gun from his waistband and stuffed it under his right leg, where he could pull it if someone made a move against him. He felt better knowing Latisha's gun was in a holster under her jacket.

Willy called one of his soldiers, "Hey Emory, where you at, man?"

"I'm in Snow Hill like I always am. What 'ya need, Willy?"

"I'm with Latisha, and we're on Route 12 headed towards Snow Hill. We may've picked up a tail, and I need you and some of the boys to run a little counter-surveillance. Call me back as soon as you and your peoples are near Route 12 in Snow Hill. I'm going to lead this tail right past you, and then you can drop in behind it. I want you to follow the tail wherever it goes after I lose them in Snow Hill. Spread out and switch places until they go to ground. Don't fuck this up, or it's your ass. You feeling me, Emory?"

Ignoring the threat, Emory said, "It's our lucky day, Willy. Two of my guys are with me right now, so we already have three cars ready to go. I'll call a couple more, but they can catch up if it's necessary. What you want us to do if the car following you stops somewhere? What kind of car we looking for?"

Willy gave him the description of the car and instructed him to do nothing but watch and record what he saw. "Emory, there's a chance this is a cop, so we don't want to be going all hostile on them. I need to know where it goes and if the driver meets up wit anybody. After I lose the tail, I'm going home and wait for your call. Don't disappoint me, Emory!"

"I won't, Willy, I won't." The call disconnected.

Emory turned to his men. "Time to get our shit together. Willy expects us to get this right, and I'll be damn if I'm gonna be da one to let Willy down. Are you feelin' me?"

The three men knew from Emory's tone this was some serious shit. None of them wanted to get on Willy's bad side. They knew what would happen.

Razor picked up on the first ring.

"How's it goin, Razor? We're almost there."

"They're going into Snow Hill, and it's getting harder and harder to keep an eye on them without hinking them up. A lot of little streets and sharp turns. I may have to drop off soon."

"We're almost to Snow Hill. Try to hang in there just a little longer." Ana hit the end button. The phone had been on speaker, so Julian understood the situation. He was driving the van about ten miles over the speed limit and was afraid to push it any harder for fear of drawing the attention of the police. His focus was on the road, but his mind was elsewhere. *Damn, this is the opportunity we've been looking for. We've got that son of bitch away from his house with only one other person in his car. If we can eliminate him today, we'll be where we need to be to take over.*

Willy spoke to Emory on his phone. "We're coming into town, and we're gonna go down Court Street to the red light at Main. Latisha will slow down and try to catch the red light. At the last second, she'll speed up and shoot us through the intersection. I want you on Main, and when you see Latisha speed up, I want you to pull across behind us so the car tailing us can't follow. Try to make it look natural as if you're just jumping the green light. Can you do that?"

"Yep. I got it."

Willy's plan and Emory's driving worked perfectly. The tail car was stuck behind another car at the red light while Latisha and Willy sped away. Latisha worked some back streets and ended up on Route 113 going north. By cutting across some backroads, they would work their way back to Salisbury. All was now in the hands of Emory and his boys.

Latisha said nothing. *I hope, for Emory's sake, he gets this right. Willy won't deal well with failure.* Willy sat there and said nothing. Lost in his own thoughts.

The cream-colored car was a Toyota 4-door sedan. Emory followed it only three blocks before it pulled into a 7-11 Store. The driver drove past the gas pumps and to the side of the store, where it backed into an empty slot. Emory watched the driver, a dark-haired female, talking on a cell phone for a minute before lowering it out of sight. She just sat. Doing nothing.

One of Emory's people spoke on his burner phone. "What you want us to do now, Emory?"

"Stay put and stay the fuck off the phone unless you got something to report. Keep hidden. I got eyes on the car, and I'll tell you what I want you to do when I want you to do it."

Emory's little army had grown to a total of five cars. The four other drivers all had their burner phones turned on but remained silent.

Five minutes passed before a white van pulled into the 7-11 and drove directly to the Toyota. It pulled past and then backed into the empty slot next to it.

Emory had his phone in camera mode and propped securely against the upper part of his steering wheel. Four people grouped near the front of the van. Two Hispanic females and two Hispanic males. The exchange of words was far too distant to hear, but the phone did an excellent job of framing the faces of those gathered together. Emory snapped multiple pictures and then viewed them by enlarging the image. Definitely Hispanic, but beyond that, there was no way of knowing who they were or their purpose.

"I lost Willy. I got caught behind a car at the red light, and they disappeared before I could get through the intersection," Razor explained.

Julian remained calm and said, "It's okay. We'll get another chance. The fact that he's traveling around with just his driver tells me he has no idea of the danger he's in. We may have to rent a couple of cars and set up again at his house, but we'll get his ass. It's just a matter of time. We must remain patient and stay smart. Let's all go back to the house and make plans for how we deal with this guy. You did an excellent job, Razor. Maybe this trip to Snow Hill is part of a pattern. We'll see, and when we get a chance, we'll strike and show the rest of his crew that no one is safe. Our hunt has just begun. Let's go home."

Dropping his Mustang into drive, Emory told his crew, "They're on the move. Every five miles, switch up on the car that's behind them. If they stay on the main roads, Tiny will get ahead of them and stay about a mile in front. I'll tell you what to do as we follow them. Just follow my directions, and don't do anything stupid."

Emory notified Willy, "Boss, a white van had shown up with three Hispanics joining the Hispanic female who was driving the cream Toyota. Both vehicles are now moving, and we're following. I'll call you as soon as they stop somewhere. We're being careful not to be noticed."

"I'm counting on you, Emory. Call me when you got something."

Emory's plan appeared to have worked as they followed the van and Toyota out of Snow Hill and North on Route 113, heading towards Berlin. The car and the van made no counter-surveillance moves.

Ten minutes later, Jonas, the man directly behind the target car, notified Emory, "The car made a left into a private driveway. There's a faded red mailbox on the left of the road, with the number 13867 painted in white. There's no name on the mailbox and the driveway's long. Both cars disappeared over a rise in the road. I'm afraid to go up the driveway."

"You did right not to follow. Everybody back off and assume positions in the area. Find places where the police won't be called. I'll check in with Willy and get further instructions."

Willy had been waiting for what was to him an eternity. "Emory, what's going on? Are you still following them?"

"Willy, I think they may be home. They went up a private driveway about ten minutes ago, and neither vehicle has come out. It's a long driveway, and we gots no idea what's back there. What you want us to do?"

"Do nothing, Emory. Just watch that driveway for the next two hours. If nobody comes out, I want you and your guys to go home and get some rest. I need to think on this and what all this means and come up with a plan to deal with it. Tell your guys to stay close to their phones tomorrow. You did well, Emory. You did real good! I won't forget it either." Willy disconnected.

Willy smiled to himself. Thinking out loud in a low voice, "I think the prey has just become the hunter. We must plan carefully and make sure we know the number of people we're up against, but be assured we will strike soon. Nobody fucks with Willy Spears. I'm going to draw this circle into a noose."

Latisha occupied the chair across from Willy. She nodded slowly and caressed the handgun she held securely in her lap.

49

I OWE YOU ONE

Kelly was in her office early. She'd been running database checks trying to find out as much as she could about Martin and Michael Hamilton. Martin had one speeding ticket that he had paid without going to court. Michael had nothing in her records checks. If he had a juvenile record, it remained sealed. She made a note to talk to Mrs. Hamilton. She would know if her boys had crossed the line and definitely more than the judicial system of Worcester County.

At 8:30 a.m., while working on her second cup of coffee, Kelly's cell phone rang.

"Kelly Hart."

"Ms. Hart, this is Carlton. Do you remember me?"

"Yes, Carlton, I do. Are you having problems with your wife and daughter again?"

"No, Ma'am, we're doing good. I get to see Shelene every weekend. My ex is treating me alright and doesn't give me any trouble when I'm around. Whatever you told her must've sunk in. She's even looking at me differently now that I have a full-time job and I'm paying my child support right on time.

You told me if I stepped up, my life would get better, and it has."

"If everything is going well, why are you giving me a call this morning?"

"I'm calling about Martin and Michael. I was with Mrs. Hamilton last night. She lives in the apartment below mine, and she's really upset. She told me you were looking for them, and I know I owe you one. I've got some information, but I don't want to talk on the phone, and I don't want to meet up anywhere around here. I can't be seen talking to the police."

"Carlton, you know I'm not the police. I'm a private investigator."

"Means the same thing to someone like Willy Spears. If you want to meet, I have a place near where I deliver parts for my job. Will you meet me in Chincoteague, Virginia? It's only about an hour from Berlin, but I know the people I worry about don't go around there."

"I can do that. When and where do you want to meet?"

"Meet me at the South Chincoteague Tavern at 1 p.m. today."

"I've never been in there, but I know where it is. I'll see you at 1. Call me if anything changes. Carlton, can you give me a hint about what you want to talk about?"

"It's bad, Ms. Kelly. I'll tell you when I see you."

Kelly frowned; *I thought this case might go south. I need to talk to Marie Barnett and tell her where I'm going and whom I'm meeting. It's a public place, but you never know what you're walking into.* She unconsciously touched the handle of the gun riding on her right hip.

50
SOUTH CHINCOTEAGUE TAVERN

Kelly arrived in Chincoteague, Virginia, at 12:30 p.m., a half hour before she was to meet up with her new informant, Carlton Chambers. *I didn't have time to vet him as an informant, but he's willing to give me information about Martin and Michael. For now, I'm going to assume he's reliable and trustworthy. He picked the location for the meeting. It's a public place, and it's broad daylight. If there's a bad or dangerous side to this town, I've never seen it.*

The island is only seven miles long and about two miles wide and has a population of under 4,000. It's well known for the wild ponies who live there and the children's story book, *Misty of Chincoteague,* depicted in a 1961 Century Fox movie.

It's a very quaint and friendly place to visit, and tourists pour in and out of the community, especially during the summer months. Recently, investors have added restaurants, housing rentals, and other niceties that are starting to change the once sparse fishing village into a summer retreat. Those resistant to change probably hate the new look.

Kelly sat across the street from the tavern for a few minutes, just watching the place. It looked kind of run down, but that might have been by design. Swanky wouldn't cut it in this place, and if it did, she doubted Carlton would have ever gone in. She checked vehicles in the area and saw no one lingering or appearing to be a threat or even interested in her or the tavern.

Since Kelly arrived first, she would now set the rules of engagement. After locking her car, she walked into the dimly lit tavern. The inside was in no better shape than the outside, but the place was clean, and there were a few folks already perched at the bar; one of several tables was occupied by three older gentlemen, all sipping on draft beers. No, Carlton. The bright light that streamed in through the open door had all eyes turned her way. *I'm sure everyone in here is a local, and I'm definitely being checked out.*

There was no reception hostess or anyone who appeared to be seating customers, so Kelly worked her way to a table that occupied the area furthest from the entrance. She seated herself facing the door. She had a clear view of the entire place.

A middle-aged woman with dull blonde hair left her seat at the last bar stool, came over, and said, "Hi, I'm Barbara. What can I get you?"

Wanting to fit in, Kelly replied, "Do you have Miller Lite in a bottle?"

"Sure do. We serve some pretty good sandwiches, the soup of the day is cream of crab, and I can offer you a house salad to go with it. I'll bring a menu with that beer. Do you want a glass?"

"No glass needed. Just cold beer, please."

"Our beer is cold, you'll see. Be right back."

"Oh, make that two menus. I'm meeting someone; I'm about fifteen minutes early."

Barbara nodded and went behind the bar. Less than a minute later, she came back with Kelly's beer in one hand and two menus in the other.

The tavern people had turned back to their drinks and conversations. Two old guys sat huddled about halfway down the bar with beers in front of them. They were talking and laughing, obviously enjoying each other's company. The two continued to look her way. Kelly chuckled to herself. *These old guys are checking out what they think may be a potential hookup. Sorry fellows. Go back to your jokes and stories of glory days. My social calendar is all booked up, and you guys are old enough to be my father. Not looking for a sugar daddy.*

Kelly sipped her beer slowly. At precisely 1 p.m., Carlton walked through the door. It took a moment for his eyes to adjust, and he walked directly to Kelly's table and took a chair to the side of her. *Guess he doesn't want his back to the door, either.*

Carlton's ass had barely hit the chair when Barbara appeared at the table. "Hey Carlton, how you doing today?"

"Good Barb, how about you?"

"Doing okay, you having the regular today?"

"Yep. A burger, fries, and a coke. You know how I like my burger."

"Yes, I do. How about you, Miss, make up your mind on what you're having?"

"How about half a turkey club and a cup of your cream of crab?"

"Sounds good. Need another beer?"

"No more beer. Can you bring me water with my meal?"

"Sure can. Be back as soon as your food is ready." Barbara turned on her heels and moved behind the bar to a service window that opened into the kitchen.

Carlton appeared a little nervous and kept checking the front door as if he was expecting someone. His eyes shifted back and forth, not settling on Kelly. His hands were on the table but clasped tightly together.

"Carlton, you expecting someone else to come in here?"

"No, it's not that. I just need to tell you some stuff that might get me killed if the wrong people knew I was talking to anybody about what I know."

Carlton looks like a very fit guy who could probably handle himself in a fight, but his fear feels real. "Okay, Carlton, why don't you just spit it out and tell me what's bothering you or what it is you know that's so dangerous to talk about."

At that moment, Barb showed up with their food, and all conversation stopped. While the food was being placed on the table, the two old guys at the bar broke out in a raucous laugh, causing everyone in the tavern to turn around and look at them. They ignored the attention and kept on laughing at their private joke.

"Carlton, who are those guys? Do you know them?"

"Yeah, that's Hugh and George. I think Hugh is Irish, and George is a Brit. They're always in here and always together. Best buddies, I'd guess. When that British guy gets going, I can't understand a fucking word he's saying. Bloody this and bloody that, eh Mate. They're pretty harmless, but in their day, I bet they raised holy hell."

Barb had walked away. "Ms. Kelly, are you still looking for Martin and Michael?"

"Yes, I am. Do you know where they are?"

"Not exactly, but I was told they're both dead!"

Even though Kelly feared this might be the case, she was taken aback by the blunt presentation of fact, "Carlton, I need you to start at the beginning and tell me everything you know about Martin and Michael."

"About a year ago, a friend of mine started hanging around the drug people in Salisbury. He told me he was making some quick money, and he didn't have to work hard to get it. He told me he would introduce me if I was interested. My baby was coming any day, and as much as I needed money, this wasn't for me. I'm scared of jail. I tried to get my friend to distance himself from the gang before something bad happened to him. He wouldn't listen to me, and we sort of drifted apart. The baby came, and I had a bunch of part-time jobs trying to make ends meet. My wife and I were in a rough spot. There was no time left for any of my old friends."

"So, what happened to your friend?"

"That's what I'm about to tell you. Two days ago, he called me. He said he was scared. Something terrible had happened, and he needed someone to talk to. Said he was stuck in the middle and in way over his head. Sounded like he was crying when he was talking to me. I'd never heard him act like that. I agreed to meet with him. He told me it had to be someplace private. He said it would be dangerous for both of us if we were seen talking. We met in a wooded area we used to go to when we were young bucks to drink beer and sometimes take our dates because it was secluded.

"He told me that he'd been riding with Slick Melvin for about six months. Melvin goes around to the stash houses and collects the money from drug sales in Sandpiper. Melvin is lazy, so he has my friend do all the dirty work. Sometimes, he doesn't even get out of the car; he just tells my friend to go in and get the money and come get him if there's a problem. There was never a problem until the day before he called me.

"He said he and Slick Melvin went to a stash house on Sixty Foot Road. It was one of the regular stops. That day, they couldn't get anyone to answer the door, so my friend found an unlocked window, climbed into the house, and let Melvin in the front door. They found Martin and Michael in the living room. They were sitting, tied to chairs with pillowcases over their heads. Both had been shot in the back of the head and were dead. The house had been ripped apart, and any money or drugs that were there were gone. My friend said he freaked out and told Melvin they needed to call the police. Slick Melvin told him to shut up and calm down. He said he had to call Willy before they did anything.

"Melvin called Willy, and after the call, Melvin told my friend they were instructed to clean up the house and make it look normal. They were to wrap the bodies up, take them out of the house, and bury them where they wouldn't be found. My friend said they were there for hours and then backed Melvin's car behind the house, put the bodies in the trunk, and buried them later that night in a field. Melvin made my friend do most of the digging, and the hole was so deep he was afraid Melvin had been told to bury him as well. He said before he was dropped off the next morning, Slick Melvin threatened him that if he ever spoke about what he'd seen or what they did, Willy would kill him. Melvin also reminded him that because he helped clean up the scene and bury the bodies, he would be going to jail for a long time if it ever came out.

"My friend is afraid Willy will decide to clean up any loose ends and kill him. Slick Melvin has been around a long time, but my friend is on the lowest rung of the gang, and nobody would stand up for him, and if he disappeared, nobody would miss him. He asked me what he should do, and I told him to just lay low and not talk about it to anybody, even Melvin. Pretend it was no big deal and just do what they tell you to do. I told him they'd be watching him to see if he was going to be able to handle what happened or if he started running his mouth. I told him I knew someone who might be able to help him, but I didn't tell him who. That's when I thought about calling you."

"You've never said your friend's name. What is it?"

"It's Freddie. Freddie Jones. He says Willy Spears is doing his own investigation into who did this, and when he finds out, he's going to go to war with them. The word is he's promising to kill whoever was involved. Freddie told me that for the first time, he was given a gun and ammunition and told to practice with it because he may soon have to use it. Freddie wants out. He doesn't want to hurt anybody. He says everything is out of control. Can you help him, Ms. Kelly?"

"I don't know Carlton. This is some bad stuff. Did he tell you exactly where the bodies are buried?"

"He said he didn't know exactly where he was but thinks he could find it again if he had to."

"Carlton, here's what I want you to do. Stop talking to your friend on your cell phone. Take him out of your contacts and remove the call you got from him. If they decide to take him out, they may check his phone and see your number. Can you get a burner phone?"

"I never thought about that. Yeah, I can get a burner. I'll call him with the burner and tell him to delete me from his phone and get a burner for himself. I'll do that right after I leave you."

"Okay, tell him to stay calm and not to do anything stupid.

Don't give him my name, but tell him you spoke with someone who may be able to give him a path forward, but no promises yet. I need to talk to someone myself and see if there's anything that can be worked out. Tell him his first act of good faith will be showing someone where the bodies are buried. Without that, I can't and won't help him. Understood?"

"Yes, I understand. I'll text you my burner number once I have it."

"One other thing, Carlton. Who is Willy Spears?"

"Willy Spears runs all the drugs in the area and is a very dangerous man. My stupid friend has good reason to be afraid."

Kelly let Carlton leave first and even paid for their meals. *If this shit is true, then he's more than earned a burger and some fries. I need to talk to Brogan. This could turn into an all-out drug war. The police need to act before Willy Spears does.*

Back in her car, she called Brogan's number, but it went to his voicemail. *He's probably up to his eyes in reports and meetings concerning the kidnapping of Patty Ryan and the shootout at sea. This information is two days old, so it could hold a few more hours.* She left him a short message asking him to call her when he got a minute. *No use getting him all fired up over the phone.*

She drove slowly, her thoughts turning to Mrs. Hamilton. *That poor woman has lost both her sons because of their involvement with a drug gang. She'll be crushed by this devastating news.*

Kelly saw a store approaching on her left side. She'd been in this store before, and without a second thought, she turned into their parking lot. She needed something to brighten her day. This might be the place to find it.

As she entered Sundial Books, she had pleasant memories of her last visit. She had found a novel about a woman who had suffered great loss in her life but found her way back and was now very happy and successful. It was a true story. Kelly unconsciously let her fingers run along the scar on her right forearm that reminded her of her loss and recovery. The bell over the door announced her arrival.

She was warmly greeted by the owners, Jonathan and Jane Richstein. Jonathan offered his help if she needed it. She declined and said she would just like to browse the store.

Kelly was drawn to a display containing books by local authors. One of them was a book she had previously read titled *Vengeance.* Kelly smiled to herself when she saw a book. A book about a damn good cop and brought back some sweet memories of their own.

Her eyes traveled to the book next to it by the same author, *No Backup.* She lifted it from the shelf and studied the artwork. The picture and the feel of the book in her hands sent slight chills through her body. A girlfriend had called her shortly after it came out and told Kelly, "It's about you and your boyfriend and your recent exploits." *I swore to myself I wouldn't go looking for this book, but here it is in my hands.* She started to put it down but then snatched it back and held it against her chest. Her heart thumped quietly against the book. *This is crazy. How can I not read a book about Brogan and me? I'm buying it, and I'm reading it!*

Kelly walked to the counter and presented the book and cash to Jane. Jane didn't know who Kelly was and may not have remembered her being in the store before.

"Is that it for today?" Jane asked while preparing to ring up the sale.

"Yes, that's all."

"You should've come in this past Saturday," Jonathan said

as he watched his wife put the book in a small bag and hand it to Kelly.

"Really, why's that?"

"We had a book signing on Saturday, and that author was here signing books. The book you just bought has a message and his autograph, but on Saturday, he was personalizing them to the buyer."

"Wow, sorry I missed that opportunity." Kelly lied and felt her face flush. *How embarrassing would that have been! Being so vain as to buy a book about myself and my boyfriend.*

Kelly quickly left the store, not knowing until much later that her embarrassment would have been a hundred-fold worse after she read the last chapter of *No Backup.* Kelly jumped in her car and discarded the book on the passenger seat. *Time to get back to work. Brogan is going to shit when I tell him he might be facing a killing war among drug dealers.*

Kelly's cell phone rang. She glanced at the screen. *It's Brogan.*

51
Recon

Latisha and Willy were alone in his house. Willy was considering what Latisha was laying out for him.

"Willy, let me call Emory. I'll meet up with him tonight around midnight, and he can show me exactly where these Hispanics are hold up. When I was in the Army, I used to go on reconnaissance missions all the time. We'd go out beyond the wire and snoop around in enemy territory. We'd identify troop numbers, weapons, and places where they were weak. Then, later that night or early the next morning, our guys would send out a search-and-destroy team using our intelligence. We killed a lot of towel heads that never knew we were coming. I'm good at this, Willy. Let me do a recon on their spot, and then we can work up a plan to take them out. Right now, we don't know shit about their setup or how many of them are at the end of that dirt road. They have no idea that we're on to them. I'll go in alone. Emory can wait for me someplace. I can't take that stumbling fool with me. He'd get us both killed."

"I like it," Willy said, "But it bothers me you being alone.

What if they see you or grab you while you're crawling around in their backyard? We've been together a long time. You're the only person I trust one hundred percent. I can't afford to lose you."

"You ain't going to lose me, Willy. They'll never know I was there. I'll make Emory stay close enough that if he hears gunshots, he and his boys can come to the rescue. It won't come to that, Willy, trust me."

"I do trust you. Call Emory and make it happen."

"Willy, I got to be moving slow and easy. This takes a lot of time, so don't go worrying if you don't hear from me until tomorrow morning. I'll get out of there before the sun comes up, and I'll come straight back here and give you a full report."

"Be careful, Latisha."

"I will, Willy. I will."

At 12:30 a.m., Latisha entered a wooded area near the dirt driveway. She was dressed from head to toe in camouflage. It was the greens and browns that matched the surrounding environment.

Latisha directed, "Emory, slow roll this rod without coming to a complete stop or hitting the brakes. And make sure the headlights and interior light are off."

Latisha virtually slid from the vehicle with only the slight snick of the door latch when she pushed it closed. Emory lost sight of her within seconds as she blended into the landscape. He had his marching orders. Before Latisha left the car, she told him, "You return to this exact location at 5:00 a.m. I'll be waiting. If I'm not here, you call Willy."

They had picked a spot for him to hide out. It was close enough that he would hear a gunshot, and if he did, he would summon his boys, who were also hidden in a van about half a mile away in the parking lot of a gas station that was closed for the night. They were heavily armed.

Emory's only concern was falling asleep during the waiting. *If I fall asleep, will I hear a gunshot, even with the window rolled down? I'm going to change the plan just a little and pick up one of my guys to wait with me. If we get tired, we can take turns staying awake. I'll take him back to the van before 5:00 a.m., so Latisha will never know. If there's a shootout, she won't give a fuck as long as we show up with guns blazing.*

Latisha had considered her ghillie suit for her creep to the target but decided it would hamper her progress through the woods. It worked better in open fields. She was confident her camouflage clothing would be sufficient with the cover of darkness.

She used the driveway as a guide to her target but remained well away from it so as not to set off any tripwires or hidden cameras. She was pretty sure they wouldn't set up counter surveillance or warning devices this far into the woods. Otherwise, they would be checking them all night long as they were triggered by critters roaming through the woods looking for food.

There were no animals big enough to be a threat to Latisha. There were coyote sightings on the Eastern Shore, but even they would avoid contact once they got a sniff of a human being in the area. But foxes, rabbits, and other small game would be taking advantage of these dark woods.

It took her two hours to travel the distance to where the woods ended, and a cleared-out area appeared. At the edge of the woods, she was able to see an old farmhouse and some outbuildings, including a large dog house. A dog would definitely present a problem. Latisha had brought a silenced 9mm handgun with her, and was an excellent shot. She used a small set of binoculars to get a better view. A chain lay outside the dog house, luckily with no dog attached. *There's no water or food bowl present. That's a good sign.*

The full moon lit the area. *The windows are curtained. But I see slivers of light being cast through a window near the front of the house. Maybe someone is still awake or is standing guard throughout the night.*

Latisha crept closer and closer to the house. Tensed and ready in case a dog attacked. Up close, the dog house appeared to be unused. *Still might be a dog living inside the house. Gotta take my time. Slow is fast in these situations.*

Finally, Latisha arrived under the lighted window. She rose slowly to a standing position and peeked into the room. With the outside much darker, it would be nearly impossible to detect her.

The living room and kitchen were open areas. A TV was turned on, but Latisha was unable to hear any sound. She doubted the volume was turned on. A man sat at the kitchen table hunched over a laptop computer. A semi-automatic handgun sat on the table near his right hand. A coffee cup sat at his left hand. *This guy was small and obviously not one of the guys Emory had seen gathered around the van. If this guy is a guard, he's distracted and not taking his job seriously. Maybe he's just a night owl or can't sleep. There's at least five of them. I don't see any other weapons in plain view.*

Latisha moved around the house, peeking in each window. Although she was as quiet as a mouse, she was sure a watchdog would have alerted her to her presence by now. No dog sounds. She peeked in each window where the curtain was separated enough to see in. A small bed with one person sleeping in it. A small night light provided enough illumination to see the sleeper had long dark hair, which matched the description of one of the women seen at the van. Another handgun was on the nightstand. *Pretty safe to assume everybody in this house has at least one gun with them at all times.* The other windows were curtained tight, and she could not see the occupants.

Latisha checked the van and car parked near the house. Both were locked. She used a small pen light and took a quick look in each. She saw nothing but empty soda cans and carry-out food bags crumpled and discarded.

On her way towards the house, she noticed a large tree near the rear of the house, some of its branches extended over the roof. With the help of the moonlight, she observed several branches scattered on the roof. It gave her an idea. She retreated to the wood line and prepared a hide, a place where she would be able to see without being seen.

I need to get the house awake and see how many people are in there. While in the open area, she grabbed a couple of rocks about the size of golf balls. Once her hide was completed to her satisfaction, she stepped out from the woods and hurled one of the stones high into the air and towards the house. Before it landed, she was back in her hide. The stone hit the roof of the house with an audible thud. She waited.

A light came on in the rear of the house. *Come on out. Show me how many of you there are.*

The front door of the house was thrown open, and the computer guy peeked out, not fully revealing himself. A moment later, a much larger guy pushed past him. The big guy was armed with what appeared to be an AR-15. He held it with practiced ease. He said something to the little guy, who then joined him outside. They closed the front door to reduce the light that illuminated them and slowly began circling the house. The little guy was checking the windows, and the big guy was covering him with his gun pointed away from the house and towards the darkened woods.

Latisha stayed very still, just watching. *I'm invisible to them.* Her gun lay near her hand but would offer very little protection against an AR-15 if it was brought to bear on her position. *Just stay still.*

The front door was opened again, and a third man and two women came outside. All of them held handguns. The man and the woman with short hair also held large flashlights, not yet turned on.

Latisha lowered her binoculars, not wanting a flashlight to catch a reflection off the lenses. *They can't see me. Even with flashlights, I'm invisible.*

Both flashlights came on and began searching the edge of the wood line. About fifty yards from Latisha's hide, a deer broke cover and ran down the tree line before darting back into the woods. All five guns came up and were pointed toward the deer, clearly visible in the beam of the flashlights.

Thank God nobody fired. That would've brought Emory and his men in here shooting at anything that moved. These people have had training. They used shooting discipline by not firing wildly at an unknown target. There may be only five of them, but we'll meet a disciplined response. This recon has revealed a lot.

The five Hispanics met at the side of the house, facing Latisha. The man pointed his flashlight up onto the roof, where he was able to observe numerous sticks and branches. The rock had apparently rolled off the roof and joined the hundreds of rocks, stones, and debris that surrounded the house. All heads were positioned so they could see the roof. An explanation had been found. They all retreated into the house, and various lights began to be extinguished.

Had we been set up in the woods tonight and used my ploy, we could've ambushed the entire group using AR-15s or rifles. They would've had no place to hide. It would've been over in seconds. Willy will be pleased when I tell him what's happened tonight. We can plan now!

At 5:00 a.m., still dark, Latisha emerged from the woods and got into Emory's idling vehicle. They drove away without turning on the car's headlights until they were well down the road.

Emory asked, "How'd it go?"

"It went good. I'll tell Willy what I saw, and he'll tell you what he wants you to do."

Emory knew not to ask further questions. He had a healthy respect for Latisha's capabilities, and he had never killed anyone, but he was sure Latisha had and would again. Willy kept her close for good reason. He would wait to hear from Willy.

52

WHAT'S OUR STRATEGY?

Kelly took the call, "Hey Brogan, I'm about an hour from home, I should be there around 6 p.m. I've got some information to share with you. It's important, but not something I should talk about on a cell phone."

"Sure, how about I meet you at your place? We can order Chinese for dinner. Will I be happy with what you're about to tell me?"

"I doubt it, but I'll explain as soon as I see you."

Brogan strode through the door about ten minutes after Kelly arrived home. Following the mandatory greeting by her dog and the requisite number of pets on his head and belly, Brogan turned to Kelly, gave her a lingering kiss, and said, "So what's up?"

Kelly held onto Brogan a few moments longer than normal after they broke from their kiss.

"You want to tell me about your day before or after I throw something new on your plate to worry about?" Kelly asked.

"My day was nothing but paperwork and meetings, so lay it on me, whatever you've got."

"How about a double murder and a festering drug war that may kick off at any time?"

"Are you fucking kidding?"

"Nope, here's what I know. I told you about the missing brothers, right?"

"Yep, did you find them?"

"Not yet, but today I was told by an informant that they're both dead and buried in a field. He said it was drug-related, done by someone who hit one of Willy Spears' stash houses on Sixty Foot Road. They killed the two brothers, stole all the dope and money in the house, and left them tied to chairs with bullets in the back of their heads. Execution style.

"When Willy's people found them, they called Willy. Willy decided he's doing his own investigation. Told his guys to clean up the house, move, and bury the bodies. When he figures out who did this, he's going to make an example by killing them. Probably make it messy so everyone will learn a lesson."

"Do you believe this informant?"

"About ninety-nine percent. My guy has nothing to gain from this. He felt he owed me a solid for helping him with a domestic child visitation issue about six months ago. I got paid, but he feels he owes me more because I talked his wife into giving him a second chance to do the right thing by her and his kid. He's stepped up, and things have turned around for him. This is his way of paying me back.

"All his information right now is second-hand from his close friend who's in the drug gang and afraid for his life. Apparently, his friend is very low in their chain of command. He was ordered to help clean up the scene and bury the bodies. He feels he may be a loose end that Willy Spears may want to clip. I think he wants out but doesn't know how to do it."

"Holy shit, Kelly. We're still filling out forms over all the bodies that piled up during that lethal treasure hunt. My new boss is going to start second-guessing himself. I seem to bring a lot of bad things with me wherever I go. Now you're handing me another case with dead bodies in the ground and a promise of more to come." Brogan sighed. "Okay, what's our strategy?"

Kelly smiled at the inclusive response, "I was thinking we test the guy looking for help. We have him take us to the grave of the missing brothers."

"Do you know how to contact him?"

"No, but my informant does. Want me to reach out?"

"Let me call Rudy Carol first and tell him what's going on. Once he picks himself up off the floor, he may have some suggestions or questions before we go off on another one of our crime-solving missions."

"We need to be careful, Brogan. It looks like some unknown has committed two brutal murders against a well-established drug gang. I'd say someone has a big set of balls." With a smile, she continued, "Not as big as yours, honey, but close."

He snickered at the funny, "We're always careful, but I believe you're right. More people are going to die if we do nothing. I've no love for drug dealers, but there're always innocent people who end up being collateral damage. We'll need to move on this now with a plan and probably a SWAT Team close at hand. Call your snitch and see if his friend is ready to take a leap to the good guys. I want to be at that grave site tomorrow morning."

Just outside of Salisbury, 7:00 a.m. the next day, Willy and Latisha sat at the kitchen table. She had drawn a crude map of the area she had surveilled throughout the night.

She told him how she had snuck around the house, looked in windows, and checked their vehicles. And how she lured the occupants out of the house to obtain their number and readiness.

"Willy, as best I can tell, there're only five of them. Three men and two women. All of them are armed with handguns and at least one AR-15. Based on what I saw, they seem comfortable with the firearms and have training and discipline in using them. They don't seem alarmed but cautious and ready. We'll hit them at their place in the middle of the night. If we can get them outside again, it should be easy, with little risk to our people. I'd suggest we use silenced weapons. There're no houses close, but the noise of gunfire will travel. They're bound to get off some shots even if our weapons are silent. We'll get a quick police response for shots fired. I think we should use a diversion to draw police away from the area before we hit them. Can you get me ten men? I'll make eleven. We want overwhelming numbers for guaranteed success. We'll hit them tonight around midnight while our intelligence is fresh."

Willy listened closely and agreed with Latisha's evaluation and loosely formed strategy.

"Alright, Latisha, put something together. I'll arrange for ten men for you and pick a spot near Snow Hill where everyone will meet. No one will be armed until we get there, and then I'll pass out the guns. You can count me in as a twelfth person who'll be there."

"Willy, are you sure? This could be dangerous. These plans

always go to shit as soon as the first shot is fired. I don't see us failing, but there's always something that can go sideways."

"I know Latisha, but I need to be there with my people. They need to see I'm not afraid and I'll stand with them when the shit hits the fan. I'll wear a vest and hang on the fringe, but I'm going to be there. These people fucked with our operation, and the message needs to be strong and permanent. We hit them hard and leave them where they lay. Make sure I have an AR-15 for myself."

"Okay, Willy. I need to get a few hours of sleep. I'll have our plan on paper by 5 p.m. I'll make sure we succeed. Should any of our people go down, we'll take them with us when we go. We can't leave any evidence behind that'll link this to us."

Early morning near Snow Hill, the last of the Calupoh Cartel gathered in the kitchen. Diego spoke to Julian, "How'd you explain what happened last night? We all heard a noise on the roof, but there was nothing but some little sticks. I don't think they could've made that noise. There wasn't even any wind last night."

"Not sure," Julian responded. "All the windows were secure, and the vehicles were okay when Tomas checked them. Maybe it was an animal, but where did it go? You and Tomas were out there in less than a minute. Maybe you can see something now that it's daylight. Razor, go with Diego and see if there's an explanation outside."

Diego and Razor began to slowly circle the house, re-checking the windows. The first window was locked. They could see boot prints in the dusty soil that surrounded the entire house where Tomas had stood in front of the window.

The second window was also locked, and again, footprints appeared directly in front of the window.

"Hey Diego, you see that?"

"What am I supposed to be seeing?"

"There's a second set of footprints at the window. Tomas's footprints have almost covered them, but see there's a different kind of tread in the dust. You can see a partial print sticking out from the side where Tomas stood. The other footprint is a little smaller than Tomas'. Someone was walking near the house before you and Tomas got outside last night. That's why Tomas's are on top."

Now, they were looking at the ground differently. They began to see the smaller footprints appearing and reappearing near and underneath the footprints made by everyone else who was outside walking around last night.

"Razor, let me see the bottom of your boots."

Razor lifted one foot at a time so Diego could examine them.

"You have a different tread design. Go inside and check everybody's shoes they were wearing last night."

Razor disappeared inside the house while Diego returned to the first window. It was faint, but he could see the smaller footprints coming to and from the house in almost a straight line. Without walking on the footprints, he followed them to the wood line and stepped inside the treed area. He saw it almost immediately. The weeds were knocked down, and a small depression was visible just inside the woods. Was this where the deer they saw last night lay? When they saw the deer, it had been much further down the wood line.

Julian examined the beaten-down area more closely and finally lay on his stomach, facing the house. Shit, this is a hide. Someone lay here last night and watched the house, then snuck up and tried to peek or get in through the windows.

When the group reassembled in the kitchen, they tried to figure out what was going on. They had all examined the small footprints and even found them near the vehicles. The hide was troubling.

"That footprint is pretty small. Maybe a kid. You think it might be some nosy kid living in the area or some pervert trying to cop a look at the girls when they're in their bedrooms?" Tomas theorized.

Diego interrupted, "I don't know who it was, but it's freaking me out, and I intend to do something about it. Tonight, I'll set up in the woods near the hide. If this asshole comes back, I'm going to get the drop on him and put him in a world of hurt."

Julian looked at his little band of desperados and said, "We'll all stay up tonight.

"Razor, you'll be with Diego. The rest of us will turn off all the lights, but the one in Ana's bedroom. That room faces the woods. It'll look like we've gone to bed. Ana, crack your curtain just a little. Let's see if we can draw this bastard back up to the house. We'll be in the living room ready to back you guys when someone comes. All these fuckers living in the country carry guns, so everybody is locked and loaded, but try to take him alive so we can find out who he is and what he's looking for."

It looked like it might be a long and dangerous night for everybody.

53

INEVITABLE CONFLICT?

Brogan had gotten his wish. The sun was just rising. He, Kelly, four crime scene technicians, Freddie Jones, and local farmer Roger Curry stood at the edge of Mr. Curry's southernmost acreage. They stood in an area designated to give Mr. Curry's farm tractors access to his crops. It was bordered by a wooded area. They were at least sixty yards from any hard surface road and about ten acres from Curry's home.

"Are you sure, Freddie?" Brogan locked eyes with the young man.

"Yes, sir. Melvin and I placed that log over the area along with a bunch of leaves and sticks to make it look natural, but I'm sure this is the spot."

Brogan and Kelly had picked Freddie up half a mile from his home while it was still totally dark. Freddie was visibly afraid but now committed to seeing this though. There was no wiggle room in the agreement he had made with the State's Attorney's Office. He was to cooperate one hundred percent by leading investigators to the burial site and giving a full written statement as to everything he knew about the deaths and subsequent disposal of the bodies. He would then testify in court whenever he was needed. One lie, one deviation from full cooperation, would send him spiraling into the depths of a long prison term from which a guy like him might not survive. His reward would be no jail time and relocation if he wanted it.

Roger Curry, dressed in his bib-overalls and straw hat, shook his head, *I can't believe someone brought this horror to my property so close to where me and my family slept, unknowing.* Mr. Curry readily agreed to sign any waivers necessary to allow the police full access to his property.

Brogan turned to Sylvia Willard, the senior member of the forensic team, and said, "It's all yours."

The team removed numerous pieces of equipment from their van parked a short distance away, including four shovels necessary to aid them in their recovery efforts. Before anything was touched, photographs and measurements were made. A detailed sketch was created. Even the distance from their location to the hard-surfaced road was measured and recorded. Crime scene tape was used to surround the area.

A vehicle moved slowly towards the scene along the edge of the field. It stopped outside the ribbon. The driver's door swung open, and Assistant State's Attorney Jim Lyons emerged, walked to the ribbon, and stopped. He and Brogan conversed, and Lyon retreated to the front of his car and assumed a position, leaning against his car while observing the activities of the crime scene techs. Freddie Jones, Kelly, Mr. Curry, and Brogan all gathered with him outside the tape. They were soon joined by Sheriff's Detective Frankie Mazzone and a uniformed Deputy First Class. This would be a Sheriff's Office Investigation. Mazzone's partner, M.J.

Callanan, was at the house on Sixty-foot Road with another forensic team investigating the alleged murder scene.

Within minutes of beginning their gruesome task, Willard reported, "We have evidence showing the soil in this area has recently been disturbed."

Encouraged, they dug in earnest but with the care necessary to preserve evidence.

Twenty minutes later, the digging suddenly stopped. One of the crime scene techs said, "We've got human remains."

Further digging would be slowed and carefully done by small hand shovels until the bodies were completely exposed. Medical Examiner Michele Vickery had been summoned to the scene. Crime scene techs would collect evidence and anything found in the hole that was not natural to the soil. Something as small as a cigarette butt or a lost button could become crucial.

After Vickery arrived and conducted her initial investigation, she huddled up with Brogan and Mazzone. "Both your victims have been shot in the back of the head. No other injuries are immediately visible, but the gunshots would've been enough. They're both males, and I'd ballpark their time of death to be at least four or five days ago. Both will be sent to Baltimore for a complete autopsy. We're bagging some of the insects that have taken up residence in the bodies to help pin down the time. Detectives, you have a double homicide to solve."

Brogan cautioned everyone at the scene. "There's to be a twenty-four-hour media blackout on this recovery. Anyone who leaks information will be met with the wrath of the state's attorney's office. We believe these deaths are part of a much larger investigation. Any leaks may lead to further deaths. Is everyone clear on this?"

Brogan looked at each person individually and waited until each acknowledged the order.

"Everyone knows their job. Keep at it."

Freddie Jones sat leaning against a nearby tree when his cell phone went off. A quick glance brought terror to his eyes. Without immediately answering it, he yelled, "Detective Brogan, it's Melvin. What do I do? He never calls me this early in the morning."

Brogan shouted to everyone on the scene, "Silence. We need absolute silence to take this call. Freddie, put your phone on speaker and answer the call." He did as he was told while Brogan stood next to him.

"Hey Melvin, what's going on? Man, do you know how early it is?"

"Yeah," Melvin acknowledged, "I know how early it is, and I ain't happy either. Look, you got the day off. I ain't coming by to get you this morning. I want you to stay home and by your phone if I should need you."

"Okay, Melvin, but what's going on? I can tell you're nutted up."

"Keep this to yourself, but something big is going down tonight. I can't talk about it except to tell you, you didn't make the top ten, and you're lucky."

"Man, what does that even mean, Melvin?"

"Willy says he got his most trusted people hooking up with him later tonight for a tall order. I'm one of those ten, but you're not. Probably because you're too new or something.

"Willy told me not to bring any guns with me, which is totally fucked up. He said he'll have something for us when we meet.

"Shit kinda scares me a little, but I know better than to cross him, and I ain't fucked nothing up, so that's what I'm going to do. You just lay low today, but keep your phone with you in case I need you in a hurry. Do you know where that closed-up chicken factory is just north of Snow Hill?"

"Yeah, I know the one you're talking about. Do you want me to go there?"

"Fuck no. Stay home like I told you. I'll call if I need you, and if you don't get a call, I'll fill you in tomorrow. Just lay low. Got it?"

"Sure, Melvin, you're the boss. I'll be beside my phone."

The call ended.

"You did good, Freddie," Brogan said, "you did really good. To keep you safe, you're not going home. We're taking you to a safe house where there'll be some detectives with you. If Melvin calls again, do just what you did. The detectives will tell you what to do after the call."

Brogan turned to Mazzone. "Can you arrange for a safe place to keep Freddie and a couple of people to babysit? S.A. will cover any expenses. Don't tell anyone other than the sheriff where this place is. I don't even want to know. Just keep him safe and have your folks reach out immediately if Freddie gets any more calls. Oh, yeah. No outgoing calls from Freddie. He talks to no one. Call me direct if there're any problems."

Frankie said, "Done. I'll arrange it."

Both men walked out of earshot of Freddie.

"Frankie, we're going to need the sheriff's office's SWAT Team tonight. I'm calling the state police for a second SWAT Team to act as backup for your guys.

"I think if we can all meet up at the Sandpiper P.D. training room at 5:00 p.m., we'll have enough time to put together our plan and be in the Snow Hill area before this thing, whatever this thing is, goes down.

"I suspect Willy Spears has identified the shooters who took out his people and intends to make his statement tonight. We may be going into the middle of a drug war. If Spears is bringing at least ten people, I suspect he's up against a similar number, hopefully less, but we need to be ready. Can I depend on your tactical vehicle, a couple of K-9s, and your drone?"

"I'll talk to the sheriff. I'm sure he'll give us everything we need. The hard part is going to be keeping a lid on this operation with all this personnel needed."

"I hoped having our meeting in Sandpiper might draw any curiosity away from our area of interest. How we move everybody into place will be part of the loop. The drone will be an essential part of how this goes down. I have to call Rudy Carol and brief him on what's going on. I'm going to have Jim Lyons listen in on the call so he knows the plan. If we need any legal advice, we'll have him to bounce things off of."

Mazzone nodded his understanding and agreement. Brogan made his call to the S.A. at the end of his briefing; Rudy Carol said, "Do you think this thing is definitely headed for bloodshed?"

"I think it's inevitable, but we're hoping to contain it or stop it if we can. I'll keep you posted."

"I trust you, Brogan, stay safe tonight." Carol ended the call.

Kelly had stayed on the periphery during all these exchanges but now spoke to Brogan. "My missing guys. My informant. My client has missing sons. Don't even think about cutting me out. I'm in this up to my eyeballs. Put away your shining armor. **Do not** even think about trying to protect me. You guys wouldn't know shit without me, and I'm going to be there for the finish. You know I can handle myself. If you need me to sign a waiver, get it out and give me a pen. Are we clear?"

Brogan raised both hands in surrender. "Did I say I was going to cut you out?"

"No, but I know you."

"Now you're the one who doesn't know shit. You're in. Get your gun and your vest. No matter what happens tonight, you stay with me. Right with me, okay?"

"Yep, I'll be right with you. Damn, I miss this shit!"

Glad I didn't tell her she was going to have to sit this one out. I wasn't quick enough, and now I'm not brave enough.

54

Hidden By Darkness

The meeting at Sandpiper P.D. was going well. The conference room was crowded with armed and dangerous men and women. Two full SWAT teams, three K-9 handlers, the sheriff, the barrack commander, and the chief of Snow Hill P.D. were all in attendance. Additionally, ten handpicked uniformed officers from the various departments lined the walls due to a lack of seating for everyone. Everyone wore solemn faces. The room remained quiet despite the crowd. Trooper Irvin Blackburn decked out in a State Police SWAT Uniform. He was the trooper from the house on fire. Brogan tapped down the urge to smile, but it reached his eyes, and Blackburn gave him the slightest of nods.

I shouldn't be surprised, but I am. This young man keeps showing up when I need him the most.

Brogan led the meeting and kept it brief.

"Willy Spears is the known head of a drug trafficking gang here on the Eastern Shore. He lives near Salisbury. Each of you'll get a photo of Spears before you leave.

"Here's what we know. There've been execution-style

murders of two of Willy Spear's people. They were killed at a reported stash house. Drugs, money, and weapons were stolen. Willy had the bodies removed to hide the murders and the existence of the stash house.

"Earlier today, with the help of an informant, we dug up the bodies where they'd been hidden. Spears ordered them hidden so he could find out who did the killings and deal with it himself.

"Spears has said he is seeking retribution for those killings. I suspect that'll happen tonight. Willy Spears is gathering at least ten of his most trusted people tonight at a long-closed chicken factory just outside of Snow Hill. I believe he's ready to strike. Because they're gathering in Snow Hill, I further believe his targets are in that area. We just don't know exactly where or when."

Snow Hill Chief of Police Leonard raised his hand, and Brogan acknowledged him. "There's an abandoned grain mill off Route 365 between Snow Hill and Girdletree. It's closer to Snow Hill and well off the road. It's surrounded by trees. It's completely fenced in, and I have the key to the gate, plus pre-granted access by the owners for any public safety needs. My people check it while on patrol. It still has electricity and a couple of large buildings where we can hide all our vehicles. There're no houses within sight of the entrance in either direction. It's available for this mission if you need it. You can be anywhere in Snow Hill in just a few minutes."

Brogan spoke without hesitation. "Perfect. That's where we'll rendezvous tonight at 7:30 p.m. There'll be a disabled vehicle with the hood raised at the entrance to help everyone find their way in. Try and space yourself out so as not to arrive in a parade or caravan. I trust everyone in this room to keep this to themselves. We'll be facing an unknown and heavily armed force, and any prior warning leaked to them will increase the odds we may be walking into an ambush.

"A final, before-action briefing will occur at the grain mill. All this'll be occurring during the hours of darkness. Darkness will be our friend. Be sure to bring all your night-vision equipment. You'll need it. Meet with your supervisors for final instructions and equipment needs.

"Every person will be wearing a vest and ballistic helmet if you have one. SWAT Teams will operate under their own protocols. SWAT leaders may want to meet briefly before leaving here today.

"You're all dismissed except the drone operator, who I'd like to meet with right now. The drone will be our eyes in the sky and, hopefully, the key to our success. Go get ready. I'll see you all at 7:30 tonight."

Men and women shuffled out of the room. Each with their thoughts about what might happen tonight. Coming home safe would be a priority. Significant others would be kept in the dark. A heightened level of worry was always there. These were violent times, and police remained on the front lines.

55
CONFRONTATION COMING

Approaching darkness surrounded the quiet town of Snow Hill. People were winding down after their day at work, gathered around as families for dinner and perhaps a few television shows before retiring for the evening. Just another peaceful nightfall on the Eastern Shore of Maryland.

Looming near the unsuspecting public were three opposing forces. All were armed and preparing for a confrontation that may end in extreme violence and possible death.

At 8:30 p.m., Diego and Razor left the farmhouse and made their way into the woods near the hide they had discovered. Both were armed with AR-15s and handguns. Extra magazines for both weapons were jammed into their camouflage cargo pants and shirts. Their faces and hands were blackened to help conceal them in their ambush sites. They both had a camouflage tarp.

The woods were cool. A slight breeze moved the dead

leaves around on the ground. The tops of the trees swayed gently, allowing moonlight to filter through. The light shifted, creating shadows and movement. Dead and rotting vegetation produced a musky, pungent odor. In the daytime, the woods were an inviting place. At night, it became more sinister and foreboding.

Diego examined the area and made a decision, "Razor, find a place down there further where you can flank this guy if he comes tonight. I'm going to settle in here. I'll have a clear shot from here. I'll tell him to raise his hands and drop his gun if he has one. If he makes one false move, I'll blow him away.

Just in case he runs, he'll be running back towards your position, and you can take him out."

"You don't have much to hide behind here if he starts shooting at you."

"Don't worry. I'll be dug in, and like I said, if he even blinks wrong, I'll blow his fucking head off. Just make sure you're well hidden so you don't spook him before he gets back to his hide."

"Okay. I won't shoot unless he gets away from you."

"You probably won't be shooting 'cause he ain't getting away from me. Go get comfortable. It's gonna be a long night. Make sure your phone is on silent and keep it under the tarp so I can text you if I need to."

Razor moved away. *Chauvinist asshole. Probably shoot himself in the foot if this guy shows up. I'm going to set up where I'll be safe from him going crazy with that gun.*

She found a fallen tree about forty yards away. It laid at an angle that protected her from errant shots from Diego and provided her cover on three sides. When the tree had fallen, it pulled the root ball right out of the ground. The ball stood six to eight feet high. She wedged herself against the tree where it met the root ball. The log was large enough and thick enough to stop a bullet. The dirt and roots were also thick enough to stop a round coming from that direction.

She laid the tarp on the ground so she could sit or kneel. She worked the foliage to completely hide herself. A black backpack was slipped off her shoulders and leaned against the tree. Razor pulled out a lightweight black jacket and slipped it on. She had brought power bars and two bottles of water but left them in the pack. Her cell phone was set to vibrate and clipped to the inside breast pocket of her jacket. She pulled the jacket closed and zipped it halfway up. The phone lay against her chest. If it vibrated, she would know.

Razor used her hands to dig out a hole through the root ball. She was able to see the hide that had been used to spy on their house. The hole was large enough to site the barrel of the AR-15 or her semi-automatic pistol to cover a wide area of ground. She screwed a silencer onto the pistol. It might hamper a perfect shot, but it would help conceal her position if she took a shot.

She couldn't see Diego, but she knew she was much safer than he was. *Always acting the macho man. I hope this guy is half the killer he pretends to be. I'd hate to be out here with some idiot who's going to lose his shit if a gun goes off. This is fucked up. He's going to kill some farm kid, and then we'll all be trying to cover for his ass.* Her hand slid to her rear pocket, where she felt the tip of her razor. It comforted her, and she grew calm but remained prepared. She sat and nestled in against the tree. She was comfortable and could remain in this position throughout the night.

At 8:30 p.m., Latisha called a female gang member who lived in Snow Hill. "Sasha, I'm going to text you a location near Snow Hill, and I want you to go there and wait until I text you again.

"When you get my text, I want you to call Snow Hill P.D. Tell them there's a shooting and a cop is hurt and bleeding. While you're still on the phone, I want you to fire three shots into the ground, scream, and tell them to hurry up. Give them your location, hang up, and toss the burner phone and gun into the pond where you are. Then, drive slowly out of the area. Can you do that when I text you?"

"Sure, I can do it, Latisha. What's going on?"

"Don't ask questions, Sasha, just do exactly what I told you to do. I'll get you a new phone and gun tomorrow. Keep your mouth shut and follow orders."

"I will, Latisha, I will."

Latisha was sure neighbors in the area would report the sounds of gunfire and create the distraction they needed. The location was ten miles out of Snow Hill and on the opposite side of town.

At 10:00 p.m., chosen members of the gang started showing up at the old chicken factory. Two of Willy's men guarded the gate. Their job was to allow access only to Willy's people. Then, to instruct, "Turn off your headlights and park near the first large building you come to."

By 10:30 p.m., all twelve gang members had arrived. They now stood near two cargo vans. The windows were heavily tinted.

Willy and Latisha stood together, and when Willy nodded to her, she raised her voice, "Shut the fuck up. Willy's got something to say."

Willy was armored up, had an AR-15 strapped across his back, and had a pistol rig on his chest holding a dark gun. He wore a black watch cap and had painted his face and hands with something to eliminate the sheen of his skin. He made an imposing figure, like some kind of Rambo. Everyone fell silent.

"Listen up. Most of you know by now we lost two of our guys. Someone hit one of the stash houses and killed them. They took our dope, money, and guns. They need to pay, and that's why we're here tonight. Latisha has found out who they are and where they are.

"Tonight is payback; we're gonna kill every one of those motherfuckers. They're Hispanic, maybe Mexican or Guatemalan. Maybe Cartel people. Don't really matter. They ain't from the Eastern Shore, and they shouldn't be here.

"We're going to send a message to anyone who thinks they can come in here and take away our livelihood. I pay you guys good. If they take over, you got nothing. If they don't kill you, you'll end up back on welfare or jacking cars to put some coin in your pocket. I'm here with you, and I'll be standing tall when we take these motherfuckers down. Anyone afraid or don't want to go with me say so now. No hard feelings. You'll be out, and you won't get back in. I need people who're loyal and willing to put it all on the line. Who's out?"

No one moved or said a word.

"Okay, I'm turning this over to Latisha. Do exactly what she tells you, and we be good. No room for fuckups. Be a little bonus in this for all you guys if this goes right."

Latisha stepped forward, and the men formed a semi-circle around her.

"Me and Willy will be in the first van. I also want Slick Melvin and Emory with us. How many of you guys been in the military?"

Five guys raised their hands. Latisha pointed to the three biggest guys and said, "You guys will be in the van with Willy and me. You other two will be in the second van."

She pointed to the guy who looked the most squared away and said, "You'll be in charge of the second van, and you," pointing to the last military guy, "will be his backup. Everybody get around the hood of that car over there."

Latisha led the way and unfolded a large sheet of paper. On the paper was a drawing of the place and surroundings where they were going. She spread it across the hood. A flashlight appeared and lit up the paper.

"Here's what we going to do."

Brogan and Kelly sat in their darkened undercover car. They were tucked in a small alley about one hundred yards from the entrance to the old chicken factory. They had been there since 8:30 p.m.; too dark and far away to see much detail, but they could see the entrance and two men standing just inside the tree line. Lit cigarettes had given away their location. At 10:00 p.m., people started arriving.

Brogan and Kelly were pretty sure Willy was already there. The drone operator, Corporal Emerson Hoopes, was at the edge of an open field approximately half a mile from the chicken factory. At 9 p.m., Brogan directed their drone to recon the factory.

Using night optics on the drone, Hoopes was able to identify two Ford vans sitting next to a large building. A Mercedes was also parked nearby. No other vehicles were visible, and no people were seen. The operator made sure he kept the drone far and high enough away so as not to alert anyone near the factory. The drone was an invisible surveillance platform. He brought the drone back and landed it in the field near him to conserve its battery.

At 11:00 p.m., Brogan ordered the drone back up for a status check. The drone had just taken a position over the factory when people began loading into the two vans. There were no long weapons visible. Any handguns would be invisible at the distance the drone was hovering.

Hoopes called Brogan immediately and told him what was going on. Brogan immediately transmitted via a tactical radio channel to the temporary command post set up in the abandoned grain mill.

"Have everybody saddle up. These guys are on the move, and we've got no probable cause to stop them yet. The drone is on them, and I'll follow them at a distance where they won't see me. I'll feed my location to you and have you direct all our personnel to head my way. No emergency lights and no high speeds. We don't know where we're going yet, so we gotta go slow."

"10-4, Brogan. We'll be at the gate and ready to go in any direction," responded Detective Sergeant Ordway, who was on the command post radio.

Kelly turned to Brogan. "What do you think?"

"I think we're headed into a shit storm. Just remember to stay with me no matter what."

The vans pulled onto Route 113 and drove North. The drone remained overhead and followed the vans. Brogan pulled out and took directions fed to him by Hoopes. He had his game face on. This was it. He lived for moments like this. He glanced at Kelly. She stared out the front window. Her look was intense. No fear. Only determination.

56

Fighting for Your Life

The drone followed the vans for about five miles before watching the first van extinguish its headlights. The second van followed suit. Without signaling, both turned slowly left into an unlit driveway. Not even the brake lights illuminated during the turn into the driveway.

Corporal Hoopes took the drone higher and with the assistance of the night vision optics saw both vans disappear into a canopy of trees covering the driveway. At the higher altitude, Hoopes was able to see a small farmhouse in a clearing beyond the wooded area. There were some additional outbuildings of unknown purpose near the house. A sliver of light escaped from one window in the house. A van and car sat near the home. Both were dark.

The drone was not equipped with heat-seeking capabilities so it was unable to penetrate the foliage or the buildings to tell if any living things were lurking there. No movement was observable, and the vans he had been following did not enter the clearing.

Hoopes notified Brogan of the situation with his educated

opinion that both vans were stopped somewhere on the driveway and hidden by the forest surrounding them.

The vans came to a stop. All doors opened quietly, but no interior lights came on. The occupants gathered quickly and formed into two teams. Latisha headed a line of seven people; Willy had insisted on being number two in line despite Latisha's warning and encouragement to take a position farther back. Emory took the third slot, and Slick Melvin was right behind him. The three ex-military guys completed the line. All were armed with AR-15s. None were silenced, as Willy hadn't been able to obtain anything to quiet them down. Now, the entire plan hinged on a quick hit and a quicker exfiltration.

Using the military tactic of every other man carrying his rifle at low port, pointing his weapon outward in a different direction, they hoped to thwart any ambush without shooting each other. Latisha would lead, and everyone else would follow in her footsteps, keeping at least six feet between them. Going in quietly was the key. Stealth over speed.

The second team was to maintain security on the vans with a driver behind each wheel ready to move out at a moment's notice. At the first sound of gunfire, both vans would race forward, stopping when they reached the edge of the clearing. They would target anyone who was still in the house or returning fire on Latisha's team. The second the Hispanics were eliminated, everyone was to jump back in the vans and make a hasty withdrawal, split up, and then drive normally back to the chicken factory. Anyone killed or injured was to be helped or carried into one of the vans. No man left behind. Everyone was gloved up, and all the weapons were untraceable, so they could be abandoned when the job was done.

Latisha cringed every time Willy, Emory, or Melvin stepped on a small twig or stumbled over a hidden root. She and the three ex-military guys moved silently as they had been trained. She was glad she had instructed everyone to keep their fingers outside the trigger guard while they made their approach. Although the noises being made were few and relatively muted, they set her teeth on edge.

Brogan and Kelly maneuvered their car about twenty-five yards from the entrance of the suspect driveway. They knew their backup was en route but would take about ten minutes to arrive.

Brogan spoke by phone to the SWAT Team Commanders, "Hart and I are going to enter the woods about twenty-five yards south of the driveway. I suggest you use the driveway and the woods on the northside during your approach to minimize the chance of a friendly fire accident. Everyone has radios, but let's remain off the air unless it's absolutely necessary."

Brogan used his hunting experience to remain silent as they entered the woods. Kelly remembered, *There was a time last year when Brogan and I were in the woods under similar circumstances. People died that night.* She kept her thoughts to herself and stayed quiet behind him as they moved forward.

After about fifteen yards, Brogan stopped. *What happened to Kelly? I told her to stay with me.* He turned slightly and glanced over his shoulder. Kelly was frozen just three steps behind him. Brogan was embarrassed that he had again underestimated her skills. *Damn, she's good.* He nodded and gave her a thumbs up, and kept going.

Diego strained to hear. *What's that noise? I can't see anything, but there was a noise. Maybe an animal.* His whole body tensed as he adjusted his grip on his AR-15. His eyes focused on the darkness of the woods, looking for any movement. *Nothing yet.*

There it is. I heard it again. It's closer. Something's coming my way. I knew that fucker would come back again tonight, but we're ready for him. I hope Razor is still awake.

Razor heard it. *Someone or something is moving through the woods. Small noises, the snap of a twig, the rustle of the leaves. I hope Diego can hear it. I hope he waits before he just starts shooting up the area.*

At first, it was a tree, and then maybe just a shadow of a tree, and then it moved. No noise, just movement. Then, it took shape. A person moving towards the hide. *Oh shit, not one person, but two of them. No, three of them. Oh shit, oh shit. They all got guns.* Razor adjusted her position slightly and pushed the barrel of her rifle through the hole she'd created. *I have to wait to see if Diego makes a move.*

Diego made his move. He had seen three figures moving forward and saw they were armed. He rose from the depression in the ground that had served as his cover and opened fire. The three people dropped like stones in his concentrated spray of bullets.

He hadn't seen the rest of the line. The fourth and sixth person in line returned fire on Diego. Diego's body shook with the impact of over a dozen rounds ripping through him. He fell back into his hide and lay dead.

Razor fired a single well-aimed shot. The fourth guy in line was dead before he hit the ground.

Incoming bullets thumped against the log that kept her safe. She stayed down, knowing she'd die if she exposed herself.

The three ex-military guys found cover and delivered suppressing fire on a fallen tree where a shot had come from. No additional shots came from that location, but they did not ignore the possibility the shooter was still there.

Without speaking, one of them began flanking the position, seeking a clean shot. The other two continued delivering withering fire on the area of the log. They dumped magazines and jammed fresh ones into the receivers.

Diego's initial volley of shots set off an immediate series of chain reactions.

Willy's second team in the vans roared up the driveway with headlights off and stopped at the tree line. All five men bailed out and took up positions on either side of the first van.

Julian, Ana, and Tomas broke from their cover in the house and moved into the darkened front yard. Julian and Ana ran towards the woods, where they knew Razor and Diego were hiding. Tomas held just outside the front door, seemingly guarding the house.

The headlights of the first van were turned on, and the entire front area of the house was illuminated. All five men opened fire. Dust and dirt flew up from rounds, striking the ground around the running Julian and Ana as the shooters began adjusting their aim.

Ana was the first to fall. A round caught her in the side of the head. By the time her legs had received the message, she staggered a couple of steps before crumbling to the ground, where she lay unmoving.

Julian almost made it to the woods before he, too, was cut down by the wall of steel coming his way. The first strikes took his legs from beneath him. He hit the ground and rolled to his stomach, facing the incoming fire. His AR-15 barked as he sent his bullets down range, hoping to find those who were intent on killing him. Partially blinded by the headlights, his bullets sailed too high, striking nothing but the trees behind the van.

The flashes of fire coming from Julian's gun actually did him in. All five shooters poured rounds at the flashes emitted from his gun. Julian died moments later.

Tomas, who had remained unnoticed and frozen by what he had just witnessed, erupted into an angry animal. "Fuck you, you mother-fuckers!" He opened fire on the van and the men surrounding it as he sprinted towards their van as a possible means to escape. One of Tomas' bullets struck one of the shooters in the face. Death was not instantaneous but would prove fatal. The remaining four concentrated their fire on the van as Tomas dove through the driver's door, and the engine sprang to life.

Tomas knew the driveway was blocked. *If I can turn the van around, I can drive through the fields and get back to a road and get away. I'm alone. Diego, Razor, Julian, and Ana are all dead. I have to keep going, have to stay alive, and get out of here.*

The van door did little to stop the incoming bullets, and the windshield disintegrated under a hail of gunfire. Tomas was hit in his left shoulder, and then a bullet grazed his neck. He attempted to pull the gearshift lever into reverse but was hit twice in the upper chest. His strength deserted him, and his hands fell to his lap. His gun fell between his legs and rested on the floor of the van. *If I just stay still, maybe they'll stop shooting. Maybe the cops will come and save me. The headlights are fading. They must be backing up. I still have a chance.*

In reality, the headlights did not move, and they weren't backing away. For Tomas, the world went dark as he took his last breath. His body slumped against the driver's door.

Brogan and Kelly had hit the deck when Diego let loose, not knowing where the gunfire was coming from or whom it was intended to hit.

The ex-military guy who had flanked Razor's position worked his way around the root ball, prepared to eliminate any threat he found hidden there. An AR-15 leaned against the downed tree and sat on a tarp spread on the ground. No dead body and an expended shell casing was all he found. He jerked around, checking the area in case he had walked into another ambush. He shouted to his buddies, "Clear. Whoever was here has hauled ass. I'll check towards the road in case he tries to circle back on us. Just hold there a couple of minutes while I check."

"Okay, be careful. Yell out when you come back so we don't shoot you by mistake."

"Roger that."

The ex-military man thought he saw signs of someone heading away from the downed tree and began covering ground, trying to catch whoever was trying to escape.

The pain in his chest was intense as Willy's eyes popped open. He was confused, and it took him a moment to assess his situation. He put his hand on his chest and felt for blood, but there was none. The ballistic vest had saved him. He remembered hearing shots, and then he blacked out.

Willy looked around and saw Latisha lying a few feet away. She was looking at him. Willy whispered, "Latisha, you good? Latisha?" She did not respond.

Willy strained to see her more clearly as his chest throbbed with pain. She was still looking at him. Her eyes had not moved or blinked. Understanding came to Willy. Latisha was dead, and her eyes were fixed. Her gun lay next to her, and her cell phone was still in her hand.

Willy looked past Latisha and saw Emory on the ground. His wound was so severe he was obviously dead.

Willy crawled away from his dead accomplices and tried to work himself deeper into the woods to hide from the person who had killed them. He finally made it to a tree, and with a great deal of effort, he was able to place his back against it and obtain a seated position. He held his gun, pointing outward should anyone come for him. His back was against the tree, so he felt safe from that direction.

His mind tried to wrap itself around his current situation. *Latisha and Emory are gone. Where're the rest of my people? Oh, shit, I think that's Slick Melvin lying over there too.*

He watched Melvin carefully, hoping to see his chest rise and fall, but he was as still as death itself.

They're all gone, but I'm still here, and I'll find people to replace them. My being alive is a sign it was meant to be. I'll rebuild and be stronger than ever before. I'll avenge their deaths, not for them, but for me. I won't be seen as weak. Hell, all the fucking junkies on the Eastern Shore depend on me. I'm the one that can't be replaced.

Willy felt a hand on his forehead. His head was pulled back against the tree. A shadow moved across his vision, and then it was gone. Willy started choking. He reached to his neck only to find his fingers exploring a gaping hole. Blood poured down his aching chest. His head fell forward and came to rest on his chest. In less than a minute, he had bled out.

Razor slipped back into the woods and disappeared.

Brogan and Kelly realized they were not the targets of the initial gunfire. They also grasped there was more than one active shooter in or near the woods, and they were in extreme danger.

Kelly heard it first, but before she could say something to Brogan, he heard it too. Someone was moving through the woods and was coming closer and closer to where they had taken cover.

Shielded by a tree, Brogan waited until the sounds of someone moving through the woods drew very near. Brogan stepped from cover and saw a man approaching. "Police, stop and put your hands above your head where I can see them."

The man raised his right arm quickly, stopping at shoulder height, and snapped off a shot at Brogan. The bullet whizzed by his head, sounding like an angry hornet.

Brogan fired the riot shotgun he held at hip level. He had jacked a round of double 00 buck into the breach as he entered the woods and taken it off safe at the first sounds of gunfire. At a range of about eight feet, missing was nearly impossible. There was little room for the eight lead pellets to spread, and they hit the man at nearly full force, lifting him up and throwing him backwards from where he had been standing.

"Kelly stay in here and keep an eye out for other shooters." He advanced on the downed man and saw that the shotgun blast had nearly decapitated him. Brogan still kicked the gun out of his reach and stayed focused on the surrounding woods.

A voice came out of the dark. "We surrender. Don't shoot us, we're unarmed and our hands are above our heads."

"How many are you?"

"Two."

"Both of you come forward slowly and side by side. Keep your hands high and empty."

Two men emerged from the darkness, complying with Brogan's instructions.

"Get on your knees and place your hands on top of your heads. When I tell you, drop to your stomachs and place your hands straight out on the ground above your heads and hold that position."

When both had assumed the position, Brogan moved

forward after telling Kelly, "Cover me while I pat these guys down and hook them up."

Kelly revealed herself and took a shooter's position, aiming her gun at the two men lying on the ground. She watched as Brogan quickly and expertly searched the two men and secured both with flex cuffs behind their backs. One at a time, he stood the non-resistant men to their feet and then used two additional flex cuffs to hook them together at the crook of their arms. They were now linked together side by side.

After both were secured, they stared at their dead companion. One of them gagged but stopped short of puking. The other quickly turned his head away but showed no other emotion.

Kelly glanced at the damage created by Brogan's shotgun. She had seen worse and made no comment. *You shoot at the police you should expect no less. We want to go home, too.*

The SWAT Teams had moved swiftly up the driveway after hearing all the gunfire. They moved with precision gained through hours of repetitive training exercises and experiences. They used night optics to enhance their view of what lay before them. When they got to the two vans blocking the driveway, the shooting suddenly stopped, but the shooters still held their positions. All were facing the farmhouse and appeared to be unaware of the approaching police officers to their rear. One shooter lay on the ground, but no one was offering aid.

The State Police SWAT Commander yelled out. "Police. Everybody freeze and drop your weapons."

The words were barely out of his mouth when one of the shooters whirled around to face the police. His gun was still at his shoulder. No one would ever know if he intended to shoot. The team's marksman fired one shot through his forehead. His weapon hit the ground only a moment before he dropped alongside of it. Trooper Irv Blackburn lowered his rifle from his shoulder.

The three remaining shooters dropped their guns and raised their hands over their heads. After a series of commands, they too were cuffed up after being searched and relieved of any backup weapons. All were placed in a sitting position with their backs against the lead van. All were instructed to keep their legs straight out. This position made it nearly impossible for them to make an aggressive move. Still, a SWAT Team member stood close covering them with his gun.

SWAT Team Commander, Sergeant Dan Hickman, texted Brogan. "All clear, three in custody, two bogies down, no injuries to friendly forces."

Brogan felt his phone vibrate in his pocket and quickly responded. "All clear, two in custody, one bogie down, no injuries to friendly forces. We're heading to your location.

57 THE DEBRIEFING

The state's attorney's conference room was abuzz with whispered conversations. Questions and theories were batted about among the attendees. The hierarchy of Worcester County law enforcement was again assembled to meet with Brogan.

As if on cue, the conference room door swung open, and Kelly Hart stepped through. She was dressed in her dark blue Calvin Klein business suit, starched white shirt, and Louis Vuitton heels. Her blonde hair hung softly on her shoulders. Her blue eyes flashed with excitement, and her wide smile warmed the room.

"Good morning, everyone," Kelly said as she took a vacant seat near the head of the table.

Multiple good mornings filled the room. By now, everyone knew who Kelly Hart was. Her history as a former police officer and private detective and her relationship with Brogan left no one wondering why she was present. Her involvement in closing several high-profile felony cases topped off her credentials.

Next through the door was the unflappable Detective William Brogan, senior investigator for the state's attorney's office. As always, he was impeccably dressed down to his recently shined shoes. Not a hair out of place. He nodded at the gathering of local law enforcement and spoke, "How's everybody doing this morning?"

He, too, received a variety of responses ranging from "Hey, Brogan" to "Good, how about you?" Brogan knew everyone in the room and shared equal respect for the jobs they were doing.

"I'm doing good. Glad to see all of you and happy you could make it. Guess you all want to know what's been going on since you decided I'd make a good investigator for the state's attorney's office. Well, to tell you the truth, I've been investigating!"

There was a low rumble of laughter and more than one "We've heard."

Someone had positioned a lectern at the end of the conference room table, and Brogan moved behind it and gazed at all the questioning faces.

Brogan first addressed the State's Attorney. "Rudy, would you like to say a few words before I start."

"Nope. These folks don't want to hear from a politician. They want to hear from my investigator about drug gangs, cartel members, SWAT teams, and all the dead bodies piling up in their county. You go ahead and tell your story, and be prepared for a question or two when you're done."

This brought a chuckle from the crowd, knowing there would be far more than a question or two.

Brogan began by saying, "I've never seen anything like this during my life as a police officer. Let me give you some hard facts and then tell you how it all came to be as best as we can figure out at this time.

"As a result of the confrontation on a farm just outside of Snow Hill the night before last, there are a total of eleven dead. Four Hispanic cartel members at the hands of the Spears drug gang. There are five gang members dead at the hands of the members of the cartel. Law enforcement killed two gang members in self-defense. Five people are in custody, and one suspect is still missing. There were no injuries to law enforcement personnel. An independent investigation has cleared the law enforcement members involved in the shooting deaths.

"It's taken crime-scene techs from three different agencies to process the large crime scene in Snow Hill. We've had dozens of officers, assisted by K-9 teams, search the area once the crime techs were done."

Lieutenant Tawana Milton, MSP Barrack V, Commander, spoke up.

"Brogan, what's happened to all those bodies?"

"The local medical examiner has released all the bodies to the Medical Examiner's Office in Baltimore. Rudy has agreed to pay for the transports out of our office funds."

Some sighed with relief, knowing this would not be coming out of their budget. "Thanks, Rudy, we all appreciate it," said the sheriff.

Brogan continued, "One K-9 alerted on the area behind where Willy Spears was found dead. The dog tracked the scent through the woods to a nearby road, where the scent was lost.

"The five gang members in custody were willing to talk when they learned Willy was dead. Spears had several ex-military guys working for him. One named Garrison Brown was particularly helpful. He said Willy forced everyone to participate under the threat of death."

"Sure they were," Chief Richards commented.

Brogan smiled, "This guy was full of shit. He and all his buddies have long criminal histories and were willing participants.

"Spears somehow found out the Hispanics robbed his stash house and killed the two Hamilton brothers who worked for him. He also learned where they were hiding out. Spears mounted a group of his men to go to the farm and attack the cartel members.

"We got onto what was about to happen at the last minute with the help of an informant developed by Kelly Hart, who brought it to my immediate attention." Brogan turned toward Kelly and nodded, acknowledging her contribution.

She smiled, "Happy to help"

Rudy said, "You're an asset to this county."

"Thank you." *Damn, I didn't expect that.*

Brogan continued, "The informant knew what was going to happen but not the exact location. That's when we mounted our force of police personnel to try and counteract the gang war that was about to happen.

"Unfortunately, we could only react after they started shooting each other at the farm. All our people, and I mean by that, your people, did a hell of a job in bringing the killings to an end. Everyone showed great courage and restraint.

"We had another one of the ex-military guys tell us that Latisha Freeman, Spear's driver, personal bodyguard, and now deceased, had briefed them at the chicken factory and told them that there would be five Hispanics. Three males and two females. He said she told them not to leave any of them alive to talk to the police. This was clearly to be an execution at the direction of Willy Spears.

"Only four Hispanics are accounted for right now. The bodies of three males and one female. The other female is out of pocket and probably the person who killed Willy Spears. We believe she left the track the dog followed to the road."

"Any idea who she is or if she's still in our area?" Chief Richards, SPPD, asked.

"No, and no are the short answers. Early investigation is showing no results when it comes to the Hispanics. Evidence we found in the house indicated two females were living there. Counterfeit personal identification was found on the four bodies. They were good but fake. The second female most likely had a fake I.D. as well. No reason to believe she's hanging around, but no evidence that she's left. All the deceased cartel members had large amounts of cash on them. The missing female probably had enough cash to aid her in getting out of our area.

"We did find a burner phone. A single incoming call was tracked to a number linked to a Mexican cartel called Calupoh. This cartel no longer exists. The Sinaloa Cartel recently wiped them out.

"Fingerprints of the four deceased have gone nowhere. We suspect that someone in the Mexican government has wiped the existence of these four people from their records. Searches of missing persons have revealed nothing."

Sheriff Mitchell asked, "How about the vehicles they've been using?"

"When we searched the van, it was found to have multiple hidden compartments containing cash, drugs, and weapons. The cash and drugs, including Fentanyl, Heroin, and Cocaine, amounted to well over five hundred thousand dollars in street value. Hidden VIN numbers on the vehicles at the farm confirmed they were stolen from the Texas area six months ago. Tags and registration cards are also bogus.

"Local drug investigators and agents of the DEA believe this group was sent here with a very sophisticated cover story and a plan to take over the local drug market. One gun recovered at the scene directly links the Hispanics to the murder of the two Hamilton brothers and seems to support a violent takeover in progress."

Chief Evans, Berlin P.D., spoke up, "What's the status of the drug gang?"

"With Willy Spears and the top members of his gang dead and five gang members now facing murder and conspiracy charges, the local drug gang is no more. The illicit drug supply on our streets will dry up within days.

"Spears controlled the Eastern Shore, so his absence will create a void. All the Narcs working the Shore have their ears to the ground to see who steps up to take his place. We'll try and nip it in the bud, but expect some clashes as the locals try and sort it out. We definitely won this battle, but the war on drugs rages on."

Brogan concluded by saying, "Local drug investigators, with the assistance of the Drug Enforcement Agency and Federal Bureau of Alcohol, Tobacco and Firearms, will continue this investigation. I'll personally contact any department impacted by what they learn.

"Any other questions?" When no one responded, he turned the briefing over to Rudy Carol.

Brogan thought to himself, *Not a single question about the recent quest for lost treasure and its death toll. I guess that's old news already. Works for me.*

Rudy Carol began, "Just to bring you up to date, the citizens have applauded the actions of all involved in the removal of drug dealers from their county. The media is in a feeding frenzy, but nothing we haven't all experienced in the past.

"We've once again made national news. Tourism will suffer, but a public relations campaign has already begun, describing how local law enforcement is always proactive in bringing criminals to justice. The message is that lawbreakers should steer clear of this area. This is not a location ever accused of being soft on crime. This is a place where everyone should feel safe."

The local news media, led by TV personality Lynn Murphy, declared the state's attorney and his newly appointed investigator as community heroes.

58

AFTER THE DUST HAD SETTLED

Two weeks after the shootout, things were finally calming down. Reams of paper and dozens of banker boxes were filled with reports describing what had occurred and the continuing efforts to identify the dead Hispanics and locate the missing suspect.

Brogan was in his new office. Both he and Trooper Blackburn had been cleared of any wrongdoing in the deaths of the two-armed gang members. Investigators and an independent state's attorney had concluded both officer's lives were in imminent danger. Their actions were declared self-defense. Brogan felt as if a weight had been lifted from his shoulders.

With that behind him, he made two phone calls, the first to his coin collector friend, Stanley Berman. "Hey Stanley, it's Brogan. I'm calling about the coin I showed you a few weeks ago. Have you explored it any further as to its value?"

"Yes, I have. I was going to call you, but I read in the papers about what happened in Snow Hill and was afraid to bother you."

"Thanks, I appreciate that. It's been kind of crazy, but things have begun to settle. What'd you find out?"

"I researched and identified a couple of reputable coin collectors in Spain and one here in the U.S. They would have to see the coin, but their estimates ranged between three hundred to five hundred thousand dollars, depending on condition."

"Wow, Stanley. More than I thought, by a lot."

"It's very rare, Brogan. What can I tell you? These are serious collectors and have the money. If they get into a bidding war, the price may even go higher. Of course, they want to see the coin before offering anything. In my opinion, the coin you showed me is in excellent condition considering its age."

"Stanley, I trust you to do the right thing. I want to call Betty Long and give her your name and phone number. I'll offer to send the coin back to her and tell her it's very valuable. Then I'm going to tell her about you and that I trust you to work on her behalf if she wants to sell the coin. It'll ultimately be her decision. I'm not going to push her one way or the other.

"I'm not expecting you to do this for free, so quote her whatever your price is for helping her. Then, she can make her own decision. I have no interest in what happens, and I don't want to know what the coin sells for if she decides to sell it. I just want her talking to someone I consider trustworthy."

"I appreciate that, Brogan. Please share my number with her, and if she decides to call me, I'll do everything I can to get her the best deal possible."

"No problem, Stanley. If she wants you to handle it, I'll have to get her to sign off authorizing me to release the coin to you." Brogan ended the call and dialed another number he had saved on a small piece of paper.

The phone rang four times before a timid female voice answered, "Hello."

"Betty, this is Brogan from Sandpiper. How you doing?"

"Oh, I'm sorry. I saw the area code and was afraid to answer. Tommy and I are doing okay. The last time I received a call from you, it was to tell me my husband had been murdered and that the guy who murdered him was also killed during a police action. Are you calling about that?"

"It's related. When you left me the note and the coin your husband gave you, I took it to a local friend, who's a coin collector, to see if it would help me in my investigation. The coin is legally yours, and we no longer need it as evidence. I'm prepared to release it to you, but before I do, I need to tell you it's quite valuable. It's so rare that it's valued in excess of three hundred thousand dollars by multiple coin collectors.

"I just hung up with my friend, the coin collector, and he said he'd be willing to assist you in getting the very best deal possible if you wish to sell the coin. If you want to retain the coin, I'll make the arrangements to have it sent to you, and you'll just need to sign a receipt when it arrives. Betty, this is totally your choice, and I don't wish to influence your decision. Take a few days and give me a callback."

"Brogan, I don't need a few days. I never want to see that coin again. I never want to touch it again. It would bring back all the pain I've felt. I would say I don't even want the money, but that would be foolish. That kind of money would change everything for Tommy and me. It would ensure we had a nest egg for when he's ready for college.

"His father didn't do right by Tommy. This would be his gift to Tommy from beyond the grave. When he's old enough to understand, I'll tell Tommy about the man I married. A good man who loved us both until he lost his way. This is what Randy always wanted for us. Please ask your friend to help me."

"His name is Stanley Berman, and his phone number is 410-555-2442. I told him you may call. He'll tell you everything you need to know and help you get through this. I'm going to text you a copy of our release form. Do you have the ability to download it and print it?"

"Yes, my sister has a printer, and we've downloaded other things."

"Okay, sign it, get it notarized, make a copy for yourself, and mail the original to me here in Sandpiper. I'll hand-carry it to Stanley and get a receipt from him. Oh, I got a promotion and now work for the State's Attorney's Office." Here's the address. "Good luck to you and Tommy. Call me if you have any problems or questions. Hopefully, time will heal your heart."

"Congratulations on your promotion, Brogan. You're a good man, and I'll never forget how you handled this situation. Good luck to you."

Brogan ended the call.

Thirty miles away, Kelly bowed her head as two caskets were lowered into the ground. Martin and Michael Hamilton were being laid to rest. Marie Barnett stood to her right with her head bowed. To Kelly's left, Mrs. Hamilton watched her two sons disappear into the earth. She remained stoic, but tears slid down her cheeks. She reached out and grabbed Kelly's hand. Kelly accepted it and gently squeezed the old woman's hand.

Before departing the graveyard, Mrs. Hamilton approached Kelly and said, "Thank you, Kelly. How much do I owe you?"

"You owe me nothing, Mrs. Hamilton. I just wish I had been able to bring you a better ending."

"No honey, I do owe you. You found my boys. Without your help, they would've laid in an unmarked grave for all eternity. I would've had no place to visit them and pray for them. Please prepare a bill and give it to Marie and she'll get it to me. You did your job well, and I can never thank you enough."

Mrs. Hamilton was quickly enveloped by her friends and neighbors to comfort and console her. Marie and Kelly made their way to their car, leaving family and friends to grieve.

Fifty miles due east of Sandpiper Beach, the water splashed around the diver who had just entered the water. Buck Savage and three of his friends, Johnny, Steve, and Norman, were spending their third day in a row looking for treasure. When Buck had shared his story with his friends, they had been held in rapture. He offered them the chance for adventure and riches.

The adventure was turning into boredom and disappointment as they had found nothing. Only Stephen was an experienced diver, and he could only dive a couple of times each day. It was Buck's boat, and the other two were just part of the support group. Johnny and Norman offered nothing beyond camaraderie.

On the third day, Johnny became disillusioned and brought a fishing rod with him in hopes of salvaging the day by catching some fish. His line hung limp in the water.

Thirty minutes later, Stephen's head broke the water, ending his dive. Three sets of anxious eyes peered down at him. A single shake of his head delivered the message.

Johnny spoke up. "What the hell, Buck? We've been out here for three days, and we haven't found a damn thing. Did you make this shit up? If there was treasure out here, how come those cops aren't out here looking for it, too?" Buck responded to his doubting crew members in an angry voice."

"I told you they got spooked by what they saw. Said there was bad karma and the treasure didn't want to be found. What we saw was gross, but I don't believe in bad karma, and I know there's treasure here. We just gotta keep looking!"

Suddenly, Johnny's fishing pole bent near the breaking point as a fish took his bait and swam hard, trying to get away. Excitement returned to the would-be treasurer-hunters. Finally, they had some action.

The fight to get the fish onboard lasted about thirty minutes. Johnny was making progress. Sweat poured off his face. "I got this son-of-a-bitch!"

His shirt was soaking wet from exertion. He was tired but refused to let anyone else take the rod. "This is my fish, and I don't need any help getting him in." Each time he leaned forward and then straightened his body, he reeled in a few feet of line. The other three kept yelling words of encouragement.

Johnny leaned back and fell flat on his ass when his line went slack. "Shit, the line broke. Fuck!"

"Hey, wait!" Stephen yelled. "The line's still moving in the water." All four moved to the side of the boat and watched in amazement as they saw the line move closer to the boat. They all leaned forward, attempting to see into the depths.

A dark fin broke the water and moved directly towards

the boat. A large head and glistening rows of razor-sharp teeth showed themselves.

All four crew members lurched backward away from the oncoming threat.

Buck was the first to react. He grabbed his knife from its sheath and severed the fishing line. "Pull the fucking anchor. We're out of here."

Norman, the fourth treasurer hunter, wrapped his hands around the anchor line and, with a single pull, dislodged it from the ocean floor. It came up in record speed with no regard for it being banged against the side of the boat before falling on the deck. Norman, who was seldom known to speak above a whisper, let out a loud yelp that scared his companions as much as the sight of the shark. "Go, go, go!"

"Hold on!" was all Buck said before he ignited the engine and turned the cigarette boat towards Sandpiper. Even though they were forewarned, his crew was thrown violently to the deck as the boat rose and then leveled out. Buck never let off the throttle until he was safely in sight of shore. Even then, he continued to glance over his shoulder to be sure nothing pursued them. Buck announced, "I'm done! I'm not fucking looking for that treasure anymore. I think that shipwreck is cursed."

"Yeah, Buck, you're right, it has bad Karma," Norm said. The other boys nodded with fear still etched on their faces.

The clotheslines sagged with the weight of the sheets that had just been placed upon them. The sun beat down without even a hint of a breeze.

Perspiration formed on the face and arms of this middle-aged woman as she went about her chores. South Texas was hot, and there was no sign of relief anytime soon.

"Madre, madre," said a soft voice behind her.

The woman turned slowly from her laundry and saw a miracle. "Sophia, is that you? Sophia, you've come home, my Mija!

"Yes, Madre, I've come home to stay. I've come to be with you and help you with your chores and do all the things daughters do for their mothers."

They quickly closed the short distance between them and met in an impassioned embrace. Both cried with joy at their reunion. The crushing hug from her mother made Sophia's shirttail hike up a few inches. The tip of her razor tucked safely in her back pocket glinted in the sun. Razor was home to stay.

Later that same evening, Brogan and Kelly rolled apart after a passionate coupling. Although beaded with sweat, neither bothered to pull the bed clothing over themselves. Smiling and breathing deeply, they stared at the ceiling, content and fulfilled. In the old days, they would have been looking for a cigarette.

Kelly rolled on her side, facing Brogan. "Detective Brogan, this has been a hell of a couple of weeks. Can we survive this pace?"

Brogan rolled to face her. "Detective Hart, I'm not sure, but I sure like the way it's ending."

"Get your mind out of the gutter and your eyes back on my eyes."

Brogan never shifted his eyes. "Do we need another trip to Greenbrier?"

"Your new boss might not want you going on vacation after only a few weeks of employment. How about we don't stir up any shit for a few months and re-visit our vacation options?"

"Okay, sounds good to me. Let's sleep on it."

They exchanged a gentle kiss before rolling onto their backs.

Brogan slapped the bed with a flat hand, and Kelly's spring-loaded dog appeared on the bed. He moved quickly between them, made two complete revolutions, and dropped into a curled ball of fur.

"I love you, Kelly."

"I love you too, Brogan."

Brogan pulled a sheet up and over all of them. Before closing his eyes, he glanced at the nightstand. His cell phone laid dark and quiet. How long would it stay that way?

ACKNOWLEDGEMENTS

I thoroughly enjoyed writing *Elephant's Trunk*, the third book in the Brogan series. I tried to embrace two stories simultaneously and bring you, the reader, along with me. Halfway through the writing, I changed the title of the book. While doing research to weave fact and fiction, the things I find often surprise me. *Elephant's Trunk* is real and is an area just off the coast of Ocean City, MD. I'm working on my fourth book but have not yet given it a title. I'll have to see where the story takes me.

My storytelling is never a solo journey. I have friends and readers who encourage me to keep writing. I'm grateful to have readers eagerly anticipating my next book.

Once again, Tobie, my wife and number one fan, created the cover for this book. Her art on the covers of my books has enticed readers to select and purchase them. People are intrigued and attempt to figure out what clues may be hidden in the cover art. She continues to make editorial and publishing decisions. All the things that make a prospective reader pick it up and decide whether to add it to their collection of reads.

As with all authors, I have spent countless hours researching, reviewing, and rewriting. Having the story flow and bringing new characters to life has been an integral part of this narrative.

A special thanks to my editor, Renae Dryer, who took on this daunting task. As a crime fiction reader herself, her insights and suggestions have added clarity. When I write,

I know what the words are supposed to say, and I know the message I'm trying to convey. When the book is placed in Renae's hand, she ensures my message is not confusing or lost. Not everyone thinks like a cop. Probably a good thing!

Thanks to my second editor Steve Geppi, a longtime friend, trooper and English professor for his grammatical edits. When I'm spinning my stories, my attention is on the story and characters and what they are doing to keep my readers following the action. Writing is truly a team effort.

For those who enjoyed this book but have not read my first two books, *Vengeance* and *No Backup,* I invite you to go back and give them a read. All my books are available on my website, authorjakejacobs.com, or they can be purchased through local bookstores or Amazon/Kindle.

Finally, but very importantly, thanks to my publisher, Salt Water Media in Berlin, Maryland. Stephanie Fowler, Patty Gregorio and Andrew Heller's combined assistance in bringing this book to its current format, selling my books, and monitoring my website is invaluable. Their guidance and support have been with me from the beginning.

To all my readers. Thank you from the bottom of my heart. Keep reading and stay safe. It's a dangerous world out there. Real-life Brogans are all over this nation and their stories need to be told. Support the Blue.

www.ingramcontent.com/pod-product-compliance
Lightning Source LLC
Chambersburg PA
CBHW050918030726
47503CB00007BB/2364
9781628064421